D0845746

The Famished Lover

Also by Alan Cumyn

FICTION

For Adults

The Sojourn
Losing It
Burridge Unbound
Man of Bone
Between Families and the Sky
Waiting for Li Ming

For Children

After Sylvia
The Secret Life of Owen Skye

NON-FICTION

What in the World is Going On?

The Famished Lover

ALAN CUMYN

GOOSE LANE

Cover photograph: Orsillo, istockphoto.
Cover and interior design by Julie Scriver.
Printed in Canada.
10 9 8 7 6 5 4 3 2 1

Library and Archives Canada Cataloguing in Publication

Cumyn, Alan, 1960-
The famished lover / Alan Cumyn.

ISBN 0-86492-448-8 (bound). — ISBN 0-86492-463-1 (pbk.)

I. Title.

PS8555.U489F34 2006   C813'.54   C2006-903465-6

Goose Lane Editions acknowledges the financial support of the Canada Council
for the Arts, the Government of Canada through the Book Publishing Industry
Development Program (BPIDP), and the New Brunswick Department of
Wellness, Culture and Sport for its publishing activities.

Goose Lane Editions
Suite 330, 500 Beaverbrook Court
Fredericton, New Brunswick
CANADA E3B 5X4
www.gooselane.com

For Laurel

One

"I'm sorry it's so cold," I said to Lillian, my young bride, who was snuggled beside me under the bearskin blanket. We clung to one another at the bottom of the old sleigh that took us from the train station at St. Simone, a tiny smudge in the woods north of the little chapel in Mireille where we'd been married some hours before. It was late in the afternoon, late in the year, and the steely grey of the sky was edging into black.

"It's not so cold," she said.

Her face was moulded to my shoulder, and silky wisps of blonde hair, escaped from formal arrangement, brushed against my cheek. Her breath warmed my neck, and indeed we were out of the wind and our trail was taking us further and further into the woods, the upper boughs of the tall, rigid pines dusted in snow. Yet I felt chilled through, as if not the thickest fur in the world could warm my bones, and I was strangely wracked with hunger, as if we had not just feasted with our families. No, it was more as if I had not partaken — of real food, of love, of life — in decades and now, at the edge of the banquet, could not control my trembling.

Our driver was a burly, bearded man who muttered to

himself in French and seemed able to guide his horse, a snorting, solid, slow-moving beast, with only the slightest of gestures. We were on our way to a honeymoon cabin procured by my younger brother Rufus, who was friends with half of upper-crust Montreal and who often had the loan of this country place or that.

"I haven't actually seen the cabin," I said to Lillian.

"Yes, I know, you explained it . . . dear." She stumbled over the novelty of the word. As I looked at her fair face and hair so close to mine I wondered how to render it — not from a distance but from these few inches. What would such a painting look like? A curve of cheek, her eyes so young and pale and blue, those hints of hair edging off the canvas, and in the background so much grey and black and old, hard brown — the timbers of the sleigh, the bristly hairs of our bearskin, the darkness of the forest beyond.

I kissed her again, for the hundredth time perhaps, but I could not stop trembling.

"Rufus has made all the arrangements, so I suppose it will be all right."

"Whatever it is, it will be all right." Just then her voice made me think of someone playing the part of a mother in a play in which all the actors were children. And for the first time — I had no idea why it hadn't occurred to me before this, in the months of our courtship — I realized that I was old enough to be her father. If not quite in actual years, then in grains of life slipping through the tightened neck of experience.

I sat up to look around. The wind felt unjustly cold on such a day. But I had faced down colder winds than this.

In the distance I saw not a cottage but a clearing with a

lonely, tall stone cross. And as we passed I could not help but read the carved and familiar list: Ypres, Amiens, St. Eloi, the Somme, Vimy, Mont Sorrel.

I ordered the driver to stop, threw myself off the sleigh before it finished moving and walked briskly towards the monument.

"Ramsay, what is it? Where are you going?" Lillian asked.

"It's nothing!" And I thought: why have they put this memorial on a backcountry trail where no one will see it? But also: they're everywhere now. A man can't even get married and run away to the wilds for a few days without stumbling into one.

I had to dust off the names from Mont Sorrel: four local boys, two named Hughes, a Duncan and a MacDonald. No regiment listed. I tried to think of the men I knew. Their faces swam before me, in the barns and other cozy spaces of our off-duty hours, and in the dugouts and the trenches of our time in hell. Their odour — mud, tobacco, body stench — rose to my nostrils, and I might as well have been back there, just for that moment. Did we have a Duncan, a Mac-Donald and two Hugheses?

It had been thirteen years. But it's an awful thing to forget even the smallest part of what you swear will line the remaining days of your life.

I suppose I stood for some time in my own stupor. When I turned, Lillian was waiting a few yards off, her red, ungloved hands folded across the front of her dark coat, the silly dessert tray of a going-away hat askew on her head from the long ride and our snuggling. The driver and his horse had both twisted round to stare at me, at the tears freezing to my cheeks.

"Were *you* in the war?" Lillian finally asked.

We had not yet talked of it, and here we were embarking on a life together.

"It doesn't matter," I said, and I walked past her quickly. I clambered back onto the sleigh and then, remembering myself, turned to pull her up. But she was already halfway in, and her face had that look — of someone not to be diverted from a path of inquiry. "Drive on!" I said, *"Allez! Allez!"* even before Lillian was seated. I steadied her against the lurch of the sleigh.

"You're crying," she said, facing me, not so much in accusation as in wonder. "Ramsay, tell me."

"I knew some men who got caught up," I said vaguely. "Sometimes I think of them. But not today. Today is for other things." I took her cold hands. Where had she put her gloves? There, on the floor of the sleigh. I picked them up and helped her on with them. They were so fashionably tight I could not imagine them providing any warmth.

"But you will tell me," she pressed. "We're not going to have the kind of marriage where people keep secrets?"

I kissed her and kissed her, and the miles slid by, and it was almost, almost enough.

From a distance the cabin looked derelict, a pile of logs thrown together ages ago and forgotten by whatever pioneer family had abandoned it in the purgatory of rocky fields, fly-infested summers and unendurably bitter winters.

"That can't be it," I said. Rufus would never have steered us this far wrong — he had such a sense of the lightness of things, that's what Rufus was good for. Some weeks earlier, when the stock market had spiralled so unbelievably, Rufus was somehow able to pull out his own holdings and maintain a good semblance of their worth, and he'd even protected a few of my investments as well — the very ones he'd urged me to buy in the first place, when all around us were profiting so handsomely and living so well.

No, this pile of crumbling logs could have nothing to do with Rufus. Yet our sleigh stopped and the driver clambered down to grab the bags.

"*Oui, oui, c'est ça*," he grumbled. Even the horse snorted in apparent affirmation. The driver wrestled our bags along the path — untrodden till now, covered in snow — then shouldered open the low door and disappeared into what looked like the mouth of a cave.

"Oh, for God's sake!" I said.

Lillian turned to me, startled. "Ramsay, please don't swear." That word especially, *swear*, came out like steam forced through a pipe. She looked at the ground, her face burning, as if her husband had publicly admitted embezzlement or adultery.

Was this the woman I'd married?

Our driver re-emerged. I was set to demand he take us to the real cottage, the charming, rustic place that Rufus had talked up so glowingly. But Lillian walked away from me, her shoulders inclined into the wind. She disappeared into the shack.

In my haste to catch up with her I slipped on some ice and was caught by the driver, who'd been drinking on the journey, I now realized — he smelled like whisky. I almost asked him for a swig. He smiled maddeningly, as if he wanted to stay and watch us. Just to speed him on his way I produced a dollar from my pocket and pressed it into his hand.

Then I plunged into the cabin after my bride. I was acutely

aware that I'd not carried her over the threshold. I was no traditionalist, but it would have been nice to have the moment of laughter. All summer, it seemed, had been full of laughter, of weekends by the stream on her father's farm, of fly-fishing those blessed waters, and capturing on canvas the rocks and trees and the sunlight on the pools, and gazing at the lovely Lillian as she emerged from the trail with a loaf of bread just pulled from the summer oven, wrapped in a towel, with a knife and home butter for us to share.

I'd married the farmer's daughter — not a stranger at all.

And perhaps the cabin was not so bad. Though ancient, much of the original mortar remained between the cracks, and the thick walls seemed to stop the worst of the draft. The one main room was dominated by a wood stove. An old pine table with splintery chairs sat beneath a drying rack for laundry that lowered from the ceiling. At the far end was a loft for sleeping, connected to the ground floor by a plank ladder.

Already Lillian had a fire burning, and now she was taking off her long coat and looking square at me. Her thick blonde hair was still mostly pinned back in the fussy arrangement concocted for the ceremony, but she'd abandoned her hat, and now I noticed her neck was red in places — from the rubbing of my moustache, I realized.

There will be things for me to learn, I thought, as a married man.

I crossed the floor and let my own coat fall onto the table, then held her to me. Her shoulders were wide and strong, and I felt her burning in my blood again, like a fire in the fields.

"I'm sorry I lost my temper. If I'd known how filthy and old and rundown this place would be —"

"It's not so bad."

"But it is! Don't you see? I've lived years of my life in awful places. No more, and not for you, certainly. I may never be rich, but we're going to live in comfort at least, surrounded by beauty . . ."

She was looking at me then in what already felt like the old way, her heart bursting just to be with me. A man can wait decades to be looked at like that. It can be the hardest thing in the world to win for yourself, and yet I'd won it at last.

"You're still trembling," she said. "Stand by the fire. I'll make us some dinner." She hurried over to the pantry. "What's to eat?" She started taking things off the shelves. "Here's some beans." She shook the container — it sounded as if it couldn't have held more than a half-dozen. "And what's this, flour?" She took off the top. "Oh!" she said, and clapped it back on. "Mice must be running all through here." She opened up the larder and we both stared at the empty shelves.

"Rufus said he'd take care of all the details," I said furiously.

"Maybe you should walk back to town and get us supplies. I'll stay here and tidy. You're right, dear. The place is *filthy*."

It would take at least an hour to get to the store, and darkness was coming on.

"Maybe I could catch us some fish and we'll make an expedition tomorrow. I doubt the store in town would be open by the time I got there."

I kissed her again, then gathered my fishing gear and walked outside. The wind seemed chillier than before, humming dully through the trees. I descended a narrow path that came out finally on a newly frozen pond. I tried a few tentative steps but the shore ice broke even under my slender frame. There'd be no walking out, no fishing, no easy honeymoon dinner. I said a few choice words to the absent Rufus. Then I trod up the hill again and ducked my head under the doorway. A multitude of beeswax candles filled the room with light and their heavy scent. Lillian had turned up some old silver too and had set the table. "I found some oatmeal," she said, indicating a door to the side of the pantry that I hadn't noticed. "And some preserves. Someone around here has pear trees. Lucky us." In the candlelight she looked like a wet vase still on the wheel, glistening and sleek and absolutely new.

I must have been staring at her, for she smiled and blushed deeply again. "Could you get us some water?" Instead we kissed once more. She put up with it for a time, then pushed me away. "The bucket's over there."

I found the pump around the other side of the house, delivered the water, then spent a satisfying time by the woodpile, though the axe was dull and I could find no file or sharpening stone. From the cabin I heard Lillian humming softly to herself in a fine voice as she prepared the dinner. But as soon as I stepped inside she stopped.

"Please Lillian, keep singing." She looked at me happily, but stayed silent.

I fed the fire and we sat down to eat — a big bowl of porridge for each of us, without milk or cream or brown sugar, but with warm and sweet slices of preserved pear. And a glass of well water each, in a chipped teacup.

"Cheers to you, my darling," I said. I drank, but she set

down her own water nervously, then bowed her head in a sudden gesture and closed her eyes over the food. It took me a moment to realize that she was praying. I bowed my own head, too late, just as she was raising hers.

Her father, a religious man, had prayed before dinner whenever I'd eaten with them. Yet somehow I hadn't expected Lillian to be quite that way on her own. She stole out so often to see me at the river when I was fishing and seemed so mischievous in the eye. But of course she was religious, I realized now. We'd simply not spoken of it. And what did it matter?

"We'll remember this meal the rest of our lives," I said. "We'll tell our children." Three weeks ago, when I'd proposed, I couldn't have been more sure of what I was doing. And she'd fallen into my arms and seemed even more eager than me to chart our course together. But now she was white in the face and silent and did not eat much of the grey food she'd prepared. I rose and stepped to her. "Are you all right, Lillian?"

"I'm afraid you've made an awful mistake," she blurted. In a moment she was sobbing with her face in her hands.

"What, darling? What mistake? No, I haven't!" I knelt by her and held her shaking body. "What are you talking about?"

Several minutes passed before I could even get her to look at me.

"I don't ... I can't ... I don't know a thing about being a wife or —" she stammered. "You know my mother died when I was so young and —" She wiped herself with the old cloth napkin she'd found, her wedding face now smeared. "I don't know what to do!" she said, finally looking at me. "Nobody told me."

"Darling" — I tried to soften my features, which I know can seem hard even when I'm simply thinking — "we'll make it up together. That's what we're here for. To help one another."

She cried in my arms, and we breathed hard together as if we had run a long way. But oh, the feel of her, my God, her warmth and youth against me.

"I'm so frightened, Ramsay!"

I held her face so she had to look at me. "I will never hurt you. Do you understand that? *Never*."

We continued to cling to one another like a shipwrecked pair floating on debris.

"Tell me about the war," she said then. When I did not respond she said, "It was hard on you, I know. You have such sad eyes. And your hands" — she wound her fingers among mine — "you have an artist's fingers. But you've done such hard work, too. Was that in the war?"

Such are the moments that life presents, and a man is either up to them or is not.

"I can't ... I shouldn't talk about it right now," I said.

"I was just a child. I hardly remember anything of it."

"And that's part of what's so beautiful about you!" I gripped her hand too hard. It took the look of alarm on her face for me to realize and shake free. "I'm sorry! I'm sorry! Another time, I promise. The best I can say about the war is that it's over, and it will never happen again." I tried to kiss her, but once more with too much force.

Lillian stood then and began clearing the dishes, her gestures sharp and angry. "I heated water, but it seems we don't have any tea or coffee," she said.

In vain I tried to help yet not get in the way. She dumped

the hot water from the kettle into the wash basin. Then she started looking around fruitlessly.

"Was Rufus going to supply soap too?"

"Let's sort it out in the morning," I said gently. I took her hand, which suddenly felt as cold as if she'd been outside in the raw wind. Her face was sickly pale beneath her teary paint, and she looked away from me, at the dishes in the basin.

"You go ahead," she said. "I'll finish this." She glanced up, I suppose to reassure me, but with a look of terror.

So I retreated to the loft. There was very little headroom and the mattress was tough and musty. But much of the warm air from the wood stove had collected around the bed, and a small, square window rattled with the outside wind to make this pocket seem hospitable in comparison. I plumped up the hard pillows and pulled off my shoes, then settled back to watch the light and shadows from the candles below play against the rough logs of the ceiling.

I longed to hear her sing again. But down below cutlery clattered, pots clanked, cupboards snapped open and shut. And I worried about the bed. The sheets were old, the blankets heavy and rough. There wasn't a lot of room for the two of us to lie side by side. Nor was there space for our bags — I'd left them on the main floor and thought now I should bring them up. Yet I didn't move. I didn't want to disturb her, to do anything else wrong.

Presently the candles downstairs went out, one by one, and I heard her footsteps carefully cross the floor. She mounted the ladder. My eyes had adjusted, and in the low light I could see she had put on a long, thick white nightgown buttoned high up at the neck. She felt about and stumbled into the corner of the bed.

"I'm here," I said.

"You aren't asleep, then?"

I thought I heard disappointment in her voice. "No. I'm right here."

Her hands groped for the bedcovers and then she was underneath them, beside me but separated, for I remained on top of the blankets. She turned her back and nearly sent me rolling onto the floor.

"Good night," she whispered.

I stared up at the ceiling. She held herself on her side completely still, her knees drawn to her chest. I put my hand on her shoulder and kissed lightly behind her ear. Her eyes were pressed shut.

"Lillian." I rocked her gently. "Mrs. Crome."

"Yes?"

But I didn't know what to say. Finally, as if to utter anything to fill the silence, she said, "Why aren't you under the covers? Don't you have your pyjamas on?"

"No, I don't." I rolled off the bed and began to unbutton my shirt and trousers. It seemed a strange and unbalanced dream. Out the tiny window I caught sight of a trio of narrow clouds lurking around a bright, cold moon whose light was now slicing my thin legs. I kept on my underclothes and slid in beside her. Her body felt chilled and rigid.

"Darling," I said, and clung to the only words that seemed appropriate. "I love you." They came out waxy, as if rehearsed and recorded years ago. "I know this is new. But we don't have to do anything tonight except hold and get used to one another. It's completely up to us. Do you understand?"

As I clung to her the chill between our bodies began to ease. Her breathing settled, and for some time it seemed to me that she had fallen asleep. I was accustomed to years of wretched sleep by then and determined I would not move, but would simply hold her like this for all the hours of the night. Perhaps I thought that in the morning we would be welded together and would rise hungry but a single unit.

In my starvation for life, even these scraps seemed enough.

I would paint the two of us like this, I decided. In her deepest slumber I would rise without disturbing her and set up my small board over there, by the little window, and paint her with shadows cutting across her young body, and the rough covers tucked under her chin, and myself beside her — thin and rugged and small, with eyes open, grateful for whatever the night would offer. For it seemed to me that's what love was, what I'd been missing.

But she wasn't asleep. I shifted my arm — it had gone dead beneath me and was painful now to move — and she blew out between her lips, not a sleeping sort of sigh but as if she'd been holding her breath and feigning stillness. "I'm sorry, Ramsay," she said finally, still turned away from me. "I do love you. I know it doesn't seem that way. I'm scared is all. Please talk to me. Tell me about anything. About the girlfriends you have had."

"What makes you think I've had any?"

"Well, I wasn't the first girl you ever kissed. Who did you love before me, and why didn't you marry one of them?"

Even a new husband can sense such a bomb in the water. I laughed nervously, and so she turned towards me. Her face seemed to glow in the moonlight.

"Was I the first girl you asked to marry you?"

"Of course, darling." I kissed her and she seemed to linger, to enjoy this new proximity.

"But who did you love before me? Was there somebody ... There must have been somebody during the war!" She began to tickle in among my ribs. She was young and strong and her legs gripped mine in the hard thrust of play. "What was her name?"

We kissed again — partly I wanted to stop her, but the fire was building once more. I held her tenderly and tried to keep my breathing from overtaking me.

"Ramsay, what's — ?" She groped around and I tried unsuccessfully to catch her wrist. For a moment she couldn't speak. She drew back until she was kneeling above me, most of the covers drawn around her. "It's like an animal's!"

I tried to cover myself.

"Let me see. I want to see it!"

I sat up and held her hands. "Lillian, my dear, it's all right. It's completely natural."

"I want to see it," she said again, slowly and seriously. So I shucked off my remaining clothes and paused before her, while she looked at what she'd ended up with: the brown skinny chest, the deep-veined arms and hands, the ancient, hardened pole at the centre of it throbbing with its own certainty.

"Is it always like that?" she asked.

"No, darling. Of course not."

She seemed to take a long time to digest the information. She didn't move, just slowly observed all my points and angles. At last she said, "Was it the war then, when you hurt your arm?"

She meant my left, which doesn't quite straighten. It's strong enough but looks withered beside the right.

"It's nothing. Yes, the war. It isn't painful."

"How did you hurt it?"

"We'll get to all one another's secrets," I whispered. But it was hardly the time for talking. I wrapped the covers around us again yet did my best to retain a distance even in the narrow confines of the bed.

"I don't want to disappoint you," she said finally.

"You're not. You won't. We don't have to —"

But she was pulling me on top of her, and her legs fell open more or less naturally, and I tugged at her nightdress. She closed her eyes and held onto my shoulders.

"It's what God wants, isn't it?"

"God?"

She opened her eyes, partly in pain, as I entered her. I tried to move slowly, calmly, but I felt rope-tied to a moving train.

Forgive me, I thought.

I closed my eyes, and a particular young woman arose in a way that I'd imagined her a thousand times before. Not Lillian at all, but Margaret — the woman I'd been trying to forget. But it would have been like trying to forget the bones in my body, the veins of my hands. Her hair was a warm brown and her skin was pale and white and smooth as milk. She smiled at me in certain ownership.

I became aware of the noise of the bed bucking against the plank floor, of tiny exclamations and hot breath in my ear, the surging sweetness culminating within. I was aware of the spasms starting in my body and the strength of the hands on my back. And mostly I was aware of Margaret's knowing gaze as she turned back to look at me from further and further away, with those eyes that would not release me.

"Ramsay!" Lillian said in a daze beneath me, and for a moment I had to look hard at her to recognize who she was.

"Forgive me," I whispered. "Did I hurt you? I am so —"

"Shh! Dear Ramsay," she said, and held me against her warm, pillowy breasts. "Go to sleep now."

Biting, drenching, endless rain, and my feet have gone through the soles of my blasted boots so that the mud and cold have invaded my flesh and bones, now rub raw my joints, suck my strength. I am reduced to a pair of hazy eyes fixed on the back of the sod ahead of me, yet with this wounded lad draped around my shoulder. He collapsed a long while ago and would have been left to rot by the bloody uhlans if I hadn't moved swiftly. And stupidly, it now occurs to me. I'm fag-tired, and my left arm was bent hard in battle, and I've no idea how many miles are still to go.

The arm might be broken, but it's nothing compared to what this lad is up against.

Ahead the uhlans ride in their polished helmets and soggy plumes, like sour gods ashamed to be assigned this menial work when there's a war on, for Christ's sake. Already I've seen too much of the tips of their fancy lances. But behind us bombs shudder the earth into the crumbling lip of hell's boiling cauldron. And every step is away, away from that disaster.

"What's your name?" I say to my burden. He's bleeding down my uniform from an unbandaged belly wound. Little gurgles of gas and bubbled pus escape with every step, and his head wobbles like a toy soldier's.

He murmurs something that I can't make out, then I feel the weight of him even more and struggle to hold him up.

"Keep walking. Use your legs!"

He responds for a moment, then returns to drunken swaying. If only he were simply drunk. I'd lay him in the ditch and he'd wake up in the morning, cold and bedraggled and with a body that only feels split open.

A man ahead drops his haversack and staggers on. I look up at the long, ragged line of prisoners disappearing into the rain. The road is littered with heavy saucer helmets, muddied greatcoats and extra boots that look so tempting. How long would it take to set this fellow aside and trade my wrecked boots for some new leather? But I can't imagine my fingers working fast enough. Some sour uhlan would just run me through.

So I walk on past, my feet bleeding into the road.

"Come on. Come on! What's your name?" I say.

My load groans.

"What's that?"

"Jekyll."

"Like Dr. Jekyll and Mr. Hyde?"

"No doctor." A grudging, exhausted smile.

"No. No, if there was a doctor you'd be all right. Or even a stretcher. Do you think the German army could afford a stretcher?" I say it loud enough for others to hear, and the English officer who thinks he's in charge of us — a captain of some sort who walks like a man who has had his horse stolen — turns to me. "Private, keep your commentary to yourself!"

Murmurs from some of the others but we're too tired, really, to take it up.

"Where are you from, Jekyll?" I ask.

"Picton."

"Where's that?"

"South of Kingston." Whenever he talks gas leaks out of him from somewhere. If I had a first aid kit I could check him over and maybe plug him up. But no bloody way. "We have a farm," he gasps.

"You'll be able to write them back on the farm," I say. "*Safe and sound, Ma! How's that?*"

"Jesus." Blood spills down his lip and chin. "I wish they'd killed me."

"None of that. Save your strength. Let's enjoy the surroundings," I blurt, then look around. Surroundings? I can barely see where to place my ragged feet ahead of me.

An eternity like this. .

Sometime, I suppose in the late afternoon, we're allowed to rest at a military station. The rain has stopped but the mud continues to grow, to take over everything, and as I let Jekyll slip to the ground near a tree it occurs to me again — the thoughts forming slowly, as if in a dream — that I need to get him medical help. I look around for anyone who might be a doctor or nurse. There are tents everywhere, and vehicles with grumbling engines, and a sickening number of prisoners collecting from small marching parties like our own. So many of them are Canadians.

I approach a German officer bent over by the entrance to a stone building, a farmhouse in another life, no doubt. He's scraping the mud off his boots with a stick.

"Excuse me," I mumble. "My friend here is wounded. He needs immediate attention. *Wounded*," I say again. The officer straightens up and looks at me in malevolent incomprehension. So I point to Jekyll slumped against the tree trunk where

I've left him. But his body is unnaturally still, and even as I gesture I know it's too late.

The officer spits past my shoulder, then stalks off. I return to Jekyll's cooling corpse in time to close his eyes.

The captain of our ragged group approaches. "Is this man dead?"

"Apparently." It crosses my mind that I should have saluted the captain and used his proper title. But those rules seem to be for some other reality on the far side of battle.

"Right," the officer says, thankful, perhaps, for something official to occupy his mind. "Strip his tags, then, and see if you can find a pay book and any effects for next of kin." He lingers for a moment. "I'll see about burial," he adds, maybe as much for himself as for me. Then he struts off in another direction and I hear his voice worrying other clumps of prisoners. "Anyone here speak German?"

Jekyll's body subsides into a different position, and for a moment I think he's alive after all. But it's just gravity having its way. I check for a pulse in his neck anyway, then feel for the leather cord and pull it off him, stuff the tags in my pocket. If he had a haversack he dropped it miles ago. In his pockets I find a soaked package of cigarettes, a few francs, a folded picture of a dark-eyed lady looking away from the camera.

For a second I think it's Margaret — my Margaret! Of course it's just a picture. She's safe back in London. But just the sudden thought of her —

"You're sweating like a horse!" Lillian said.

"Huh?"

"Why are you breathing like that? Ramsay?"

I looked wildly at her face, at the dark, rough walls of the cabin, our own breath misting in the cool air.

"What's wrong?" she asked.

"Nothing, darling. Has the fire gone out?"

"You were all clenched up." Tentatively she reached out and brushed some of the moisture from my brow and cheek.

"Just a dream. I don't know what it was." I wrapped my arms around her, and she continued to run her fingers along my face and neck. "Go back to sleep. Often I have . . . troubles at night. So I'll just hold you."

She looked ready to poke and pry until she'd loosened the wrappings on this new husband and truly riled the hornets within. But it was terribly late, and it had been a long day and night, and I suppose even then she was not entirely awake. In a moment her eyes closed, and I felt the sleep take over her young body even as mine remained wounded and cocked for war.

Two

A few months later we were sitting in the kitchen of the punky apartment I'd found for us in Montreal. Winter's ice seemed to have settled for good — the bottom half of our meagre kitchen window was coated inside and out, blurring the black iron fire escape directly outside it. I watched her from my seat at the unsteady table. In oblivious moments she was as graceful as a horse dipping her head to drink from a stream. But now she held her body tight, and she breathed in little gasps as if there was not enough time to accomplish all that was slated. She banged the dishes into the cupboard, wiped up the saucepan while looking at the counter stains and then at me, sitting so still.

I sipped my tea and glanced down at yesterday's newspaper. The world was devouring itself with an accumulating series of layoffs and failures, forfeitures and devaluations, suicides, stock collapses and windy promises that were sounding less and less plausible. I had my lump of savings but was afraid to spend it. Our kitchen furniture consisted of a card table and two folding chairs. Yet from the safety of my position at

Justin Frame Graphics and Advertising I felt, I suppose, like a man sitting onshore watching a faraway ocean liner sink beneath the waves. What possible connection could it have to me, this interesting disaster in the distance?

"I don't see how it can last," I said. When you have survived certain things, other people's panic can seem ridiculous and overdone. "The big money boys are so used to making it hand over fist, they won't stand for many more of these losses. It's all a matter of confidence."

"What is?" Lillian asked sharply, still banging about in the kitchen. "We're going to be late." She was in a dark blue Sunday dress that she'd made herself from catalogue drawings. The collar had a scratchy bit of lace that never sat properly. But in those days it only made her look more refreshing and beautiful. She was about to untie her apron and put on her coat and hat.

I said, "I'm not going. I'll walk with you, but I won't take in the service."

That stopped her. She turned in surprise and I braced myself.

"What do you mean?"

"I will walk with you," I repeated slowly, "but I won't take in the service."

"Don't talk to me like I'm a child! Why won't you go to church? I can't sit alone, without my husband!"

"It would be hypocritical of me," I said, rooted in my chair. Her eyes narrowed in their way, and I said, "It means two-faced. If I go I would be proclaiming a belief in a god that I don't have."

"But you've already been with me plenty of times. And we were married in a church!"

"Yes. And I regret that. The church, not the marriage." I had a strange feeling of watching myself to see what I might do. As if to confound things further I reached to her then, pulled her onto my lap and tried to bury my face in her shoulder.

"Whenever you say crazy things, I know it was the war that did this to you," she said, and freed herself from my grasp.

"You know nothing of the war."

"How can I when you won't talk about it?" She pulled herself angrily into her coat.

"What the war taught me," I said, "is that God is not the church. Or the church is not the building, not the fancy robes and mumbo-jumbo. You go to your church and I'll walk in mine and look at the snow on the branches and the shadows of the clouds on the buildings and the patterns of the ice on the windows. That will be my church. You go and sing your hymns and say your prayers and I'll walk around and feel the blood in my muscles, and when we come home here we'll eat and I'll carry you onto the bed and we'll celebrate the god-fire in us all afternoon and into the evening if we want. And we'll be religious in our devotions to our separate gods."

She was standing by the door, ready to go.

"I don't understand you," she said. "You're talking non-sense."

"Yes, and I love it! I'm tired of following everybody else's rules. No one knows *what* the rules are. I've been in realities far beyond any rules you can imagine."

"Stop talking like this, Ramsay."

"It *was* the war! The war ruined me! But it made me too. I walked out of it and here I am."

I stood up like a fool.

"Why are you acting this way?"

"Because I am in love," I said, and I grasped her by the wrist. "Don't go to the stuffy old church. Stay here with me in this stuffy little flat, and we'll make it our own church."

She pulled herself free. "Really!" she said, and looked around like a flustered bird.

"Come on!" I reached for her again.

"We can't be thinking of that all the time!"

"Why not? We're married now, and the world doesn't care what we do within our own walls."

"Well, *I* care! I care very much!" Her chest was heaving, her face red with fury. "Are you making me go alone?"

"I'm not making you do anything."

She pulled open the door, and an icy blast drove all the heat from the air.

"I was a prisoner in the war!" I blurted.

"What?"

"My brothers died, but I was a bloody fannigan prisoner rotting in German camps. That's why I don't talk about it. That's why I feel as if I've wasted too much of my life already."

She let the door fall shut and stepped towards me.

"You were a prisoner? No one said a word to me. You never —"

"It was long ago, and everything changed when I met you."

I took her in my arms then and steered her towards the bed on the other side of the curtained-off sleeping area. It wasn't much better than the dusty cabin offering of our honeymoon: a rickety old frame with shot springs and a mattress so lumpy it might as well have been made from newspapers. The previous renters hadn't bothered moving it, and from the time

I'd laid eyes on it I swore I'd replace it as soon as prospects looked better.

I eased her down on the bed.

"Who were your brothers, Ramsay? What were they like?"

I tugged off her coat and hat and gloves and began to unbutton her dress.

"Please don't do that."

I slid her shoulders free before stopping. I could see her collarbone and slip, the curve of her neck, the quiet freckles on the tops of her fine breasts rising and falling.

"Will and Thomas," I said. "They were older than me, and everything they did I wanted to do. And Alex was a year younger, the wildest of all of us —"

The outline of her nipples, the right one soft, the left hardened by the cool air. I could see the dark, relaxed join at her shoulder where the flesh of her arm met the slope of her chest, and how the shadow from the window fell across a portion of it. I could feel already the soft shading I would give to that spot.

"Everything Will and Thomas did I wanted to do. They rode horses — we all did — for some of the local farmers, and we ran wild in the woods near our home, and Father packed us all off in a skiff one summer and sent us up the Chemainus River." To the unspoken question in her eye I said, "Vancouver Island. That's where I grew up. Don't move."

I got up quickly, found my sketchpad and pencils, then settled back where I was. But already the shadows had shifted, and she had switched the angle of her arm and now it was the fall of her throat that looked so intriguing, especially when she turned her head that way.

"You're not going to draw me like this!" she said in sudden

31

anger. She rebuttoned the top of her dress. "You were telling me about your brothers."

I reached across and undid the first few buttons again.

"I'm your wife! You can't go drawing me like I'm some sort of —"

"Gift of nature? Blessing upon my eyes and soul?"

I wanted her so much to be the young woman at the sunlit stream who'd stopped my heart the moment I saw her.

"Thomas and Will," she said. "And Alex."

"Thomas was the tallest of all of us. And he had a punch" — I made a fist with my free hand while still sketching, setting out the turn of her chin — "like an iron bar. And he had sharp elbows. When you played football with him" — the lace on her slip, the twist of the strap on the left shoulder but not the right, the shadows of her hair. I started to pull at one of the clips.

"No, Ramsay. We're going to be late." She sat up again and began rearranging herself.

"Church again."

"It is the Sabbath."

I followed her into the main room where she picked up her coat.

"Don't be like this. Put your suit on, please. We have to hurry!"

But instead of following orders I found myself seated again at the table, the newspaper before me. I set my sketchpad on top of it and filled in more lines: the soft mound of her shoulder and rise of her right arm, the tiny hairs near the edge of her hands, the promise of her lips. I was driving her to tears, I knew it, but I couldn't stop myself. "I'm sorry. My church is here. I know you can't understand it, but you are more beautiful than any god to me. And when you come back —"

She hurried off, leaving the front door open.

Forgive me, forgive me, I thought.

The train bumps and swings to a halt, and we wait, the silent, mumbling mass of us, for the cattle doors to swing open. Please God, I think, let there be water. It's been hours and hours since we stopped for a time in a strange little town — well, it seemed little, though we could see almost nothing from where we sat. We stink like livestock, and the corners of the car are rank with shit and piss.

I stagger to the door and hope I won't fall out and land in a heap on the station platform. It's a few yards away and my feet are a pulpy mess inside my rotten boots, though my arm hardly hurts if I keep it in a certain position. I squat at the edge, dizzy, while the press of tired men behind me builds. A shabby crowd of civilians looks at us in silent loathing.

"Damn your bloody eyes!" Witherspoon yells from our group. "It isn't our fault. Ask your Kaiser Billy about the fucking war!"

He jumps down ahead of me — an enormous man, even with the bend in his back from this hard travel. His hair has gone white just in the last few days. As soon as he hits the ground he turns and offers me a hand. I reach out, and he settles me down like a father helping his young son from a tree. He's bleary-eyed like the rest of us, his uniform filthy and torn, face unshaved. We turn and help the others while the guards look on, stony-faced.

A group of women hand out alleged food — a pail of

dreadful soup and slices of black bread hard as wood.

"I wouldn't feed a dog these rations," Witherspoon mutters.

We march away from the station, weary defeated men. My feet have no business walking anywhere, but other men are worse off and yet still stagger forward. We're supposed to remain in single file, two paces between each prisoner. Soon enough the fifty of us are strung out like an accordion. I am in the tail, either standing still, trying desperately to stay upright, or running to catch up as the wave of delayed reaction moves up and down the line.

Then, apparently, we lose our way and the head of the line twists back to collect the tail and stagger away in a new direction, off the road entirely and across a ploughed and impassable field.

"For the love of God!" Witherspoon cries. "Get us some bloody transport if you don't know where the hell you're going!"

And I think: they're going to shoot him. They'll leave his body in the furrows to fertilize their wormy food. But even the guards seem exhausted into deafness, and we walk on and on together.

They let us drink for a time from a small brook that runs alongside the endless field. I cup my hands and pull the water to my mouth as if I will never drink my fill.

How I long to rip the clothes from my body and slide my feet in the cooling water and slip away. Somehow I'm certain that one plunge would bring me back to myself and wash away this nightmare. One desperate, deluded act, which I cannot bring myself to try.

Finally I turn away from the creek and sit back on the soft

green grass. The sun beats down with pitiless good cheer. We lounge in shade and no one wants to get going again. Witherspoon has cigarettes and matches that work. His big face curves slightly to the left, like a rain-softened football kicked too often. "See those soldiers there," he says, meaning our guards, who are smoking in their own shade not far away, rifles slung on their shoulders, their faces perspiring in the heat of the afternoon. "They're beautiful women and we've caught them by the swimming hole. It's so hot they can't keep their clothes on."

Some of the soldiers have their collars undone, that's all.

"You're barmy!" someone says.

Witherspoon closes his eyes. "They're undoing their stays. Their breasts are falling free. They're wriggling their bottoms to get out of their bloomers. They can't see us, but we can see them."

He eases his long body back on the grass and puts his hands behind his head. "God! What a beautiful day!"

Five or six of us keep looking at that sorry group of guards, as if they might be the naked ladies Witherspoon is talking about.

"I have a girl back in Toronto," Witherspoon says. I'm sitting closest to him and I suppose he's talking to me, but his eyes are closed still and he seems to be addressing himself as much as anyone. "That Beatrice. A kiss to her is like a glass of wine. She just can't get enough."

A shadow starts to pass over the field, and Witherspoon opens his eyes.

"Who's your girl?" he says to me. "Come on, don't keep her secret. Not now. We need a bloody great harem to get us through these days."

The shadow deepens rapidly, a huge cloud, I suppose, blocking out the sun. I close my eyes.

"Margaret." Just saying her name makes me feel as if I'm dropping a coin down a well. So I say it again. "Margaret with the dark brown hair —"

"God, it's a Zep!" someone says. An airship glides over the field, enormous, a giant floating ship of war, and we all stand as if we might have to defend ourselves against it. The German soldiers who've been lounging like us are now on their feet too, being ordered about, and begin struggling with cables to tie the ship down.

"Been out bombing London, have you!" Witherspoon calls. "Bloody murderers!"

We might as well be ants. There's nothing we can do to touch that huge machine.

But then a gust of wind comes up, and not much wind, either, but some of the cables must have been poorly secured, because the airship launches itself again, just as the crew is climbing out of the gondola. A dark shape in the distance falls as the Zeppelin rears over and starts to bounce — that was a man, I think dully — across the field, the remaining cables snapping now and whipping out at the tiny figures running after her.

"Hooray! Run, you fuckers! Run!"

We all yell as the Germans bumble after their now ridiculous airship. If only the wind were stronger! But it's hardly more than scattered puffs. Some minutes later the beast is secured properly, and we are on the march again, tired, filthy, hungry men. The day is cuttingly hot and bright.

Step and step and painful step. But because of Witherspoon and his reveries Margaret now is loose in my imagination.

Margaret with the tiny, perfect nose. Margaret, whose dark eyes linger far too long, and whose lips I kissed, once straight out in public on a bridge when we were both overcome and once in the darkness outside the hospital my last night in London.

My last free night before the seams of the earth split open.

Step upon step. How quickly the day closes in. But I see her suddenly in the fog. She's walking beside me now, gripping the hem of her dress to keep it from the mud of the road.

"I didn't expect you to get captured," she says in her clever voice, almost kidding.

She can't be here, of course. But her body seems close enough to touch.

"What happened to your boots?" she asks.

My feet. My feet are in shreds.

"You'll have to get new ones. I'd give you mine, but they wouldn't fit. Don't laugh!"

I can't help myself. Suddenly it seems amusing, the idea of me having Margaret's feet, wearing Margaret's boots.

"You have to look after yourself, Ramsay. I'm serious now. Get up!"

For some reason I'm on my side, entangled in a bush.

Her expression is serious. Her hat has fallen off, some of her hair has come undone, and her white hands are clenched in little fists. "Get up!" she says, and kneels down to shake my shoulder. "You can't rest here. They won't let you."

I pull at her wrist, and she topples onto me. It hardly takes anything, she was balanced so precariously on her knee. I kiss at her, but she tears herself loose.

"Not here! Ramsay, for God's sake! Get up!" A guard

37

shoulders her aside then. I'm so angry I snap to my feet and yell at him. He raises his rifle to club me, and I glimpse Margaret standing behind him. "I'm all right!" she says.

The guard barks out something.

Somehow Witherspoon is standing beside me, and I recognize it's his hand keeping me back.

I step along, steer my bleeding feet back onto the road.

"Don't be an idiot just for me," Margaret says from somewhere. I can no longer see her, the fog is so thick. I look around and around, everywhere, nearly twist out of Witherspoon's grasp.

"That was her!"

"Who?" Witherspoon's voice is low, as if he wants me to stay quiet. Of course — the guards are all around, and if they see her too —

"Margaret," I whisper in his ear.

Sometime later I heard Lillian's feet on the stoop, but she did not come in. I waited and waited, but the door did not open. Finally I pulled on my coat and found her leaning against the iron railing, looking down at the snowbound street, at the other tenements, the mountain in the distance, a cigarette in her hand.

I'd never seen her smoke before.

"What are you doing? You must be freezing!"

She did not turn. "I don't really feel it."

I rubbed my hand up and down her back. A dog came racing out of one of the back alleys, chasing a snowball some boys had thrown. Then the boys emerged too and ran around the dog, while the dog ran around them.

"I didn't know you smoked," I said.

"I don't." She took another deep puff, then handed the cigarette to me to finish. She held the smoke in her lungs, then slowly let it stream out of her nostrils — exactly as Margaret used to do when she thought she could get away with it.

"How was church? I'm sorry. Of course I'll go with you in future. I don't know what got into me. I think this whole economic disaster is starting to —"

"Your father is a hard man," she said then. "He was nice enough at the wedding, and I enjoyed meeting your mother, though I wasn't sure how that would go. I'd never met a Colombian before, and she was sweet to me. But I could tell I disappointed your father. And he asks a lot of his sons, doesn't he?"

"He isn't disappointed in you! But of course he's hard on his sons. Any man would be."

"You too?"

She still didn't look at me, but we were standing together at least, gazing out in somewhat the same direction.

"When I was all of seventeen he packed me on a train, and we crossed the country together. I couldn't wait to get away from home. Mother was the one who raised us, you see, mostly on her own because of Father's work overseas. We only saw him a few times most years. He didn't get his papers, and in North America an engineer without a certificate is hardly worth more than a ditch digger. So he went wherever they'd have him — Peru or Bolivia or the Far East.

Much as now. Whenever he came home he was like a god, filled with such stories of the jungle and the high pass. We idolized him. Now I thought he and I were heading off together somewhere tropical to drain a lake or excavate a mine. But he abandoned me in the train station right here in Montreal." The word "abandoned" finally got a rise from her — she looked at me straight on in some alarm. "In the midst of the crowd he handed me fifty dollars and an address where I might find a bit of work. 'Write your mother,' he said to me. 'She'll want to hear from you. And if you should ever find yourself with a—'"

I faltered then. For I suddenly realized I'd told the same story many years before to Margaret and her family in London, got to the same spot and encountered precisely the same problem. For the briefest moment I seemed to be dizzily in both eras.

"Well, it doesn't matter," I said quickly.

"Find yourself with a what?"

"Nothing. Shall we go inside? It's so chilly out here."

"How am I supposed to learn anything if you won't talk to me? What was it your father said to you in the train station?"

Lillian's will could be like a horse pulling a plough. In that moment I did not have the strength to resist it.

"He said if I ever contracted a ... a ... particular disease, I was to get in touch with him immediately, and he would send money, no questions asked. That's all. And I never have. Contracted one, I mean. Let's go in." I turned towards the door.

"What disease?"

"It doesn't matter! You don't need to know about it!"

"I hate being a child around you," she said quietly.

"There are particular diseases that a man can get from a

woman — and vice versa — from sexual contact. That's what he was talking about. I'm sorry I brought it up. That's all."

Lillian shivered but made no sign that she wanted to move inside.

"Will you be like your father, do you think?"

"Well, I don't know. I'm not sure I've ever thought about it, really. The discipline was good for us, I suppose. Whenever Father arrived home after a long absence he would line us up and make us bend over. He would say, 'This is for the grief I'm sure you've been giving your mother —'"

"So will *you* do that too?"

"Father never beat my mother. No matter how long they spend apart, whenever he comes back they are like two rocks cemented together in the same wall..."

Lillian was shaking her head at me, and slowly her meaning began to penetrate my skull.

"You're not — you aren't — ?"

Her nod was almost imperceptible.

"But how do you know? Have you been to the doctor? When did you — ?"

"I know, Ramsay," she said softly. "Tomorrow you're going to bring me to the doctor. But right now you're going to tell me ... everything about the war. About being a prisoner."

"Darling, I —"

"I want to know the man I married," she said, slow and steady, powerful beyond her years. "I want to know the father of my child."

41

Three

We slipped inside the apartment, but I did not feel like taking off my coat; the chill was gripping me as it did in those bitter days. But this time it was a frigid wind within, and I felt as if there was no withstanding it. Lillian boiled some water for tea and we sat at the rickety table and clinked cups. "To our child," she said, and then added, "Drink quickly, dear. You look like you're going to break of cold."

The first sips did warm me somewhat.

"How were you captured?" she asked.

"I was taken in the Battle of Mont Sorrel. Are you sure you're interested in this? There's hardly anything to say —"

"Mont Sorrel was after . . . Oh, I wish I'd paid attention in class! I remember Second Ypres, and the big one, the big Canadian victory —"

"Vimy Ridge," I said. And I thought, it's just names now, facts for people to forget. "Mont Sorrel was in early June, 1916. Near Ypres. It was just before the Somme, our big offensive that went so badly, so it has mostly been forgotten now. But Mercer was killed — he was a major-general, our commander. And a brigadier was captured — Williams — and

Ussher, a lieutenant-colonel. They came by and inspected our positions that morning. We'd been up all night working on a dugout, and Shipley came round with the rum ration and told us we were going to be inspected. Well, bloody hell — I'm sorry, Lillian, I can't talk about this in completely polite language."

"Just talk about it, then," she said quietly. She was warming her hands on the cup, and she looked small and terribly pretty. Let's stop this, I thought. I'll get my sketchbook. We'll think about what's really important.

But instead she asked, "What's it like being in a battle?"

I hardly had to think of a reply. "Like being in an avalanche. There was nothing anyone could do, really. The earth is suddenly moving all around you. I was buried for a time in a hail of bombs —" I was conscious of the inadequacy of such words, as if they could come anywhere near describing it.

"Did you kill anyone?"

"Some. I manned a Lewis gun for a time. And the Germans were pouring over the fields by the thousands, it looked like. You know, you imagine for a moment it's the end, you personally are losing the war. Slip past us, then the town of Ypres would be open. So yes, I killed some. Then I got blown out again and I wandered around — I must have been unconscious for a while — and then it was as if I was in a dream. I was staggering and eventually was taken."

She was hanging onto my words, but I couldn't really tell her, not so that she'd know.

"A German fellow called out to me. Who was I? A Canadian? Then: 'Have you ever fished the Chemainus River?' He was a baron and he'd spent many years in British Columbia, and he loved fishing."

She couldn't possibly know. Not from these words. Not from anything I told her.

"So you were held in a camp?"

"Raumen was the main one, then I got transferred to a different one near Münster. We were starved, mostly. The food was a disgrace. And we were made to work, though we dragged our feet a lot. You see, I can tell you, but —"

"Who was Margaret?"

I was so stunned I sat with my mouth open.

"You say her name sometimes at night. When you get in your sweats, and I am lying awake listening to you. You say — sometimes you say, 'Margaret!'"

Lillian was studying my face so closely that there was no use trying to lie.

"My cousin. In London. I stayed with her — and her family — for a short time before Mont Sorrel. It was my only leave in London."

"Were you in love with her? Do you love her now?"

"Why would you ask that?" I said, incredulous. How could she possibly come to that conclusion from a few things mumbled in the night? Yet she was looking at me as if she knew a great deal more than that, even. As if she'd taken out and laundered my thoughts and now was set to wring them clean and dry.

"You say her name," she said slowly. She looked away and I guessed it even before she could mouth the words. "And there are those paintings."

"What paintings? What are you talking about?" I said, as if I could take back what her eyes obviously had examined — without permission. Without a thought to my privacy. "I've

shown you everything I thought you should see. You had no
right —"

"Well, what am I supposed to do?" She stood up then,
and so did I. "This is my home! Am I not supposed to go in
the closets? Should I ask your permission every time I want
to get the broom?"

"That's my work! You had no right —!" I grabbed her.
She would have had to move several boxes to get at those
canvasses, which I'd never told her about, which were mine
and mine alone. She would have had to untie the strings and
separate them one by one, then tie them again and replace
them at the back for me not to have noticed. All while I was
at work.

"What are you going to do?" she blurted. "Hit me?"

I pushed her aside to get her out of my grasp, to try to
keep a grip on myself instead.

"You painted her *naked!* Picture after picture. Was that
Margaret? Did she pose for you? Getting out of the water like
that? Sitting on the rock? What kind of cousin is she? It's the
same girl over and over. It must be Margaret, and you must
love her or you wouldn't be so upset!"

"She never posed," I said. Burning coal sat behind the
space between my eyebrows. "She knows nothing of those
paintings. They are not for you or the world. They were . . .
exercises . . . "

"They're indecent!"

"They're not that, either. I know you can't understand.
But in private I need to be able to go anywhere . . . freely . . .
in my imagination. There can't be closed doors. That's what
my art is for. If I lost it —"

She started crying, her fists at her sides. "They're horrible, Ramsay. If I thought you were that kind of painter I wouldn't —" *Wouldn't what?* I thought. "Everything you showed me was so beautiful. The stream. The rocks and flowers. You painted *me*. You made *me* look so beautiful."

I took her in my arms, for she was sobbing now and I could see it was my fault. She was carrying our child, and she was so young herself, and this was such a shock. And clearly she hadn't looked at all the paintings, for she would have mentioned them by now — the Russians standing like starved cattle by the fence, the hollows of their cheeks empty caverns, and the bunkhouse at night in deep shadows with the hunching fannigan forms like lumps of men on every bed, and the twisted grey corpse by the side of the road with the single empty boot glistening beside the stump of an arm — all those images torn from memories no sane person now wanted to witness.

If she'd seen them she might not have asked with so much energy about the German camps.

"You love her, don't you?" Lillian said. "This Margaret. This cousin of yours."

I tried to brush the tears from her face.

"I did love her. Yes, of course I did. I would have fallen in love with any young woman I met in London in that week away from the front. It would have been inhuman not to. And the thought of it, the memory of it —" *her* I thought; I should at least say *her* — "did help me through some terrible times. More than I can say. But it was ages ago, and I love you. I've *married* you. And we're going to have a child. That's all that matters. Let's talk no more about it. We'll move forward from here. It just stirs things up for me to think about those days, and it's upsetting for you. Yes?"

She buried her face in my shoulder, and I had a hard time keeping the waterworks from my own eyes as we stood in the middle of the draughty flat and did our best to keep away the world.

"Tomorrow we go to the doctor's, and after that we'll see about moving. I don't want our child's first view to be this sorry box filled with bad air."

"But we have so little money!"

"Maybe I'll sell some of those paintings. Spread a bit of Margaret around this dirty old town —"

She gazed up at me then, aghast that I might actually do it.

"Not to worry. Enough said. We'll find another way."

"Maybe we could move to Mireille," she said. Her voice was suddenly far less timid, and I realized she must have been thinking of this for some time, just as she must have been thinking of the paintings, choosing her moment to be most upset. "There's room with my father. We could save the rent, and he certainly needs me."

I felt my dander rising again. "Lillian, I couldn't just walk away from my work. Not now, not when most of the commercial artists in the city are out banging on doors —"

"There's the train," she said. Another card falling. Another calculation.

"Riding in every day and night, how much would that cost us?"

"A lot less than rent. And the country air's better. We'd have our food and so much more room than here. And Papa's not going to last forever —"

47

"No!"

"He wants us to take over the property. You wouldn't even have to farm it. We could hire others —"

"My work is here! I don't want to be travelling every day and night and never see you and the baby. Frame is a decent man, he'll push me more salary. I've been with him eight years. That's settled. All right?"

She looked ready to say more, but I didn't want to argue, not on a Sunday, not this day in particular.

But the murk in the water had been stirred, stirred.

"What are you doing?"

As soon as I speak the needle drives far into my wound and my spine whiplashes, though my legs are being held firm. I have a vague sense of the darkness of the room, how shadows stretch along the ceiling like mounds of earth waiting to cover me up.

He unleashes a torrent of German, and for a moment I see his dark, heavy hair, the cowlike eyes, too big even for such a large head, the hands that look meant to steer lumber down a fast-flowing river.

"Jesus!"

The pain settles like fish hooks inside. His whisper is the gentle sliding of a knife being withdrawn from its scabbard. I close my eyes, lie as still as possible, as if such stillness might fool him. But someone shrieks in another room, followed by other wails of distress and the cursing of ill men too pained or hungry or bored or scared to sleep.

She's in the room somewhere. I can't see her but I know she's here.

Later I hear a voice whisper in the gloom beside me. "He said you're lucky to still have your feet." I look over at a bandaged wreck, one arm suspended from above by a wire stretching towards the ceiling. "I understand a little German. They were going to amputate when they first brought you in, but Schreider wanted to try you out on something."

"Try me out?"

I don't remember arriving here at all. The last I know I was stumbling along the roadside, bleeding into the dirt.

"He has things he wants to test. That's what I heard, anyway," the man says.

He sounds British, but not from London, perhaps. Somewhere else. I introduce myself and he replies, "Bill Chesterman." He blinks hard — the small section of face around his eyes is nearly his only unbandaged bit of flesh. "Caught a taste of the new gas," he says. "How about you?"

I tell him I'm all right, practically ready to be up and at it. "Who told you this doctor wanted to cut me up?"

"The last guy in your cot. They took him out yesterday dead as a post. Nice chap, too. Australian."

And he starts to laugh, a wheezing, slightly crazy gurgle.

She's in the room but I can't see her, can't turn my head enough for the bloody straps.

"He came in with a broken jaw. Some fight or other. *Herr Doktor* Schreider mucked about with his mouth. We could all hear the screaming. Crushed a bunch of teeth with a pair of fancy pliers, then rooted around with a nail to get out all the scraps. Blighter died of fright."

Towards morning *Herr Doktor* comes back and pumps my other leg full of something equally excruciating. He rubs the feet up and down, digs his fingernails into the wounds. "Ya? Ya?" he says. I scream to blow the glass out of the windows.

"Ya? Ya?" he says.

If I had a saw or knife or a stretch of sharp wire I'd hack off my own feet to stop the pain.

I don't tell him about my arm. I don't tell anyone.

Some days later the poison subsides, and gradually my feet begin to heal to some semblance of working order. Schreider brings in a phalanx of white coats to surround my cot and examine the miracle of my limbs. They're stern, quiet, respectful men, all but one younger than Schreider. Some have bloodstains on their coats. All have eyes that look as if war is teaching them more than they want to learn. They prod and sniff and turn my feet from left to right and back again while Schreider talks at them in his way, a machine-clanking sputter. Some of the words are directed at me. Schreider waits for a time, sneering, evidently expecting a reply.

I don't say a word. But Schreider and his colleagues leave finally, and Chesterman translates for me afterwards. "You're lucky to be alive. But now your feet are healed, and *Herr Doktor* said it's time for you to work for the Fatherland."

Sometime later a British sergeant arrives, trailing a scowling German guard. "Crome, is it?" the Brit says, and shakes my hand. He is carrying a bundle of clothes for me but turns to chat with Chesterman first. "How are they treating you then, Bill? Rotten as always?"

"And always rotten," Chesterman sings back. "How about you, Collins?"

"Hardly keeping my head above the shit," Collins says

cheerfully. He's a small man, even shorter than me, though less wiry. Perhaps in his forties. The crescent of his hairline sweeps to the rear of his head.

"Collins has been in camp since Second Ypres," Chesterman says. "Practically runs the place."

"Oh yes," Collins shoots back. "And you've been delusional ever since they wheeled you in. When was it?"

"The Charge of the Light Brigade."

I swing myself out of bed and totter on shaky legs.

"I was told you were fit for duty," Collins says.

"I'm fine," I mutter. "Are those for me?" Collins has brought a faded dark tunic and black trousers painted with a red stripe down the leg, and wooden clogs to replace my ruined boots. I hold onto his shoulder and lift one leg at a time, doubtfully, while he helps me. Fortunately the trousers come with rope for a belt. The clogs have no splinters — that's perhaps the only good thing about them.

"Can you walk, Crome?" Collins asks. "Or should I try to make the case for you to stay here?" He nods ever so slightly in the direction of the guard who's taking it all in with malevolent silence.

"I'd sooner roast in hell."

"Let's not rush ahead of ourselves," Collins says.

Chesterman laughs painfully. "You two get out of here," he gasps. "Before I bust a seam."

I take a few tentative steps, which brings upon me a flood of verbal abuse from the guard. But Collins bolsters my arm. "Just keep walking," he whispers. "I'll fill you in." We march beside the guard along the grey corridors, out of this damn hospital. While the guard sputters Collins says, "You're going to *Arbeit*, see, *raus raus*, like a good *englischer Schweinehund*, and some more things that he's talking about, or there will be *Strafe*, understand, punishment for all the *Kriegsgefangene*. Not just you, but all of us. Nod your head, yes, that's it, since England *kaputt*! And keep your nose clean or it's the hoosegow for you. *Verboten*! Precisely. Now we all understand."

Down the stairs and out into the blinding sunlight, and along more passageways between high fences of barbed wire. Across an infinite distance to an open section near what must be barracks — squat, sorry-looking cabins with black-topped, shallow-sloped roofs. Towards about thirty ragged men at attention in the dirt compound, watching us approach. Even from a distance I can see Witherspoon towering above the rest. I hope they've not been standing long on my account. I hurry, try to keep up with Collins and the guard. I spot a machine gun trained on us from an overlooking tower, as if we might bolt en masse and fling ourselves at the barbed wire.

"So you will salute the lamppost beside Sergeant Agony here. Yes, not at him but at the lamppost, good, and march over by Cuddihey in the rear of the second row. And if we're all good children we won't have to stand here for hours listening to more of his prattle. Now *raus!* Yes, make a show of hurrying, but not too quick."

Collins winks at me and nods slightly, his face a strange mixture of restrained fury and kind humour. I fall into line beside Cuddihey and try to stand somewhat straight. But I'm exhausted from just that short walk out of purgatory.

And into something else.

Agony marches in front of us, his face flushed, spouting more harsh words while Collins provides the appearance of translation. "No sick days, either — *nicht Kranke besuchen!* Because of the wonderful food. Steady, men, humour him.

And more things that he's saying, *nein, nein,* no to this and to that or we're going to have to answer to *Herr Kommandant* Farmer Bob. Don't laugh at my jokes! Stay British or it's *Strafe, Strafe, Strafe!*" Peering between the shoulders of the men ahead of me I see in the distance a ghoulish gang of prisoners forming on the other side of a barbed wire fence. Ragged as we may be, they are in tatters, the skin shrunken around their skulls, eyes dull as caves, shoulder blades propping up the worn fabric of their uniforms.

"Who are they?" I whisper to Cuddihey beside me.

"The Russians," he whispers back. "They've been here the longest. They only have what the Germans give them."

What the Germans give them is the same as what the Germans give us. At dinner I line up with the others for another round of anemic soup and half-slice of petrified bread. The water comes from a pump in the compound and smells of sewage.

"Easy on the champagne, there, fannigan," Collins says to me. We are sitting with our backs to the hut, faces in sunshine, as if the heat of the afternoon might make up for the paltry and disgusting food.

"You can call me Fannigan if you want, but I'm not Irish."

"Everyone's fannigan here," he says, smiling. "*Kriegsgefangene!* Prisoners of war." He dips his bread in his soup then rolls it around in his mouth to soften it. "Don't eat too much of this swill — not that you'll ever get a chance — but never skip a meal, either. If it's horrific just have a little. You have to keep something in your stomach." He has brought some forms for me to fill out. "They want to know what you are in real life. Be careful what you answer. They're looking for miners, machinists, farmers — anyone who might be useful to their war effort."

"I'm a lion tamer," Witherspoon says. "And Milne is a magician, and Findlay —" he searches among the group of lounging men till he catches Findlay's eye. "What are you, Findlay?"

"A dance instructor!"

Others begin calling out their professions.

"Butler!"

"Bullfighter!"

"Bellhop!"

"Sausage fitter!"

"A what, McGuire?" Collins calls back.

"I fit the sausage into the skin," McGuire answers. "And if you don't believe me, give me a whopping big helping of sausage and I'll fit it into my skin before you know what's happened."

Good-natured laughter. Great God, I think, we are almost men again. A band of fannigans.

"So what are you, Crome?" Collins asks.

"I'm an artist," I say with pride, and write in the word, then look at it in the hard sun of this dismal place.

Four

Justin Frame kept his offices in a tired little building off
Dorchester, about a forty-minute walk from our cold and
crummy flat. In the slush and ice of that winter, in an old
pair of shoes with rubber galoshes, my hat pulled down, coat
collar scarfed and buttoned, I made the trip a perfectly round
twelve times per week. I could have taken the trolley car,
but I was saving to move us up in the world. When I was
single I used to buy lunch quite often with the other fellows
from the office — with Gil Jenkins and Howard Lineman and
old Bruce Bannerman, who'd been working for Frame for
twenty-two years. Bannerman could sketch a woman's face,
hat, dress and gloves for a quarter-page advert in the *Gaz-
ette* in eight minutes while carrying on a loud conversation
about last night's boxing matches. Almost all Bannerman's
women had the same face — those imperial eyebrows, the
hard lines of their cheeks and lips — so they became known
as "Bannerman girls." Clients asked for them specifically.

Yet he was the first one old Frame let go. In the winter of
1930 all kinds of businesses were throwing out the engine
coal to keep from sinking further. Bannerman had a soft,

pillowy face red from drink, a nose that looked punched-in ages ago. Everything for his retirement had been in northern Ontario gold stocks that had evaporated the season before. But his daughter had married a banker, still employed, and they were going to take him in. The day old Frame told us the news we stood around Bannerman's cluttered desk and drank Scotch, and I thought about other winters I'd endured in other years.

"These times are not so bad," I said to them, and we all grunted and agreed. Even old Frame stood with us and drank. We might have been a herd of bison gathered around the water hole, shuddering out of the wind. I'd told old Frame about the pregnancy months before, and he'd shaken my hand and said how much he'd like to help. He would look at the books and see. If I'd just be patient . . .

Jenkins went next, towards the end of March. He'd been the last one in the door, hired in the spring of '28 when Frame was turning away contracts, we were so busy. Frame gave him the news at the end of the day — and mid-week at that — and there was no Scotch, we did not stand together like bison. "Oh no," Gil said simply, in a scared little voice, and his face grew pale the way I'd seen men's faces blanch in other circumstances. "Oh no," he said again and again.

A hard, late-season snowstorm had blanketed the city and clogged the streets and sidewalks. I walked Gil partway home. The snowbanks rose above our heads, and we slithered and slipped like slapstick figures from a blurry movie.

"You're lucky!" he said to me bitterly. "You've got Lillian and the baby on the way. Old Frame would never let you go."

"You'll find other work," I said. "I've seen this before. While everyone else is moping around, you figure out what needs to be done. It's panic and black thoughts that are so defeating."

"It's never been this bad."

"Of course it has. And worse. I know."

We floundered together until we reached his street, then I shook his hand and said that we'd keep in touch, though I knew I'd probably never see him again.

When I told Lillian the news she wiped her hands on her apron but did not turn to me. She was at the counter dealing with dinner.

"I think that will be it for the layoffs," I said lightly. "Frame's keeping the rest of us pretty busy." And I told her what Gil had said to me about my position in the firm, even though I didn't fully believe it. Howard Lineman had five years of seniority on me, three children and a sick wife. Frank Wilbrod had four kids. John Kent was looking after his mother and three aunts. But I thought perhaps Lillian would take heart.

"We should move to the farm," she said. "It'll be spring soon. Papa needs the help and we need to save money, in case." She didn't finish the thought but changed gears instead. "You were going to get us out of here anyway."

"I am. Just not yet. The price of everything's going down. Men with jobs look pretty shiny." I kissed her on the neck from behind and put my hands on her belly, which was in its first swollen bloom.

"You're all wet!" She pushed me away and I stood looking at her, so radiant with life.

"I want to have this child on my family's farm," she said in her plough-pulling voice.

"But Mireille is nowhere. It's got hardly anything — a few streets, the mill, if that's even still going."

"Of course it's still going!"

"But what else? What's there for me?"

"Everything it had last summer! You could still paint and fish and walk the trails. I thought you fell in love with Mireille when you fell in love with me."

"I did. I did. But let's not rush into anything. The patient man keeps his head."

"In the meantime what's his wife supposed to do?"

I held her then and waltzed her out of that darkened little kitchen. "Dance with me," I murmured in her lovely, tender ear. "Dance with me and enjoy the day."

We shuffled for a time. My dancing years were spent doing other things, and it showed. And there was no music, and the potatoes started to boil over on the stove. The whole worthless apartment smelled of the wet, of our bodies and clothes and our cheap, steaming food. Of our closeness, and of the hard, smelly city leaning in on us from all directions.

Lillian left my arms to tend the dinner. Sometime later she looked up and said, "What are you doing?" I suppose I looked as if I was just standing there, gazing off at nothing.

In the swampy fields outside of Raumen my prisoner clogs sink into mud and slip from my feet, until I kick them off and carry them. We have shovels on our shoulders and walk at a dead-slow fannigan pace.

"Drag your heels, boys," Collins says. "Slouch those shoulders. Bellies out!"

The air is slow, my limbs sluggish from hunger. Breakfast — awful acorn coffee and not much else — ran through me like a greasy splash of rain. At the far end of the field we come to the manure pile and the row of empty carts. A farmer greets our second German sergeant, Blasphemy the Great, a meaty slab of a man far larger than Sergeant Agony, who has stayed back at camp. Blasphemy confers with the farmer, while we lean on our implements and three guards with rifles watch us from a distance.

Then Blasphemy sputters his orders to us, pointing at the manure, the carts, the rutted pathway over to another field. Collins provides the translation.

"Now that's pretty clear, gents. We move the manure into the carts, and the carts along to the next field, then we empty the carts and return. *Nicht langsam*, understand? No foot-dragging. Our dear sergeant doesn't want anyone to lose their shovels like the last time. Williams, what's wrong with you? Where's your shovel?"

Williams looks around in bewilderment.

"It was here just a minute ago, Sergeant."

Collins sputters off in his own crippled German to tell Blasphemy that Williams has *already* lost his shovel. Blasphemy strides over to Williams and screams for a minute in his face, while Williams gazes around like a dumb animal. We all begin looking for the shovel.

"Now gents, we mustn't start losing the Kaiser's equipment like this," Collins says. We search under the empty carts and along the edges of the fly-ridden manure pile. McGuire and Witherspoon head back, slowly, along the path we've just come on.

"*Halt! Halt!*" Blasphemy yells, and then three guards train their rifles at them. They stop, their hands raised, and peer around innocent as crows.

"We thought he might have dropped it back here," Witherspoon says.

Blasphemy orders us all to start work immediately. Williams will have to dig and carry the manure with his hands. We head listlessly over to the pile. I stop to put my clogs back on. Some others lean on their shovels. Findlay carries a load of manure over to one of the carts, but spills the contents onto the side of the wheel.

Blasphemy explodes, with Collins beside him.

"Careful, gents! I don't want to see any more spilling of manure, and all of you there, *schnell, schnell!*"

Some minutes later Witherspoon announces that his shovel is gone, too.

"*Es ist verloren,*" Collins says to Blasphemy, shrugging his shoulders along with Witherspoon. "Has anybody seen Witherspoon's shovel?" Collins calls out, so we all begin looking on the ground. Findlay grabs my elbow, and together we start back down the rutted track.

"*Halt! Halt!*" Blasphemy yells again, and we stop and throw down our shovels, thrust our hands in the air.

Witherspoon's shovel is found, eventually, snapped off at the neck.

"This is certainly what I call shoddy materials," Witherspoon says, holding the broken handle and the shovel blade in the air for all of us to see. "Look at that. Rotted right through!"

"How can they expect us to shovel manure with faulty equipment?" Jenson says.

We all gather around to look at the miserable excuse of a German shovel. It's too much, finally, for Blasphemy. He races into us and grabs Witherspoon, then strikes him across the face with the back of his hand. Witherspoon staggers back, his nose bloodied, and smiles dopily at Blasphemy.

"Gently! Gently! Back up now, lads. Take it easy!" Collins says. The three guards with rifles ready surround us while Blasphemy vents.

Witherspoon picks up the broken shovel blade, sticks it into the manure pile and carries the slop over to one of the carts to dump it in.

"That's the spirit, gents!" Collins says. "*Nicht langsam!* We must fill up eleven carts of horse shit today. Eleven! That's *elf! Elf!* All in one day!"

Slowly we carry the shit over to the carts. For every two or three of us working, another four or five lean on their implements and share a smoke. Blasphemy goes over to stand with the three guards, who smoke and watch us with contempt.

We shovel and dump, shovel and dump, as slowly as we can get away with.

"I heard from Beatrice," Witherspoon says to me dreamily. "She's aching for me. *Aching.* She said she was walking down the street to her new job. She's doing the figures in the office where I used to work. Got a great head for figures." He is conjuring her for us with his singsong voice, as if the words could bring her out of this boggy field. "And the kind of figure that turns heads. She glimpsed some blighter in a uniform across the way and this is what she wrote. 'My knees fall a moment beneath me, to think it might be you.'" Our shovels deep in it, the flies building now because we are here. Witherspoon turns to me. "How about your Margaret? Are her knees falling beneath her when she thinks she catches a glimpse?"

"All the time," I mutter. "I cut such a romantic figure."

I throw my load onto the cart with extra vigour. The sweat seeping down my skin feels like the closest thing to a bath I've had since London — the dream of another lifetime.

"Don't we all cut romantic figures?" Collins says happily. He grins through a smear of slime on his cheek.

I stop talking because she — Margaret — is standing by herself some yards off, looking at me in her way, her face tilted as if about to ask a question, her gaze steady and firm. She shimmers in the air and does not speak, so neither do I.

The first of the carts is finally filled, and Witherspoon, Findlay, Kingsley and some others volunteer to push it over to the next field.

"Hurry up, lads! Come on!" Collins exhorts them with more dash than usual. "You can do it!" They burst into a run, the cart bouncing and chasing down the rutted lane.

"Sprint, you lazy bastards!" Collins calls, and the rest of us start cheering them on as well. Halfway to their destination the cart suddenly pitches into a pothole. Then, as the men keep pushing, it tips over and spills its horrible contents onto the grassy banks of the lane.

"Oh no. Oh dear!" Collins says, and with him we all trot over to view the disaster. For a time, Blasphemy simply stands at a distance, apparently unable to believe his eyes.

"How are we ever going to make our quota for the day?" Collins asks, while two wooden wheels of the upended cart spin slowly in the air in opposite directions.

I turn to see if Margaret is laughing. But she's gone, of course. Sunk into the rot of my brain.

Five

Mid-August, the sun so close and streets so cramped and steamy that all of Montreal felt like a kitchen endlessly boiling jam. It was a Saturday just before noon and I walked to the station directly from work. I tried hard to stay in the shade and strode as a man fleeing the city. The streets that day seemed even more filled than usual with milling, luckless men whose faces I did not want to see — men who shuffled dirt with their toes and stuffed hands in their pockets as if somehow holding themselves up, and who, from time to time, glimpsed themselves inadvertently in darkened shop windows.

"Ram!" someone said, but it did not seem possible that anyone could know me there. Not that particular day, when Lillian was meeting me at the train station, and we were heading down to Mireille for probably our last visit with her father before the birth. Lillian's belly was the size of a late-season watermelon by then, but she'd insisted I didn't have to come all the way home for her. There wouldn't be time anyway. The Mireille train left at 12:25.

"Ram!" the voice insisted, so I turned, although I didn't

stop walking. And I didn't see anyone who appeared to know me, so I walked on. But then a big hand on my shoulder brought me to a full halt, and attached to it was a strapping fellow in a fine suit, wide as a barn door, his meaty face covered in sweat, as if he had run several blocks to catch me. "It is you!" he said. "I thought so. Good Lord, I don't think I've seen you since Trafalgar Square. Your brother Rufus said you were here in Montreal, but I guess you don't go to any of the right parties."

I couldn't for the life of me remember him. Trafalgar Square? I'd only once in my life been in Trafalgar Square. For a moment I thought it was Johnson from my old unit. I'd met him in London that week of leave, but not at Trafalgar. Anyway, Johnson died in the slime of Mont Sorrel along with everybody else from my platoon. Everyone but me.

"Bill Kelsie," the man said, finally. "I was skinnier way back when. How are you doing?" It came back to me, but he kept talking anyway. "I lived just down the street from you in Victoria. I was a couple of years younger. And when I ran into you in London you were just back from — where was it?"

"Ypres."

"And I hadn't gone over yet."

I really had to keep moving. But Bill Kelsie was holding me still on the sidewalk.

"Isn't it funny what you remember?" he said. "When I met you that time, you were with three of the loveliest ladies I've ever seen. All to yourself! I wasn't going to bust in, but you could've given me a little something to work with —" He was kidding, squeezing my shoulder still.

"They were my cousins," I said. "My aunt and two cousins."

64

"Even worse!" He laughed as if it was unforgivable, our little moment in London on the far side of everything. I looked at my watch impatiently. I really was going to have to start running soon to get that train.

"Listen, Bill —"

"Rufus said you were taken prisoner. Same as happened to me, practically."

"I have this train to catch. My wife and I are going down to see —"

"It was before the Somme." Nothing was going to stop that mouth from spilling over. "I was doing some extra bayonet training with my friend Hayshaw. I figured we hadn't practiced enough, you know. Nothing can prepare you for what a real battle is like. But we had this freak accident. His bayonet went right through some important bones in my foot." He lifted up his shoe to show me, as if I might be able to see through the shiny black leather. "It's never been right since Hayshaw. They had an inquiry and everything. All above board. Everyone was cleared. Just one of those things. So in a way both of us got lucky. We both missed the worst of the war."

For a second I wanted to stamp my worn heel on his fortunate wound. Something in my face must have telegraphed my disgust.

"Anyway," he said nervously. "I do get into town from time to time. I'm in import-export." He fished a card out of a silver pocket case and thrust it at me. I took it and resumed walking towards the station. I couldn't help but notice that he didn't have too much trouble keeping up. His wind started to go before his foot. "And I heard about the new commission that's been set up to give you boys compensation," he said.

"Commission?"

"Government operation to get money from Germany for the prisoners who were mistreated. Apparently some were. Mistreated."

I told Bill Kelsie again about the train, about Lillian.

"You hurry on then," he said. "Don't want to hold you up. But you weren't mistreated, were you? Rufus said —"

"Great to see you, Bill." I shook his meaty hand, then legged on past him.

"Might be worth applying anyway," he said. "You never know. Nothing like government money in tough times. Rufus said you're working as an artist. That must be some trick!"

"I wouldn't touch it with iron tongs," I said to him, meaning the government money.

At the station Lillian was sitting all alone on a big, polished bench surrounded by our bags, biting her cheeks and staring at the door. When she saw me she dipped her head and rose — two hands under her belly to help lift herself up. "Sorry I'm late!" I said.

"I would have bought the tickets," she said in a quiet, angry voice, "but I didn't have enough money after the cab."

I picked up the bags — four suitcases and a hand basket — and hurried off to the wicket. I couldn't think of why she'd packed what must have been half the house. But I didn't want to say the wrong thing, so I stayed as quiet as I could.

"If only you'd left me enough money this morning," she went on. "But you said you'd be here in plenty of time." She was working up to a good, hard blow. I knew it yet couldn't help myself.

"I ran into someone on the street and couldn't get him to stop talking," I said.

"Who was it?"

We were almost at the wicket now. Two elderly women stood in line in front of us, chattering like a couple of crows on a telephone line. I glanced at the station clock: 12:22.

"Excuse me, ladies," I said. "My wife and I are late, and it's all my fault. I wonder if we might be allowed ahead of you? Our train leaves in three minutes."

They turned to eye me suspiciously. But when they saw Lillian in her enormous print dress they stepped aside.

"*Bien sûr*," one of them said. "*Après vous deux.*"

I paid for the tickets in a heat of urgency, but even as the ticket master was handing me my change I knew we weren't going to make it. "Let's wait for the next," I said.

"But we can still make it!" Lillian cried. She started struggling with the luggage herself while the crows and the ticket master looked on. I threw him a questioning glance, and he checked his watch doubtfully.

"You'd have to run."

I opened my hands. "Lillian, you're in no con —"

But she was already scrambling, with most of the bags clutched to her. I grabbed the basket and the one small case, which she'd left for me, and galloped after her. When I caught up to her I tried to wrestle some of the other bags from her, but dropped the basket in the confusion. Instantly, Lillian stopped to pick it up.

"We can catch the next train!"

"You catch it if you want!" she hurled back, then she was running again. She had the basket now, so I took the heavy bag. I was conscious of a crowd watching us with too much interest. At the platform the Mireille train was already pulling out, but slowly. I sprinted ahead and threw on what bags

I had, then ran back and took what I could from Lillian and threw those on as well. She just had the basket now, but the train was speeding up.

I wasn't sure she was going to make it. But our luggage was leaving. "Hurry!" I said. A conductor blew his whistle at us. Then I had her arm, and the car slid by us with no time to decide. I leapt for the moving step, pulling Lillian with me.

"Ramsay!" she said, struggling. She seemed to be trying to pull away. But then she grabbed the handrail and I hauled her up. Just in time as it turned out: the platform ended a few yards further on.

I hadn't been watching that part of the near-disaster, but Lillian had. Somehow we'd gotten away with it.

We found seats, and I hurried off to secure the luggage in a proper rack. When I got back Lillian was staring out the window as if she might never speak to me again.

"That was bloody reckless and stupid," I said. "I'm sorry for my part of it. We should have just waited."

"Why didn't you just give me enough money this morning?" she said, without looking at me. "You treat me like a child. Why couldn't you just come on time?"

My heart was still hammering and I found myself clenching my fists. "I might have left work early. But I don't want to give Frame any excuses —"

"Thank the Lord we're all still in one piece." She stared relentlessly out the dirty window as we chugged past the baking, steamy streets of the city, the tenements with their laundry waving over the fire escapes, the darkened, still factory buildings with half their windows broken in, the dusty patches of weed and rock lining the railbed on the way out of town.

I explained again about Bill Kelsie and the delay. When I finished I listened to the blessed clattering of the rails, and for a moment I thought she'd just leave it. But finally she said, "London again. Everything happened to you in London."

"A lot of things didn't happen in London." I was too riled up. I should have just stayed quiet.

"You yearn for her, don't you?"

"What are you talking about?"

She turned her gaze on me full bore. "Why didn't you marry her if you wanted her so much? Is she too close a cousin?"

"I married you," I said in a quiet fury. "I love you."

"Yes, the fat cow!"

We were picking up speed now, climbing the bridge over the St. Lawrence before hurtling south. The sun on the wide water shone painfully silver, and all the ships looked rusted and old. We wouldn't get to Mireille soon enough. Not for me. I could not stay quiet and I could not fight. I took Lillian's hand and held it warmly between my own. "You are more beautiful, more full of life now than even when I met you, and when I met you I thought I'd never seen anyone so radiant. Anyone. All right?"

She looked down at our hands together.

"But still you pine for her. What did she do for you?"

"Nothing!"

She turned her gaze out the window again, and I turned my body away and glimpsed, with my rattled eyes, a man I was certain, for a moment, was Collins making his way up the aisle. I almost called out. But it wasn't the Collins I first met who'd come to get me in the hospital, or the Collins at the manure pile leading the lead-footed fannigans. It was the later Collins, after the guards had beat him for our schoolboy pranks, after his days in solitary. It was Collins suddenly old and spent, Collins in defeat, Collins broken but still standing, a sad rumour of himself.

The ghost of that Collins shuffled past. I stared at the space where he'd been, Lillian kept her eyes trained out the dirty window, and we did not say another word the next fifty miles.

"Now then, lads," Collins says softly, his weak voice barely carrying to the back row where I stand out of the bitter wind. I'm trying to stay still but my limbs are in a ragged retreat from the cold. "There is mail, apparently, but we must earn the right to see it. If we can all stay still and silent —"

"Oh, Jesus Christ!" Witherspoon kicks at the dirt two rows ahead of me. Others turn their heads and mutter.

"Shh! Quiet!" Collins pleads. "The more fuss we make, the longer we'll have to stay out here. I was told —"

He is such a small man, and his cheeks have fallen in from the hunger of this winter, from that and worse, what the guards have done to him, but his eyes are in a desperate dance like the last candles on a Christmas tree.

"Why the fuck aren't Agony and Blasphemy standing with us, then?" someone challenges. I crane to see who it is: Napier, a new arrival who stands half a head taller than even Witherspoon. It's a wonder either of them survived the trenches.

"They want us to think about our conduct," Collins says, pronouncing the words carefully. "Now, we can stay out here and freeze or we can get our mail fairly quickly, I imagine, and go back inside to read it. Which would you rather do? Let's pick our battles, gents."

The moaning and muttering dies down. It's impossible to stand still, though, in such a wind. We have to shuffle our feet to keep from freezing, slap ourselves and shove our hands into pockets. Our ranks close slowly, unconsciously, as we become one organism against the cold, one man's heat reaching out to another's, a wall of backs sheltering those behind.

With Collins standing bent and alone out front. I don't know how he stays upright. Even the Russians have gone inside to get away from this chill, and they're so desperate they usually stand through anything just to watch us get our mail and parcels. Someone always slips them something.

A man collapses in our front rank — Lennox, who is pulled to his feet again but can barely manage to keep standing. Collins orders Williams to shift places with him, and some of the others help him back to the relative protection of the inner ranks.

"There better be bloody good mail," Williams mutters, and the rest of us take it as an excuse to begin talking again, to openly stamp up and down, to slap our arms and blow breath on our freezing fingers.

"Lads! Calm now," Collins says in alarm, almost ready to shout. "I'm sure it won't be too much longer."

It is long. It's as long as the war, as any of our lives. The dull excuse for a sun crawls its way across the painful sky, and our teeth clank together, our blood abandons all but the core of our most vital organs. In one of the windows of the administrative building across the compound, tucked safely behind barbed wire, we spot the two tiny figures, Agony and

Blasphemy, who appear from time to time to look out at us.

We call. We yell. We scream our lungs out and jump and wave our hands.

"Lads, lads," Collins says again in a failing voice. "We've been out here this long. I'm sure they'll come. A few more minutes!"

"Who gives a shit about mail?" Sherwood says.

"There probably isn't any after all," someone else calls. "They threw it away. If I know those —"

Two grey-clad figures appear in the distance, slowly marching towards us. The larger one, Blasphemy, has a sack over his shoulder.

"Steady up, lads!" Collins says.

The closer they get the slower they walk and the colder the wind seems to blow. Collins salutes just over Agony's shoulder, straight to the lamppost, and reports in his fractured German. Blasphemy lets the mail sack slip onto the ground. Then Agony begins one of his standard harangues, pausing occasionally to let Collins provide a minimal translation.

"It's all about obedience, boys," Collins says. "Discipline. A modern army is based on discipline and we haven't any, which is why we're all prisoners and why Germany is winning this war so handily. Humour him, lads. It's all about *Arbeit*, this life is *Strafe, Strafe!* We'll make it much easier on ourselves when we learn to follow orders. And on and on, more words than I can follow. Look concerned, lads, look like the sharp fighters you are. That's it. That's bloody it. If we weren't such bloody fannigans we'd have our mail by now."

Agony begins pacing, and even Blasphemy starts to look uncomfortable in the biting wind.

"Now we're on to the Fatherland. Bear with it, boys, it

can't last forever. But the Fatherland is full of genius scientists, you see, and other great minds . . . and they know about discipline. They're all champion athletes, you get the idea, yes, yes, the Fatherland. Look reverential."

"Why don't you cut the fucking crap?" Napier calls out.

My eyes are on Collins, on how his shoulders shudder at this new trouble.

Blasphemy drags the offender out of the ranks and throws the tall man on the frozen dirt. Three times quickly he kicks him in the groin, then methodically, several more times, in the stomach and ribs. Napier lies groaning and spitting blood and we stand and watch, unable to move.

Collins turns his gaze slightly away in the practiced manner of a veteran fannigan.

"The German soldier," he says softly a little later, when picking up the translation, "is so much superior to any English mercenary swine. That is why the war will eventually be won by the Fatherland."

Hours later, it seems, the letters are distributed. Blasphemy hands them one at a time to Agony, who examines each envelope minutely, then hands it to Collins, who reads out the name. Then the soldier marches to the front, salutes the lamppost, receives his envelope and marches back. The name on the next envelope isn't read out until the previous man is all the way back in ranks, even if that next letter belongs to the very same person.

"Crome!" Collins calls finally, and I march out, determined to make a show of it. But my limbs feel stuffed with frozen straw, as if they'll crack away with too much movement.

The halt, the salute. I look steadily past Agony's face. Wait for the proffered envelope before extending my hand. Not

Mother or Father's handwriting. *Hers.* In a second it's as if hot oil has flushed through my system.

I march back, the envelope waving in the cold wind like a talisman to ward off all evil. My first letter from Margaret. I'm dying to tear it open immediately. To hell with it all! A letter from Margaret!

Instead I stand still as a post. Napier remains on the ground, moaning dully, and Witherspoon has received three letters from Beatrice. He is muttering beneath his breath, "Come on, fuck, come on, get this *over with.*"

But only when all the mail is distributed are men allowed to carry the fallen Napier off to the clinic, to read their messages from home.

Finally we march into our smelly compound with the one bare light suspended from the bleak board ceiling, the oppressive rows of rough lumber bunks, the overflowing shit buckets fore and aft. The paper of the envelope is so thin and delicate I am fearful of ripping it to shreds in simply holding it. But I manage to pry it open and then gorge myself on her words like a starved wolf tearing into a carcass, swallowing down whole paragraphs without reflection, just to taste the fact of it: a letter from Margaret has arrived here in hell.

Then slower, slower, I read the words again, sitting on the edge of my straw mattress, up above Witherspoon with his mound of mail, over which he is weeping like a man who has dug up lost treasure. My one blanket is wrapped around my whole shaking body.

Dearest Cousin Ramsay,
   I have written to your father in Victoria and now
he writes back with this new address for you which I

hope is the correct one. As soon as we learned that it was possible that you were captured rather than killed, Emily, Mother and I sent off packages in your name to a number of different camps that we know of. You will remember that our foundation has been involved in sending packages to prisoners, but I can tell you that is no guarantee of our knowing anything or being able to help promptly. It is often a nightmare to get packages to the proper men even when we know for certain where they are.

I can't tell you how overjoyed we were when we learned the news that you had survived. Father paced up and down the hallway bellowing (in his way), "He's alive! He's alive!" when the cable came from your mother. We cried and laughed and Mother spilled the potted plant she was holding.

So much bad news arrives by cable these days.

The first word (perhaps you have heard this) was that you were dead. Father was certain you had given your life defending General Mercer. The accounts of the battle in the newspaper were at the same time horrific and so sketchy as to drive one mad for want of facts.

I am devastated to learn of Thomas and Will. I know your parents have written to you already and so this is not news. But I regret terribly that I never met them, and —as you well know —that this awful war ever had to take place. The losses for all of us are incomprehensible.

But you are safe! Please know what joy the news has brought us, even though we are concerned for your health and welfare. I am sending under separate cover a package of food and basic necessities. Please write as soon as you can —I fear I cannot believe the news until something has arrived in your hand.

I am sorry this is such a frazzle. I will compose some-
thing more worthwhile at another time. But let me speed
this to you with all our love.
          Sincerely, your cousin Margaret

p.s. Emily is sending her own letter separately, and I
imagine you will hear from Mother as well, and perhaps
even Father, who was so taken with you while you were
here, Ramsay. He would never say it but I'm sure he
now thinks of you as a son.

I've had many weeks already to absorb the news of Thomas
and Will, yet it still doesn't seem real. Now the mention of
their names freezes the air in my throat. And then — *He's*
alive! He's alive! — I can picture Uncle Manfred in his sus-
penders, his jowls flapping, eyes bright with excitement.

We cried and laughed and Mother spilled the potted plant
she was holding.

But what about you, dear Margaret?

Please know what joy the news has brought us.

What about you?

I fear I cannot believe the news until something has arrived
in your hand.

"Witherspoon!" I call down. "Do you have any extra
paper?"

Witherspoon lies buried in pages. "My mother-in-law is
complaining of the gout. Beatrice is thinking of joining me
here. Crome, would you give up your bunk for her?"

"Trade me some paper and the bunk is hers!"

Witherspoon hands up a measly single sheet, and then I
borrow the stub of a pencil from Bildersley, who smells as if
he is coming apart and will soon be simply a pile of ooze on

the floor. Against my knee I write *Dearest Margaret,* and look in astonishment at the raggedness of the letters.

> *You mustn't worry about me. I am safe where I am and cannot complain — at least not too bitterly — about the treatment I have received.*
>
> *Far too much has happened to be able to write. But please write to me — write anything that comes into your head. Write whatever would make me feel as if I were sitting next to you in conversation on a pleasant day in the park.*
>
> *But I must know — how is Boulton? I got a letter from Emily before capture — it seems like a hundred years ago — and she mentioned you are now engaged. Is it true?*
>
> *My thoughts are yours, war or no war. I feel …*

I am at the bottom of the reverse side of the tiny paper, the words getting squished further together.

> *… as if there is everything to talk about and no way to do it. Love, Ramsay.*

An envelope costs me my last four cigarettes.

I read her letter again and again, marvel at certain phrases, at the look of the words, the feel of the paper in my cold hands. Of course I think of Boulton, the lucky blighter with his banged-up knee — injured at a meeting of conscientious objectors, of all damned things — going off to his government office every day. What could Margaret possibly see in him?

He's there with her, that's all. He's there and I'm not.

Just before lights out I gaze up at the crowded, smoky, suffocating barracks, at all of us huddled in our blankets, our ragged clothes, the one little wood stove at the opposite end of the room barely sending out heat. The quiet in this room could fill a church, I think, could trick death for a moment into passing us over as already claimed.

Six

"There's Papa!" Lillian said. For a moment I looked out the train window at the old blue hills rounded like shoulders hunching to the south, at the quiet little station with its fading paint the colour of rotting leaves, and at the dirt road leading up the rise away from the lot where no one waited but a thick man in a straw hat and dusty clothes, sitting high on his tractor. "Papa!" Lillian yelled through the opened window, and waved and laughed when he waved back, arcing his hat high over his head.

I waved and laughed along with them, relieved to be there at last.

As soon as the train stopped Lillian bolted from it like an unbroken horse while I collected the bags. I called after her to be careful, but she might as well have been that horse. "She's going to drop that baby if she keeps running like that!" a matronly woman clucked behind me. She was encased in a woollen suit stiff as armour, and her legs looked as if they could support a piano.

"It's going to be our first," I found myself saying.

In the lot Mr. McGillis gripped my hand. "It won't be long

now," he said grimly. "What do you think, Lillian?" His face was pale and faded as an old cedar post, not sunburnt earth-brown the way it normally looked.

"The doctor says three weeks yet," Lillian called back. She was already in the hay wagon behind the tractor, and hauled up the luggage I handed her. All the tension of the train ride seemed to have evaporated.

I pulled myself up beside her. My father-in-law started us off, the tractor spewing black smoke and moaning like a sick beast.

"What's wrong with it?" Lillian shouted over the noise.

"The bank wants her, that's what's wrong!" Mr. McGillis called back.

We topped the rise, then churned down into town, the old Mill Road winding as always past the tavern, the leaning frame of the general store, past houses huddled together like old men playing checkers, past the river, so brown and slow at the first curve, then so suddenly narrow and swift by the old stone mill, past the bridge and up the hill on the other side, away from the town centre.

"Everything all right in the city?" Mr. McGillis called back without turning around.

"It's fine, Papa!"

"Still got that job, Ramsay?"

"Still employed!" I called back.

Lillian touched my face, then. We were lying back in the hay. We might have been on our honeymoon again, heading to that wretched cabin — but before we knew that Rufus hadn't even seen it for himself, that he'd taken someone else's word for it. Before we figured any of this was going to be difficult, disappointing or bitter for either of us. Her clear blue eyes were nowhere but on my face, scanning it for something. "I'm sorry," she said so quietly I had to strain to hear. "I'm sorry I get so angry."

"You've got an excuse," I said, patting her belly. "And I should be looking after you better. Maybe we shouldn't have come."

"But this is exactly where I need to be!"

We followed the road out of town, past fields and wood-lots till we came to McGillis's farm. It all looked much the same as it had the first day I'd blundered onto the place, a little more than a year before. Sam, a greying German shepherd, sniffed his way out to greet us as the tractor and wagon stopped before the swaying front porch, with its worn, cracked boards. Lillian nearly hurled herself off the wagon to embrace him. "Careful!" both Mr. McGillis and I called, but she just laughed and rubbed her face in the dog's old mug.

The screen door still sat ajar, with even fewer traces of ancient green paint than it used to have. The mottled rocker still looked as if it would turn to dust if anybody tried to sit in it.

"Ramsay, walk me down to the stream! Before we do anything else."

"Before lunch?" In the rush to make it out of the office I hadn't eaten.

"Before anything! Pa, will you come with us?"

I unloaded the luggage and basket and moved it all the few feet to the porch, then dropped it by the steps.

"You lovebirds go ahead," Mr. McGillis said.

She was Lillian again at a stroke, like some wilting cut flower magically replanted and brought back to life. We almost ran down the trail to the stream. The hot August sun reached through the tall branches of the pines and poplars and dappled the soft mosses. It was past mosquito season then, past blackflies, a respite. When we broke through the forest shadows to the stream edge the sunlight hit us as if bounding off a new tin roof.

"That's the rock where you were sitting!" Lillian said, and she went over to it and sat down, half-facing the cool waters where the stream pooled. "You had a trout when I came up."

"Yes," I said, and approached her as if she were me and I were her.

"Then you heard me coming." She stood suddenly on the rock. I reached out my hand immediately. "It's all right! You stood just like this. You didn't know whether to concentrate on the fish or on me."

"Be careful."

"Then the fish went over there —" She pointed to the spot farther on, where the current picks up.

"Lillian —"

"Then you twirled like this —"

She spun herself and I grabbed for her but felt my shoes suddenly slipping on the wet rocks. It was her grip that held me up — again.

"And I caught you! Just like this!" she screamed. "And that's when you asked me. You just blurted it out."

The sunlight on the water was so bright it nearly sang, just as it had been the year before. A day almost exactly like today.

"You don't regret it, do you?" she asked suddenly.

"Of course not, darling."

She looked away, and the greyness of the city seemed to

settle again between us — the knowledge of it at least. I took her hand. "The sun is out. There's enough to eat at home. We're having a child. How could I be happier?"

"I don't know, Ramsay," she said quietly.

I threw a rock in the water and waited a decent time before suggesting we head back.

At supper that evening Mr. McGillis scraped his bowl like a fannigan and sopped up the last dribs with Lillian's biscuit, murmured and slurped and smacked his lips. Then he spooned out more for himself before either Lillian or I were even halfway through our first helpings. "You found your mother's recipe," he said.

"It's just tomato soup," Lillian said. "And it's my recipe."

"Well, it makes Maisie's taste like bilge water."

"I'm sure hers is perfectly fine. And you'd starve if she didn't feed you. Any meal I've ever had with her was absolutely fine."

"The woman has her notions," Mr. McGillis said darkly. He paused for a moment and let his eyes lift from his bowl. "She considers herself the only one doing the Lord's work. She'd elect herself chief apostle if she could and send all the rest of us down to hell."

"Well, she hasn't charged you a cent for all the meals she's cooked since I left," Lillian said.

"Yes, that's right. She hasn't charged a cent. It's all going into her heavenly bank account." Mr. McGillis turned to me. "I try to keep the Lord in my thoughts as much as the next, but some take it straight up the flagpole and try to live there.

This Maisie Campbell doesn't want me to have any other book but the Bible in my house. She spoons out the stew, then tells me how soon I'm heading down into purgatory if I don't start cleaning up my —"

"Papa," Lillian blurted, "Ramsay and me want to move in with you!"

I dropped my spoon.

"I'm sorry, I just have to say it, it's so obvious. We could save a lot of money even if Ramsay takes the train, and I'm already cooking for Ramsay, and I will be for the baby, so I might as well cook for you. And there's lots of room. I could work the garden and help with the —"

"Lillian!" I said. "Who decided all this?"

"I'm just saying it!"

"Children," Mr. McGillis said.

"I don't want my baby growing up in those sickly rooms!" Lillian said to me. "I can grow vegetables a lot cheaper and a lot better than what I can buy in sorry old Montreal. And it's easy to keep a few chickens and a pig, and there's so much room here. You said so yourself! Maybe Frame would let you do some of your work from here." Lillian's face looked pinched and red, as if she were determined to head-butt her way through every obstacle.

"Children," her father said again.

"It all makes sense and I know I'm right. It's what you want, I know," she said to him. "This farm is too much for one person."

"This farm is not mine anymore," he said. We sat stupefied, as if a sudden wind had blown off the roof and opened us up to the evening sky. "I'm sorry. I knew you'd be upset, so I wasn't going to tell you right away." He broke off some more biscuit, lathered it in butter, then wiped his bowl clean again. "It's the bank, of course. The money for that blasted tractor, but also some more that I borrowed to build the new barn — which, you're right, I never did build. Instead I gave it to Peter Grimsby to invest for me in a surefire thing. Which sure did fire, it surely did."

Lillian hit the table with her palm. "What are you talking about?"

McGillis's eyes looked like swamps in the cold light of morning. "The farm is gone," he said. "I'm out at the end of the month. Don't worry, I'm not coming to Montreal to crowd up your little place. Maisie Campbell has offered to room and board me. All I have to do is listen to her. It's a sentence I deserve."

"Who's Peter Grimsby?" Lillian asked.

McGillis drank down his water and tore off some more biscuit and the evening unravelled like a ball of barbed wire as we disentangled each cutting truth. He'd laid it all out in the beginning, but we had to go over it again and again — the explanation of Grimsby, of the loans for the tractor and the barn, of the mishaps and miscalculations, the risks, the sudden collapse of the house of cards. For all our questions and his explanations, for all the tears and trouble, it always worked out the same.

"So you see, I'd love to have you come and live here with me," he said sadly. "But that's not God's plan, now is it?"

That night we lay awake in the small bed in Lillian's old room. The mattress was just large enough for us to spoon together on our sides, Lillian holding herself rigidly, her back to me, staring holes in the wall.

"We'll be all right," I whispered. "I have work, we're not in debt. We won't live for long in that crummy flat. We can buy a place out here — maybe even this property. The bank will own it, but I don't know that a lot of people have extra money these days. It'll just go to weed for a time, that's all. And if we can't buy this place, then another nearby."

She was shivering now, her body somehow cold in the heat.

"I know this is hard news. But there are ways through it. With a few breaks, if we keep working ... "

"I wish the baby wouldn't come," she said suddenly, in a wounded voice small as a bone in the throat.

"You don't mean that."

She willed herself still, still in the grey shadows.

"Of course the baby's going to come. Now we have something to work for. I didn't see it before. But you were terribly right. We'll make it back here. It's a perfect spot to love and grow. Now we both know it. And that's a step right there. Do you understand?"

She didn't even seem to be breathing. I placed my hand on her belly and felt, with relief, the soft kicks and turns within. I kept talking gently, holding her until the shadows were too long to contain and I could not fight anymore the pressing silence of sleep.

Letters, food, work. Hunger, love, sweat. Fatigue and hatred. This bloody cold bunk rife with fleas and mould and rot. And the ragged edge of want cutting at the throat like a rusty razor sewn into your collar.

Just little cuts. But every tiny movement worn with blood.

Dear Margaret,

I am enclosing a charcoal sketch of our barracks. If for some reason it is deemed a military secret, here's what you'll have to imagine. The wooden bunks ranging in rows are so crowded together there is barely floor space for a man to stand. The sleeping pallets are filthy, ragged and losing their straw. One thin blanket is folded in precisely the same way on the foot of each bed. The window has cracked or broken panes. There is a single, dull bulb hanging from the wooden planking of the ceiling. In the far corner is a small wood stove that throws no heat and in the foreground a bucket too small for the night sewage. What I could not show: the stench of an open toilet, unwashed men, rotting linen; the despair of endless days; the sanctuary of night and sleep; the unspeakable joy of receiving mail.

Unspeakable joy? For a few moments, perhaps, while the envelope is being held, while all is possibility still and not actual words on tangible paper. Father writes with his curt list of practical advice — the importance of staying clean, of maintaining one's sense of perspective, of remaining realistic about the future course of the war. *For it will not last forever, and there will be rational life again, perhaps in just a few months. But I know how fast a collection of hard men lumped together*

*in rough circumstances can turn rancid. So you must keep
your head above, no matter how dismal the surroundings.*

And Mother writes her few words at the end: *Loving and
hope from all of us dear, dear Ramsay* on pages wrinkled from
tears. And young Rufus says, *You must know from the news
that we are whipping their hides daily, and I'm sure you'll be
home soon! In the meantime I am using your bicycle to deliver
groceries to which I'm sure you won't object.*

And this from Margaret's sister Emily:

*We think of you constantly, especially Margaret,
though she would never say it. She seems so set on
martyring herself in marriage to Henry, as if that act
alone could bring the world closer to peace, though of
course it is breaking her spirit, and if you were here …
Well I don't want to say too much, although as you
know discretion was never my forte. But if the war did
end soon — not that it will, but if it did — and you
came right away, then I'm sure the sight of you would
shake her back to her senses. For something did happen
between the two of you when you were here, didn't it?
Margaret will not say a word to me, even in strictest
confidence, and yet after you left she moped about so,
and when the news came that you'd been killed — well,
you've never seen such a fit of carrying on. When Lord
Kitchener died at sea we got the barest comment from
Margaret over breakfast. But when your black news arrived — if the house had been bombed by Zeppelins she
would not have been more upset. She loves you, Ramsay
— I'm telling you plainly because she never would.*

Witherspoon, who makes it his business to keep up with my love life, reads over the letter, his hairy legs swinging from the edge of my bunk, his big eyes squinting in the poor light to make out Emily's cramped words.

"Sisters," he says. "Very tricky waters. But let me see if I've got this straight. Emily is the older, ugly one, right?"

"No — she's younger, maybe even prettier. In a conventional way. She has reddish, curly hair and thinks herself a bit of a painter too. I'm afraid I criticized her work before I realized it was hers. It was hanging on the wall, one of those fussy landscapes the eye passes over."

Witherspoon digests this information without taking his eyes off the page. "So she hates your hide," he concludes finally. "Now, where's your latest from Margaret?"

"Actually, I think Emily fancies me."

"That's why she's telling you all about how Margaret loves you?"

Witherspoon is hard to resist like this. His dark eyes press in, and for a moment he makes me feel as if talking like this might somehow bring the better world right to the gates of the camp.

"The last night I was in London, she threw herself at me somewhat."

"Somewhat?"

"She crept into my bed in the middle of the night. I had to kick her out."

"You threw the young, pretty one out of your bed the night before returning to the front? Because she wasn't Margaret?"

Trust Witherspoon to frame the stupidity of it.

"Would you sleep with Beatrice's sister?" I ask quietly.

"At the moment I think I'd sleep with Beatrice's dead Aunt

Gertrude!" he says gleefully before returning to the letter at hand. "So, Emily is in love with you and is jealous of her older sister. Why would she write to say how much Margaret is pining for you?"

"Because Margaret *is* pining for me."

"No! No, no, no," he says, shaking his head. "That's too simple and straightforward and honest. We're dealing with women here. Sisters at that. Emily is writing to torment you because you kicked her out of bed your last night in civilization. And she wants to punish her sister for being happily in love with what's his name."

"Henry."

"Henry the civil service shirker, who's not only going to have body and soul together after this war, he'll be employed too and miles ahead of any poor returning sod. Emily can't even get herself a Henry, so she's poisoning her sister's well and persecuting you at the same time."

Witherspoon wipes his hands with the satisfaction of a great psychological detective. "But," he continues suddenly, "the young, pretty Emily obviously also still cares for you a great deal, and one encouraging letter from you and she'd agree to marry you in a heartbeat. You'd have someone in the flesh, beautiful, charming, passionate, an artist at that, waiting for you at home when you get out of this hellhole. Instead of pining for her older sister who's marrying what's his name anyway. *And,*" he says, his eyes darkly lit with this last thought, "you'll have someone to dream about while you're here. She'll send you gushing letters and marvellous parcels stuffed with chocolate and bully beef and good English cigarettes. And when you get back to London you can see whether you still like her or not."

Witherspoon slaps my leg in self-satisfaction. "How did you leave things with this Emily? I hope you apologized over breakfast or something. She isn't really furious with you, is she? Can it be overcome?"

"I painted her portrait."

"Excellent!"

"Her nude portrait," I say quietly.

Witherspoon laughs suddenly, and others now stir and stop what they're doing to listen in. Card games pause, other fannigans hesitate in their cigarette-rolling, their letter-writing, their mumbling to themselves as they stare off into the gloom or pore over the same tired novel they have read and reread time and again.

"She posed for you in the nude?"

"No. But I painted her that way."

"You are full of surprises," Witherspoon says. Then to the others he calls out, "Crome kicked her out of bed, but then he painted her in the nude!" Roars of laughter. "So she really does despise you. That's why she's writing to torture you over Margaret!"

"She told me she liked the portrait," I say quietly.

"Ah." Witherspoon subsides into silence, then calls out to the others, "The plot thickens!" He snaps his fingers. "Let me see her most recent letter," he says suddenly. "Margaret's, I mean."

"No."

"Oh, come on. This is too delicious to hoard."

"It's not for publication all over the screaming barracks!"

He becomes the humble Witherspoon, the apologetic one with the low, confidential voice. "You know how overexcited I get sometimes. Of course I'll keep it to myself. Completely. I'm sorry, man, sorry."

Several minutes of this, and so I hand it over finally.

Dearest Ramsay,

What a balm it was to receive, finally, something written in your hand. I can understand that you are unable to say much of your treatment and well-being, but if I may read between the lines it seems that at the very least you are away from the carnage at the Front.

You know my feelings about the war. You know too, I think, some of my feelings towards you. There is no sense in saying any more at this juncture than perhaps to thank God for providing some small personal relief in the midst of international calamity. I think I shall not sleep soundly until you are returned whole in body and the cannons have fallen into slumber.

I could fill pages I suppose of small details of our petty lives. We saw Chu Chin Chow *the other night, a show of great whimsy that almost was enough to divert our minds.*

And yes, Henry and I are officially engaged, although he seems more eager than ever to overcome his knee injury and enlist in some branch of the fighting service. He feels the lack of uniform keenly. All men like him are made to consider themselves cowards, even though he is doing important Ministry work, as you know. The theatre lobby the other night was lined with red hats checking men's papers and dragging off those unfortunates without an official excuse for being out of khaki.

Perhaps I have broken some kind of law just setting down that last sentence. We've been warned not to say much lest we give away secrets so I will stop.

Please write often and tell me as much as you can, of your feelings especially if the actual details of life must be left out. I sometimes think what is the point of our being here if we cannot share deeply what's in our hearts with our fellow men — with some special others at any rate.

Forgive me, please, my fumbling and incoherence. I find myself thinking about you for days on end as if I too were a prisoner.

Write!
Yours in captivity,
Margaret

Witherspoon absorbs it all in deepest silence. The card games, the cigarette rolling, the reading and staring and mumbling all resume.

"What are you going to write?" he asks finally, in a quiet little voice, not quite like his own.

Dear Margaret,

Paper is in great demand so I will not waste this sheet on the ugliness of life here. I wrote a letter to you once before going into battle — it seems ages ago now. But it's with my pack still, I imagine, buried in mud if it hasn't yet been blown to bits. In it I said that if I were at all whole and not a hound of hell as I have become (thanks to this God-fearing war) then I would urge you to forget about Boulton, to marry me, to be my muse and wife and confidante and the mother of whoever our children might be. So you see, those are my feelings, blunt as I have laid them out, but the hopelessness of stating them seems even more profound now than it did on the other side of the Kaiser's guns.

So, dearest Margaret, keep your Boulton out of the war, and love him as much as you can. But whatever happens please write back to me — your words are oxygen to my blood in this forsaken spot.

With love, Ramsay

Seven

Hard before dawn the damn rooster split the air with his squawks and screams, and I sat up suddenly in bed as if bombs were falling. For a moment I didn't know where I was. Nothing looked familiar: the needlepoint portrait "Our Lord & Saviour" on the wall, slightly sinister in the shadows despite the woolly white lamb and the calm blue eyes; the faded flowery chintz curtains trembling in the cool morning breeze; the white chest of drawers with the silver mirror lurking in the corner. Briefly, I imagined I was back at Stokebridge Street in London, that either Margaret or Emily was going to come through my door, perhaps with a tray of breakfast. That I could set my life here and wait in drowsy comfort before being dragged back to the present.

Then I heard Lillian and her father downstairs and forced myself out of the warmth of the sheets and into some proper clothes. The heat of the summer felt so broken it might never have existed or was at best a vaguely remembered sensation, the tailings of a dream. I hurried down the stairs and greeted father and daughter in the kitchen, which looked chaotic: the floor and counters were strewn with boxes and crates of dishes and glassware and old pots and pans, with cutlery and cutting boards and hand-knitted table mats from generations past. It would all have to be moved, sold or given away.

Lillian was frying bacon over the old black wood stove, and the smell of that and of the coffee percolating beside it ran through me like the memory of riches. I kissed my wife on the neck and asked how she had slept.

"I almost fell asleep," she said without turning around.

Mr. McGillis was at the counter with a screwdriver, scraping the rust off an old apple corer. He too looked as if he had not slept.

"I wish I didn't have to rush back to work. I should probably stay here and help with the" — I stumbled over the word. What was going on? A move? An eviction? — "transition," I finally said.

"There'll still be plenty to do when you get back," McGillis muttered.

Still Lillian did not turn around.

I walked outside. Sam, half-asleep on the porch, thumped his tail at my approach but did not lift his head. Some chickens were pecking in front of the house. I didn't know if they were supposed to be there or not. The whole world, even the outhouse, carried a silver coating of dew, and a careful mist hung low in the trees and bushes, brushed the tops of the fence posts and turned distances ghostly. When I got back inside Lillian had poured warm water in a basin and set out my shaving things.

"Will you come back tonight?" she asked. Her eyes were low, as if my face might be somewhere on the floor.

McGillis kept scraping at the apple corer.

"Of course. I don't want you to overwork here."

I reached for her, but she turned back to the bacon. She lifted the cast iron pan and poured the grease into an old mug on the stove. So I left her and wet my face, then quickly lathered the soap. This was McGillis's shaving spot, and the little mirror hanging on the wall was about half a head too high for me. I tilted it this way and that and managed to somehow see to scrape myself clean. Then I towelled off and dumped the water down the sink. I had to step around my father-in-law, who remained intent on cleaning up the apple corer.

"Why don't you just throw that out?" Lillian said to him.

"It's still good. Somebody could use it."

"Who?"

He didn't lift his head.

Lillian's father would not sit with us. I gobbled down the toast, bacon and eggs while Lillian sipped her coffee. It felt as if the food was falling into an empty well, as if I'd never be full or satisfied. Soon enough I had to go. Lillian held on to me for a time just a few paces from the spot where I had kissed her that evening, not quite a year before, when McGillis had given his permission and we were alone for a moment.

When I marched off for the train the air felt cool and fresh in my lungs, the sun washed the fields in a brilliant shine, and the entire morning seemed to propel me away from that sinking farm.

Witherspoon is going to escape. The news is passed to me in a whisper as I dig holes for fence posts in wet sod. The shovel is wet too; my legs are wet; the sod seems to extend into my foot, up my leg, into my blood and bones the wearier I get.

I stay quiet. A guard stands behind us not eight paces away.

Two feet down and water starts to seep into the hole. My shovel blade disappears into the mud. I listen hard, but can't hear anything more than the pelting of the rain, the grunts and mutterings of famished, exhausted men.

We walk back in our ragtag single file, guards at the front and in the rear as hunched and rain-chilled as the rest of us. I try to make out Witherspoon. Is he ahead of me? Most of us are indistinguishable, like so many soggy brown rats. But Witherspoon is so tall and walks with an unmistakable bobbing gait. He'll be missed immediately, I think. When's he going to go?

He must be behind me. I half-turn once, then stop myself — no use drawing attention. Just ahead of me is Collins, walking with his head down as he does now after his time in *Strafe*. His left eye has started to water and must be infected, but he will not go for *Kranke*. He's convinced the doctors would purposely blind him, and probably he's right. Witherspoon will be in for it as well if he gets caught.

Does he have extra food on him? Did he manage to get a map? A weapon of some kind?

Where is he?

The guards aren't watching particularly, but there's nowhere to go — fields stretch empty and desolate in every direction, with hardly a bush or fence post for cover.

So I lower my head, slog along and try not to think about it. But that is impossible. We're several days from the Dutch border, that much at least we know. Several days for a fit man, rested and fed.

Weeks maybe for the likes of us.

As we pass along a lane I look up just in time to see Witherspoon huddled in the bordering hedge. He winks at me, and I have no time to react. For a moment it's insanely difficult to not acknowledge him in some way. But then I'm past. My ears prick up, but I hear no whispered remark, nothing out of the usual. Someone coughs several paces back, but we are all hacking and wheezing these days.

We just keep walking. I wait and wait for the call of alarm, for the rifle shot, but we remain a soggy, smelly, moving mass of fannigans with our guards in tow, dulled themselves from work and weather. Maybe half a dozen of us could have slipped into the hedge and we wouldn't have been seen.

Back through the black and sorry gates of camp. Blasphemy assembles us as usual in front of the compound and begins the count. He is nearly asleep on his feet, and as he is walking past the back row Napier slips in from the middle, then forward again when Blasphemy makes the turn. Collins is talking to Agony about something — the *schlechtes Wasser* — the bad water, I am guessing. He holds his stomach in a pantomime of being sick. Agony listens for a moment, then unleashes a barrage of verbal abuse which Collins docilely absorbs. When it is done and Blasphemy is now on the front row with his counting, Collins starts up again about the *schlechtes Wasser*.

His voice is small and respectful and he keeps his runny eyes tilted away, as if Agony might slap him, which is quite possible.

Everyone else is silent, except for Blasphemy with his mumbling count.

Another torrent from Agony. Collins bows his head. *Danke,*

danke! he says and steps back, then salutes the lamppost behind Agony. He turns back to all of us.

"The water is perfectly good!" he announces. "Any illnesses we have must be the result of our poor personal hygiene habits. We will all wash more vigorously and try to keep vermin away!"

Blasphemy finishes his count and makes his report. The rain whips across our faces now. It is just as cold on them as it is on us.

Turn and go, I think. *Dismiss us.*

But Agony looks too long. He squints out from left to right. We never stand this still for him. We're never this polite.

"Come on, for Christ's sake!" I mutter — just loud enough for my voice to carry. "Let us get in and dry off."

"What are we waiting for?" Napier chimes in. "Noah's ark?"

The men begin shuffling, slapping their hands against their chests and legs. That's better, I think. Don't overdo it.

"Steady up, men!" Collins barks out, just before Agony explodes. We come again to a reluctant attention, then Agony launches into one of his favourite themes, the Fatherland's march to victory. Collins does his best to keep up.

"It doesn't matter what we throw at the German soldier," Collins translates, "one German division is enough to slaughter millions of English mercenaries. Look at what has happened at the Somme! And the French at Verdun — pathetic. The Allied generals might as well open mass graves for their own men and march them in. That is what is happening now at every battle. We are the lucky ones, yes, we received mercy. Nod your heads, lads. Yes, look grateful."

100

We are grateful. There is no recount. Agony works up our enthusiasm for the *Vaterland* for just a few more minutes, then we are on our own at last, trying to contain ourselves.

On the hill a few hundred yards away from the station I heard the whistle and the rush of the train as it approached from the south. I sprinted into the railway yard, past the dusty parking lot and through the old building and got there in good time, just as the train was pulling in. There wasn't much of a crowd: a few ladies in fine hats obviously heading off to town for a day of shopping, some other businessmen on their way back from their own country weekends, a couple of rough lads in working clothes perhaps going in to try to find a job for a few days. I already had my ticket. I had plenty of time and the sun shone so brilliantly just over the trees that I had to shade my eyes.

I suddenly felt no hurry at all. The ladies and gentlemen and rough lads boarded. I stood staring at the warm, blue hills. The engine puffed and snorted. It was a perfect morning for a train ride.

The conductor called, the train lurched ahead, I stepped aboard. The wind chilled my cheeks.

Last fall, catching this very same early train, I'd felt swimming at sea in a rock suit to be leaving Lillian behind. Why was I now in such a godawful hurry to put distance between myself and my wife?

I kept my eyes fixed on the platform. It was passing more quickly now, becoming a blur, rapidly running out. At the last moment I leapt off and staggered a step or two, then recovered myself. A few seconds later the last passenger car was past, then the caboose. The train disappeared around the bend, its black smoke curling still into the sky above the distant hills.

What was I doing?

I turned and walked back to the station. Nobody had seen me. I might as well have been completely alone in the universe, a puppet turning this way and that. The train whistle sounded — already a mile or more away.

I walked to the telegraph booth and composed and sent a message to Frame:

FAMILY MATTERS STOP WILL MAKE UP TIME
STOP THANKS CROME

"All right. Everyone calm down!" Collins says when we are safely back in barracks. "We have to give him a stumbling chance. Does anybody know anything about this? Did Witherspoon plan it all by himself?"

Nobody knows. Napier thinks Witherspoon had a knife and a compass stuck in his mattress, and they aren't there now. McGuire thinks Witherspoon was hoarding food and might have been sewing a pouch for it that he said was for tobacco. Findlay says Witherspoon got quiet all of a sudden after the last mail. "He only got one letter from Beatrice."

"One letter!" Eastman says. "That man gets more mail from his bloody Beatrice than the rest of us combined. So what if he only got one letter?"

"Maybe he'd had enough of the fine cuisine," Findlay says.

"Listen," Collins says, his voice still low but stiff enough

102

to bring us to silence. "We're all going to fry for this, and that's all right. But it does no good to keep bloody secrets. If anybody else wants to leg it home, then let us in on it so we can help and prepare. I've seen these solo skylarks before. They usually come to no good, and we all get *strafed* whether we knew anything or not. So we might as well know. Understood?"

Napier fishes something out of the little heating box, a half-burned envelope with Witherspoon's name on it. "Hold on!" he says, waving it in front of us even as it crumbles to ashes. "This is it! The note from Beatrice! She's either broke his heart or promised him something so wild he's chasing after her."

"Bring it here," Collins says, with enough steel chain in his voice to drag Napier to him. He takes the letter and examines it briefly. Then he returns the envelope to the heater and blows on the coals until it all goes up.

"Let's not become fucking animals," he says.

I could hear her cries some distance from the farmhouse, and began running then, although something else must have been tugging even before then. Why else had I gotten off the train?

Lillian was screaming as if her body were being torn open by machines. Yet her father sat on the front porch sorting through a box of rusted tools. "It's all right," he said calmly. "Maisie Campbell's on her way. And I've sent for the doctor."

"Is no one in there with her?" I yelled.

It seemed he pitied me, getting this upset over something like a birth. "It's not our place," he said.

I stormed into the bedroom. Lillian was kneeling on the bed screaming into the pillow, her hindquarters hoisted into the air.

"Lillian! What can I do?"

She'd shut her eyes and her muscles seemed coiled like twisted rope. She huffed and groaned, and the sheets beneath her were soaked.

"Is . . . is it coming?" she moaned.

I looked, but didn't know what I was seeing. A flash of pink amidst blood and hair.

"I think so."

A spasm drove the breath from her lungs. She grasped my arm and moaned again rapidly into the pillow. When the tumult had passed she said in a tiny voice, "It's killing me."

"You'll be all right."

She had not released her grip. She screamed again into the bed.

"You'll get through it. You'll forget how much it hurts."

She reacted then as if struck in the belly and sat up suddenly, then leaned against me, thrusting her chin hard into the flesh of my shoulder. I straightened up to bear the load.

When the spasm had passed once more she said, "What makes you . . . such an expert?"

She snapped her weight against my shoulder again so hard I nearly folded. I leaned into her and held on.

"Maybe . . . you should lie down."

Again and again, spasm after spasm, and where was the bloody doctor?

Her limbs were shaking. I eased her back onto the bed. Her

eyes were shut tight now and her face looked greenish. For a moment she seemed to loll back into a ghostly stillness. Then suddenly she screamed as if being torn within by shrapnel.

When the terror passed I looked again to see what I could of the baby. The pink slit was more pronounced now.

"That's better! The baby is coming. Slowly, darling, but the baby's coming!"

I don't think she heard me. I moved around to grasp her hand, and she lashed out suddenly and walloped the side of my jaw. I staggered back.

"Gaaaaawwwdd!" she screamed.

"That's better! Lillian, hang on, it's coming, it's..."

I could see more clearly now. The pink slit was a heel, not a head.

Maisie Campbell entered the room then. "What are you doing here?" she said, and I swear I could feel the cold wind on the back of my neck. "This is not your place!"

She was a tiny woman, brown hair twisted on her head and the tendons in her neck taut as wires.

"I'm the husband!" I declared.

"Then go boil water!"

She looked at Lillian splayed upon the bed. "I'll call you when the Lord has finished His work," she said.

Blasphemy bangs through the door just as I am shivering myself to a semblance of sleep. He comes with dogs and other guards, all of them barking. We shuffle as slowly as we can out into the rainy night. Then we stand, as ordered, in muddy pools and stare at the barbed wire growing grey in the dying light and listen to the howling of the dogs sent out to bring back Witherspoon.

The searchlight scans our features as the screaming of the dogs recedes further and further in the distance. I try to think of becoming a fence post — of planting myself far down in the ground and letting the stiffness of my limbs hold me up, whatever the elements.

Finally men begin falling, and we are allowed inside the barracks to moulder and shiver in our beds. The dogs come back to camp. The rest of the night I hear them sounding in and out of my dreams. When the bell rings in the morning and we are herded out — *Raus! Raus!* — I feel as if I was the one who'd been scuttling about in the wet and cold, waiting for snarling beasts to snap at my throat and haul me down.

Once again we stand as they count us over and over. Blasphemy in particular looks as if he's going to be assigned to shovel shit in a field himself — or much worse, to feed cannons at the front — if a single further one of us disappears into the dreary countryside. When he screams at us now his face is blood red.

It seems certain they will send us back out to the fields to work another day without any food whatsoever. Suddenly the barking resumes in the distance, but it is clearly different — yelps of triumph and self-congratulation. We stand and listen to the sickening approach. Gradually they come into view: this army of grey-clad guards with their pack of beasts on leashes and the stumbling, muddy, wretched soul, bound and hobbled yet made to march and kicked back to his feet whenever he falters.

There is nowhere else to look but at the spectacle of Witherspoon's torment.

Blasphemy goes on a tirade. Prisoners of war are bound to follow orders, to obey the German officers as if they are our own, to report for duty, not to violate the generosity of our hosts.

"Tolerate, lads," Collins says in a calm undertone, as he is translating. "Humour the misguided fool."

We are being fed and housed and protected while our fellow soldiers are dying in the slaughter of the Western Front. It is our great privilege to be afforded such treatment.

"To starve and shiver like rats," McGuire mumbles.

"Look grateful about it, boys," Collins says, his bad eye running, the rain giving his face a terrible sheen. "Think about what you're going to do with your lives when this nightmare is done."

The doctor finally arrived, later in the morning, and locked himself in the bedroom with my shrieking wife and that apostle of God, Maisie Campbell. Mr. McGillis puttered about the ruins of his farm, moving boxes of bits from here to there, then back again, and winding up odd coils of loose wire and stacking rotting lumber in corners of the barn unvisited since the invention of the automobile.

I stood by.

The water I boiled did not seem to be needed, the soup I heated went uneaten, McGillis seemed content alone with his boxes.

And Lillian's shrieks pushed like glass shards beneath my skin.

"This is the way the Lord has arranged it," McGillis said

to me on the porch, when I could not sit and I could not stand and the hours scraped by. "A breech birth could last all night. You might want to walk into town and have yourself a drink."

"I won't abandon her!"

"She might abandon you," he said ruefully. "All depends what Jesus wants."

A day and a night passed, and Michael George Crome was born, a scraggy kid with crow-black hair and a healthy set of lungs and wide, blue, irresistible eyes. Lillian lay back in the shadows, chalk white and exhausted, still as death. I sat with her hour upon silent hour, holding her hand, gazing at the boy, sick with love.

"I thought I was dying," she said to me, and felt my face with her chilled hand. "I thought I was going to be all alone."

"No. You were never alone."

She touched my cheek where she'd struck me. "You said you would never hurt me. Do you remember, on our honeymoon?" She searched my eyes. Of course I remembered. "Now look what I've done to you. We can harm each other terribly, can't we?"

"It's nothing," I said. "I hardly feel it."

"I can't bear to go back to Montreal. Do we have to bring Michael to those awful rooms?"

I stayed silent.

"Surely we can rent something better now. Frame will pay

you more now that you have a baby. I'll help you look. As soon as I'm stronger —"

I silenced her with a kiss.

"I just need a little bit of a garden. And Michael will need a yard to run around in. It doesn't have to be big —"

The boy was snuggled in my arms, wrapped in a blanket and sleeping like an old man.

"Ramsay, look at me! What's wrong?"

I didn't want to tell her. It felt as if we were all wrapped in our blanket.

"Why can't we get a better place? We have the money, I know we do!"

I kissed the baby and stared at his scrunched-up, brown little face.

"I just got the wire today," I said, as gently as I could. "Frame's gone under with all the rest."

Eight

I'd been out of work about eight months and was trying to make a thin pair of trousers last through another season rather than spend on a new pair now. But the cold March wind cut through them. Out of optimism I'd neglected to wear galoshes as well, and so my shoes were soaked by the sudden slush of a bad storm, and I had to fight my way up the street with my hand on my hat and my face lashed with wind and snow.

I was in no way prepared for what was waiting at the hotel. Father's message had said simply to meet him there. He had given his room number. When I knocked on the door he was a long time answering, and when it finally opened I barely recognized him: a shrunken, pale gnome, his body wracked with coughing even as he stood before me in his shirtsleeves.

"Father! Sit down!" He was so diminished he followed orders and meekly sat on the edge of the bed. In the dismal grey light by the window I could see better the craggy outline of his skull beneath a sagging face: the great beaklike nose, the prodigious steel grey eyebrows, the drooping ears and long teeth of age. His eyes were the most changed: their usual fierce light had given in. His hands were shaking and cold, his shoulders as thin as those I'd seen years before on starved men of many nationalities.

"How long have you been here? Have you seen a doctor?"

His chest heaved just to draw the slightest breath. I tried leaning him back on the bed, but he fought himself upright again and through motions with his hands, while hacking and spitting into his handkerchief, he made me realize that he needed to sit up to keep from drowning in his own fluids.

"Just ... just in ... from Managua," he said. "I was much better ... in the warm air."

"Does Mother know where you are?"

"I sent her a letter ... from New York." He hacked and coughed again, and the terrible shuddering recaptured his chest and shoulders. I drew the blanket round him and again felt the iciness of his limbs.

"I was almost done with the railway there ... in Rivas. But they ran out of money and then ... this hit."

"Have you eaten?"

He nodded then fell into another weak-breathed round of coughing. After it subsided I brought up a bowl of broth from the hotel kitchen. Gradually, as he sipped, he gained control of his voice and breathing.

"Have you found work yet?"

I shook my head. "I've heard of some openings. We're fine. Lillian and the baby are well." I did not tell him how little of the savings remained, how fearful we had become of each month's remorseless expenses.

"Everybody healthy?"

I assured him we were. "Except for a certain lack of sleep. Michael is a cherub by day and a howling terror at night."

"Montreal has always had rotten air. I'm sorry I brought you here when you were young. I suppose you've gained an attachment of some sort."

"There's work here. Or there will be again."

He looked at me dubiously. "It's a bloody awful system. And I'm not just saying that because I never won for long." He winced then as some stabbing pain ripped through him. Finally he let out a deep, exhausted sigh. "I've spent half my life waiting to get paid by one group or another. Bridges, harbours, tunnels ... those I can build. But trying to get paid ... now that's terrible work." He looked around as if just discovering his surroundings. It was not the finest hotel but not the worst either. The mattress was sunken and the curtains looked rat-chewed, but it had heat and the sheets were clean and pressed.

"Live in the country if you can," he said, and started wheezing again, his great fists doubled in a gesture of fight. Perspiration now bathed his face as if the soup had gone straight to his pores.

I found a towel by the sink and wiped his brow, and for some time he closed his eyes. He marshalled his considerable will to smother the cough into submission.

"Have you room for an old man?" he asked weakly. "And Mother too, when she arrives. I don't expect I'll last more than a couple of months." He stared coldly into his chilling bowl of soup.

"Yes, of course," I said. "Plenty of room."

He turned his gaze out the window. "I hate it when the workers are starved," he said finally. "I could have finished that line and the backers would have made their money." He took another deliberate sip of the broth. "Those rich bastards, they're not entirely ignorant men. They don't expect horses to work if they don't get fed."

Some days later Rufus arrived from Boston in a black coat and tie, as if he expected to be attending a funeral. As always his face shone like a polished apple and his eyes were full of the easiness of things. He had brought his new wife with him. She wore a cloche hat and pearls and fashionable brand-new shoes, and her eyes scanned our sorry flat quickly and with undisguised pity.

"You must be Vanessa," I said. "Hello, Rufus."

We'd missed the wedding. And now Lillian stood with the baby beside those two shiny, rich young lovers, looking as if she should be sent out to wash the potatoes. I was aware, acutely, of how tired her dress was, of the unwashed plainness of her hair, the hardness that had crept into her face over the accumulating months of bad news and rotten luck. She fit in now with the poverty of our surroundings, with the darkness of the room, the lack of running water and toilet facilities, the sheet pinned across the main quarters to make a stab at privacy. We both did.

Rufus too was examining things closely. "Are you *all* living here?"

Mother came out then from the other room where Father was sleeping. She'd grown stout in recent years and was not as easy in the limbs as she used to be. And with Vanessa she too looked nervous, afraid of offending. She shook hands formally with the tall, slender, pale young woman, then embraced her youngest son, Rufus stooping to envelop the round brown body that was so far from the Colombian plantation where Father had first spied her as a striking young girl.

"I'm so glad you coming," she said. She had been crying and crying for days, ever since she'd arrived from Victoria, and had hardly left Father's side. For hours, while he lay sleeping or semi-dazed, she would sit stroking his hand and weeping. And when he was awake he would insist that she pull herself together and read to her from Shakespeare and Homer, quietly nudging her when she dozed off.

Now I sat outside and smoked on the stoop while Rufus and Vanessa visited with the two of them. The sky was as blue and clear as it gets in Montreal. A group of children played stickball down on the street. The best hitter was a skinny girl with long legs who knew how to put every ounce of her little body into smashing that ball. They cheered and yelled and laughed while I felt numb inside, as if all my blood had turned to grease.

Rufus came out and sat beside me. He refused the offer of a cigarette. "Vanessa doesn't like me smoking," he said lamely. But his face was full of another thought. My cigarette was hand-rolled, not the fancy kind he was used to. I had a sudden memory of him showing up at my door shortly after he'd landed his first job: night accountant at the Ritz-Carlton. He was green as lettuce and I'd been to the wars and somehow he thought he would impress me with his new position. I asked him the pay — it was pitiful. "But think of the wealthy men I'll meet!" he said, his face already full of the accomplishment. Just the way he was looking now. Like a young scamp desperate to prove himself the better man.

He put his hand on my shoulder. "I'd like to bring Father and Mother to Boston. We have a much larger place, and the staff to take proper care — though I know Lillian is taking care. Of course I do. She's wonderful. But you have a baby, and this place is —"

He took note of my withering look.

"Why did you wait so long before telling me your firm went down? You know I still have contacts in this city. Or you could come to Boston. Not every business has been flattened, you know."

"The work will pick up," I said grimly.

He reached into the vest of his expensive suit. "At least let me leave you some money for expenses, for doctors and medicine. I know this must be draining and I'm certainly in a position to —"

"Your money is no good here," I said coldly.

"Don't be ridiculous! We're family."

What can you say to someone who has prospered in hard times by marrying well and charming his way through a world sick with troubles?

"I am the oldest now," I said stiffly. "I've handled far worse than this. Now put your pocketbook away before I rip it up."

The hand went back in the vest. The pocketbook was replaced by a silver cigarette case.

"Try one of mine."

I almost sent the case flying but looked away instead. The clatter of children increased. A young boy scooped up the ball expertly and hurled it back towards the flat rock that was serving as home plate.

"Just for a moment I saw Will," Rufus said. "Throwing to

115

Thomas. God, they were good together. I idolized you guys."

I finished my skimpy fag and took one of his fine, store-bought brand after all.

"That summer of the war was the very worst. Till now, I'd say," Rufus murmured. "First you were captured, and we were told you were dead, you know. Mother fell apart. You should have seen Father concocting schemes to get you out. He was going to study German and pose as a wealthy industrialist. He almost went crazy with it. I think he loved you the best. He saved everything you drew. Maybe you didn't realize —"

"Stop talking about him as if he were dead!"

"He was hard set against Alex joining. But with you captured and still alive there was no way to stop him."

The same boy had the ball again. He chased down the skinny girl, the one with the powerful swing.

"I knew I wasn't old enough to serve. I couldn't be a hero like you and the others. But I swore I would never let this family down. And I haven't. Ramsay, look at me! I'm in a position to help."

I flicked his cigarette away. Thomas and Will were swallowed in the soup of battle. Alex fell from dysentery behind the lines. I was a bloody fannigan. There wasn't a lot of heroism any way you sliced it.

Rufus shifted his weight. "Father tells me there's this commission for war reparations for the prisoners. You *must* sign up for that. There will be money for what you went through. You deserve it, Ramsay. You need it."

Now even the old man is grasping at straws, I thought. Government money! As if there could be any hope in that.

Without comment I stood up and left Rufus on the stoop to finish his smoke.

Father was in a bad way, tossing with the pain. Vanessa had taken over trying to do something for the gang of us on the coal stove. She was surprisingly dextrous in the kitchen — in such a pitiful kitchen — considering the most she probably did at home was give orders to her staff. Lillian stayed in the back room, feeding the baby, and Mother was wiping the old man's brow with a dampened cloth. He jerked his head suddenly and eyed me in a fit of clarity.

"Come here, boy!" he said in his old way, as if he had just set foot at home again after months of being off.

I stepped to his side.

"Leave us, Mother," he gasped. She did not move until Father tore the cloth from her hand and hurled it at the far wall. "I need to talk to my boy!"

She got up then, muttering in Spanish, and went to help Vanessa with the food.

"Mother and I are going to stay with Rufus in Boston," he said bluntly. "That's the end of the discussion, all right?"

My eyes fixed on the small holes in the wall close to the bed that we'd packed with newspaper to keep out the draft.

"What about your work?"

I mumbled something about the different leads I'd been trying, what I'd heard from some of the other commercial artists I used to work with in the better days. "It's bound to pick up."

"I mean your real work. You've got all this time, but I don't see any space here for you to paint."

"I can't work here, of course."

He continued to stare at me. "Have you been approaching galleries? You could use more of Rufus's drive in this respect."

He started coughing then, and I reached for a blanket for him.

"It's not money that runs the world, it's people," he sputtered. "People who have money. And you've got to show your face to them. They have to respect you, respect what you've done. If you keep hiding in here no one will know and you won't make a cent and you'll go on being bitter. There, that's my lecture." His hand gripped my wrist. He closed his eyes and went rigid for a spell.

"Write to the English relatives," he said finally. "Perhaps they know some of the right people who can push your work forward. Be a big man in London, and Montreal will come begging to you."

He grimaced then and once more clutched my arm with fingers as cold as icebox meat.

"I know, you'll never be Rufus," he said. "I guess that's what I like about you." He looked around the gloomy space for a moment and then said, calmly and with precision, "Damnation. Would you send in the women, son?" I looked at him with concern. "Unless you want to wipe me yourself?" he added, and turned away in disgust.

In the late afternoon, in our hour in the yard, I sit in a small measure of sunshine sneaking its way past the guard tower and the kitchen hut and stealing through barbed wire. I am trying not to think about food, or about the agony of waiting for parcels that always seem delayed or tampered with or outright stolen by the Germans. I try to make it enough to sit in a small spot of warmth, to use no energy, to close my eyes and will myself elsewhere.

But the hunger squeezes upon my brain, and my hands can't stay still. I have one sheet of paper for a letter and too many people to write to, one stub of a pencil that will soon be too small to fit in my own shaking hand. And so to stop it, to take my mind away for a while, I quickly sketch a dark-haired girl with hard questions in her eyes and a fine, lovely face and a mouth just slightly open, getting ready either to offer argument or to plunge into a kiss.

A desperate sketch with something of the woman captured, I suppose. Something of the way she is in my mind.

Witherspoon finds me out and sits beside me. He closes his eyes in the sunshine. He has come back from *Strafe* nervous and trembling in the limbs. Like all of us now his face is gaunt, his eyes ringed dark, and his skin reeks of something sour — of a body slowly eating itself to nothing.

"She's beautiful," he says, his back against the barracks wall. "Looks like my Beatrice before she gave me the heave."

"You probably don't want to see her, then."

"I'll trade you tobacco for her," he says in a voice like a snaggle-toothed saw. I can't tell if he wants to gaze at her adoringly or rip her face to shreds.

"I have tobacco," I say.

"I got some extra socks in my last home package."

"I don't want socks."

He keeps looking at the picture.

"Make her nude, I'll give you three pieces of biscuit."

119

"Five."

"Done!"

I tell him to bring me another sheet of paper. "And I need something smooth — a board for backing." I've been drawing against the flat of my knee, and the lines are faint in places.

Witherspoon comes back in minutes with a fresh sheet of paper and an almost smooth piece of board pried from inside the barracks wall. I quickly sketch a form I've seen in one of the French postcards circulating among the lads: a woman with a leg up on a chair, bending over to pull up her stockings. I give her long, curly hair falling over one shoulder and have her look up with a bit of womanly blush on her cheek, as if distracted by someone who has just come into the room.

Witherspoon snatches the paper from me as soon as I finish. Then he pulls my pieces of biscuit from his pocket. I put four of them in my own pocket and nibble on one, letting it dissolve slowly. My tongue is so swollen and painful from the bad food I can't hurry the procedure. And my spot of sun has moved on — the cold is quickly returning to my limbs, to my core.

I suck on another biscuit.

Collins comes by later with a chunk of chocolate he has somehow managed to keep from devouring.

"I need another pencil," I say. "This one's shot. And bring your own paper." While he's gone I imagine myself deeply sniffing the chocolate before swallowing it. Despite the biscuit my hunger is, if anything, worse than before.

"My wife's name is Helen," Collins says when he hands over the rough sheet of paper and the pencil, its point newly carved at that. "She wears her hair up. None of this bobbing nonsense. And her cheeks are —"

I haven't seen him this animated, this full of fun since before he was thrown in solitary and beaten to mash. So maybe Witherspoon will pull out of it as well, I think.

"Her cheeks are, you know, womanly."

I've already started to sketch. Several others have gathered round — Wilkens and Jackson and Cuddihey — seeing what I'm up to.

"Does she have large eyes? Is she sort of a Lillian Gish?"

"Yes! Yes, Lillian Gish would be all right. With a decent set of knockers."

I give her a pert nose and dark, dramatic lips and long eyelashes, and the breasts that he is looking for. Collins too becomes impatient to own the sketch as soon as I'm finished.

"Does it look anything like her?"

"Not really," he says with a big laugh. And the others too, all of us, stupid with hunger, laugh like little boys. "I love her anyway," Collins says. "She's my girlfriend now. I'll call her Marietta!"

I savour the incomprehensible luxury of the chocolate, close my eyes and think of my Margaret — of Margaret, rather, who isn't mine except in the deluded few cubic inches between my ears.

"We *are* a bunch of sorry buggers," Collins says as the last of the chocolate seeps down my throat.

"If anyone has bully beef," I say, "I will do a nude in any position that's anatomically imaginable."

Nine

At first I thought the place was closed, it was so poorly lit, and the door stuck badly. It wasn't W. Scott & Sons or even the fine art gallery at Eaton's, but a smaller outfit, more welcoming, I assumed. I pushed and pushed at the door and peered in past the displays of muddled English landscapes: quaint hedgerows and cobbled lanes and misty gardens with muted roses. The man at the back was reading a book and seemed at first glance annoyed to have anyone interrupt him.

He squinted at me from a distance through heavy glasses, then half rose and made a pushing motion with his hands. So I gripped the handle and lowered my shoulder and stumbled into the shop like a barbarian bursting through the gates.

"It always sticks, that door, in the hot weather," the proprietor said. He was even shorter than me but with a large head and a perfectly rounded pot belly. I followed his eyes as they took in the bound stack of stretched canvasses under my arm. His face hardened under the realization that I was not a prospective customer.

His gallery looked as if it hadn't had one of those in a good long while.

My fingers shook as I untied the strings. He was kind enough, anyway, to have a quick look. I'd included a bit of everything: some landscapes which I thought might be of interest, a few of the Margaret nudes, a portrait of Father as a young man perched atop a railroad trestle, even some of my grimmer work about the war.

"You've nothing framed?" he said finally.

"Not at this point." There was no need to confess that I could not afford it.

"Nobody is buying art these days," he said wearily. "Except the very rich, and they are few, and they only buy good British art, you understand." Despite myself I looked around at all the good British art cluttering his store.

"Are any of these painters still alive?" I asked.

It was much easier to do the knots up again and put away my work.

"I run a commercial gallery," he said. "Some of the Montreal artists I know, the local people, have joined together in various groups. They aren't trying to make a living at it. That's impossible, certainly in these times. But they teach, and sometimes they exhibit together. You ought to get in with a group like that. For the exposure and whatnot. I think I heard some of them are doing Christmas cards. A penny each. That sort of thing." He looked at me then as if the next bit of advice was practically cutting his own throat. "I've heard of some artists selling on the sly from the lobbies of the bigger hotels. You'd have to frame your work, of course. But some people have money."

I had a hard time again with the blasted door, which was stuck now from the inside.

"Much of your work is very good," he said to me. "But

you must understand — I get ten of you a day and I'm not running a charity."

At last the door opened, and I felt the concrete of the sidewalk through the hole in my shoe.

Dearest Ramsay,

I know it has been quite some time since I have written to you. Please know, that silent as my pen has fallen, you have never been far from my thoughts and prayers. Sometimes I wonder what this war has done, how it has ravaged our inner lives. There must be millions of us in homes and families around the world whose every moment, waking and sleeping, involves the extraordinary effort of mentally caring for someone thousands of miles away. We are all prisoners of hope and contemplation, clinging to thoughts, memories, fantasies of what is to come, the day when the world will be set right again.

Will it ever be right again?

I'm sorry, I should be more of a brick about these things and write to you in certain hope etc. etc. Your cheerful cousin Margaret ever stalwart. But it is hardly the way I feel. I have had such curtains of darkness draw around me, and my poor family tries to jolly me out of it. They say, "Dear Margaret, come now, get out of bed! Look at that clear sky!" And I roll over and look at the dismal, dreary, suffering clouds and know in my heart that I have the least to complain about of anyone. I think to myself, what hardships is Ramsay enduring at the moment? What of so many others? And why? Why?

Enough of my blackness. If you can stand to write

back I of course yearn to hear from you. For now, please excuse your pathetic cousin Margaret. I am looking for bootstraps with which to pull myself up, but all I seem to find is more heavy woollen clothing to weigh me down.

Forgive me, Margaret

Dear Margaret,

In your darkness walk with me — we are in Hyde Park again. Do you remember that day? That blue sky is forever. We'll walk and walk, and this time we'll talk about the way the light bounces off my little board as I write this. It sneaks in through the broken window and scatters itself over all the greys and muted browns and yellows of our teeth, the hard black scrabbiness of our beards. We will talk about the sketches I am making for nearly all the men in camp, the little echoes of femininity that help us remember the lovelier world beyond the wire. And we will talk about how in this weird and upside-down place an artist like me is suddenly wealthy. For men will trade with me all manner of things — their chocolate, even, their cakes from home, tinned meats, books, long underwear — for a scrap of paper with certain lines.

And since we are in our heads and not reality, for your part you won't be an idiot about loving Boulton (and you will forgive me for saying it. In hell one says what one feels like saying).

Damn the consequences. And damn my jealousy. It is before all that. It is just a sunny day in late May and we are walking in Hyde Park and the war is somewhere else.

Yours, Ramsay

I wandered by myself down St. Catherine Street, lugging my work like some necessary burden. The cold winds of early spring knifed through me and through all the other unemployed men with no particular place to go, their hats pulled down, defeat etched on their faces. I'd seen too many of them for too long and felt as if I were re-entering a dream in which the trap I thought I'd escaped was closing in again and again.

On a back street a crowd of men lined up for free haircuts sponsored by a good works committee. Those who weren't in the chair with a sheet around their necks stood against a brick wall, sullenly smoking. For a moment I thought of joining the line. Maybe if I'd had a fresh haircut the gallery fool would have agreed to take on some of my work.

Then again, perhaps he'd have shown more pity if I'd looked as ragged as some of these sods.

Around another corner men were playing pitch and toss in a vacant lot. The board with the target rings was hung on a wooden fence, and I watched as two lads took turns and ten or twelve others bet on the outcome.

"Are you in for a dime?" someone asked me, and I shook my head. "I never bet," I said, but I stayed to watch for a while until I began to cough. Ever since my father had left for Boston my lungs seemed to be tearing themselves to shreds.

I ended up in a bar on St. Denis, one of the last to still give credit to regulars. I stood with my foot on the rail, not looking into the mirror. The whisky was bitter and slow, and the others in the place did not bother me.

Sometime in the late afternoon I gathered my hat and made a show of checking through my pockets to see what could be offered against my debt. I left some coins on the counter behind me and turned to leave, but I fell into another fit of wretched coughing. When I straightened up again I saw someone I knew but couldn't quite place. He'd changed utterly, whoever he was, but he knew my name, at least.

"Well!" I said, and shook the man's hand. "Fancy seeing you. How have you been?"

"Yes, it's been ages," he said. It was Gil Jenkins from my old office. So we sat back at the bar. I collected my change since the keep hadn't yet noticed it, and another whisky slid down my ragged and impoverished throat. Jenkins nodded at my portfolio.

"Trying to raise a little interest?"

He'd been keeping busy, he said, and had quite a few leads, and everyone knew the downturn wouldn't last.

"The government won't allow it," he said. "I mean, we can't just leave all these men on the streets with nothing to do. There'll be work camps, I'm sure."

I shuddered at the thought.

"You fought in the war," he said. He was younger than me, much better looking even in this down-in-the-mouth, somewhat drunken state. "A lot of men fought, and now look at the way you're being treated!"

Some of the others stopped to peer at us through their own hazy eyes.

Gil Jenkins lurched to his feet. He fumbled in his pockets, then thrust a much-folded piece of paper at me. "This is a job I heard about. They need a great bloody artist. I was going to go myself but you need it more than me. You're married. And you've got a kid."

I took out a small notebook that I carried with me and copied out the address, then handed him back his slip of paper.

"We'll both go," I said. "How old is this job, anyway?"

He pushed his slip back to me.

"Look, I've made a note," I said, but he wouldn't touch the paper. I took out my few coins once more to lay on the counter. As I turned to leave I felt him pulling on the bottom of my jacket.

"I haven't worked all year," Gil said, "and when I sit down to do anything now my hands won't stay steady." I watched them quiver as he held them out for me.

"It's just the drink," I said, and steadied them with my own hands.

"I can't draw a bloody thing," Gil Jenkins said.

"Crome has money," Collins says. It is late and I am huddled under my filthy blankets, turned away from the glare of the lone light bulb hanging from the barracks ceiling.

"Crome has everything," someone else says.

"Crome! Ramsay!"

I try to ignore them.

"Come on — we're having a fucking contest and you're the only rich one in the room. You be the bank, all right?"

I've been working days in the adjacent officers' camp, painting the scenery for the production of *Hamlet* they are trying to mount. They are not made to work, of course, being officers, and are fed somewhat properly, and I have missed several days now of ditch duty to work on the flats and fill in at the officers' kitchen.

Witherspoon shakes my shoulder. One side of his face has hardened into a squint, as if he is perpetually bracing himself to be punched. On the other side a scar stretches from the jaw hinge across to the front of his throat — an altercation with Sergeant Blasphemy that I didn't see.

"I have very little money," I say.

"Too good for us now? Going to move in with the officers and leave the likes of us to shovel frozen shit for the Fatherland?"

"Calm down," Collins says to Witherspoon. "We *want* a man in the officers' kitchen." I've been bringing them what I can — bits of sausage sometimes, apples and potatoes, nearly edible bread. "Besides, you are going to join in, aren't you, Crome?"

Reluctantly, I roll onto my feet. I haven't been out in the bitter wind like they have. The relative warmth of the kitchen has made our ice-locker barracks that much harder to take.

Wilkens's bed has been cleared. In the centre is a plate with a small round blue design in the middle. Already men are combing the seams of their filthy clothes for chatts — lice — to find the liveliest ones.

"If you don't have cash, the ante is at least five cigarettes," Collins announces. "We'll accept almost anything: books, combs, chocolate, biscuits. Hurry up! Agony's going to be here soon. Baldwin, are you in? I covet your mirror! Two chatts for Baldwin if he wagers his mirror."

"How much for my wristwatch?" Findlay asks.

"Three! Three chatts for a wristwatch! Winner takes all.

Come on, Crome, you're the rich man here. What can you put in?"

I rummage up some cigarettes to make the ante.

"Not good enough. Spread the wealth, man, give us all hope!"

"How about that jackknife the captain gave you?" Witherspoon presses. "Give us all a shot at that, won't you?"

It's a bone-handled beauty and perfectly illegal, and I'm happy to put it up for others to take off my hands.

"Three chatts for the jackknife," Collins says. "Come on, who else is in? We're starting in two minutes. Two minutes!"

I pull the knife out of a hiding spot I've devised in the floorboards. Others flood in now with their marks, their spare bits of food, their woollies from home. I am allowed three chatts to work with but can only get two from the seams of my shirt onto the central blue spot in time for Collins to start them off.

"That's it! Bidding's closed! They're off, gentlemen, all hands away! You cannot touch the plate or anything on the bed. You cannot blow or —"

Collins is soon drowned out by the yelling. These German chatts are tiny, red, slow-crawling monsters that spit blood — and not their own — when cracked between fingers. But now they're our racehorses, confused little beasts at whom we scream our hopes and agonies. About twelve begin in the centre, while three times their number in men crowd around to view the spectacle.

"Come on, you bastard! Move your fucking body!"

"Roll over, for Christ''s sake! Get away from him! Get away!"

"That's Crome's chatt! Bite him! Bite him!"

The first to make its way off the edge of the plate wins the entire jackpot for its owner.

"Bleed a little! Run! Get going!"

The early leader is one of Findlay's chatts, which seems frightened of all the noise. We scream, as if the sheer volume will force the chatts to flee in the desired direction. But Findlay's chatt turns around, and two or three others edge slowly outwards past it. One of them is mine.

"Bite that bastard! We can't let Crome win!" Witherspoon leans over the mattress and elbows me out of the way.

"No interference!" I scream.

Others too lean over, the plate is jostled, then straightened, and Collins hoarsely calls on everyone to move back.

"Fucking Crome is going to win," Witherspoon moans.

But my lead chatt starts to turn back and someone else's on the other side seems to have decided to move off the plate. More screams and urgings. We are completely mad with it. All the months of bitterness and deprivation are packed into this one small, capricious, arbitrary competition that none of us can win. Not really.

"It's Crome's again! Stop him! Stop!"

My chatt tumbles off the edge of the plate and all the winnings suddenly fall to me.

"He's a fucking dago cheat!" Witherspoon spits, and in a second the plate is hurled across the room. The chatts spin off to find new homes amongst the crowd.

"Calm down!" Collins says.

"He's a fucking bloody dago cheat!" Witherspoon's fists are doubled now and he looms above me.

131

I gather up the eccentric winnings in my arms. "Take it all," I say.

"Why is a fucking dago allowed in our barracks anyway?" Witherspoon says.

"Shut your mouth. Take the goddamn stuff. I don't want it."

"Why do we have to put up with a dago?"

Collins separates us. "Cool heads, lads," he says. "Nobody cheated. Now Agony's on his way and —"

"You have no right —"

"He smells like a dago, he's got a dago fucking nose —"

I drop the loot, go for his head and miss with a right. Collins ducks out of the way just as Witherspoon's fist ploughs into my stomach. I stagger back, my breath gone. Witherspoon crashes me once on the side of the face and again in the belly.

"Ten fags on Witherspoon!" someone yells.

I get in a few blows of my own, then am stopped again by a hard punch in the side. I fall to the floor. Suddenly everyone is stepping back to make way for black boots. Blasphemy and Agony. They haul me to my feet and I lunge once again at Witherspoon, who looks for all the world as if he wants to get hit, and harder than I can manage.

"Fucking puny dago artist." He holds the knife, which looks like an odd extension of the ragged bones poking beneath his prisoner clothes. When Agony knocks him on the shoulder from behind he folds like a tent.

I see the blur of a rifle butt move towards me but can't quite get out of the way. It smashes my bad elbow. I fall to the floor with the pain but am immediately returned to my feet, Agony yelling in my face as if the world has come to an end.

"Fucking dago bastard," Witherspoon mutters to the floor as we are both dragged out into the bitter night.

Lillian was waiting for me on the stoop, Michael in her arms. She held a telegram and looked as if one more thing would break her. I thought to say to her: *You are stronger than you think.*

I propped my portfolio against the door and held the two of them in silence. I kissed Lillian as tenderly as I could, and I fought back a cough that was building in my chest.

"Is it my father?" I said finally.

You wait to receive the news, and you wait, and you expect you to know exactly how you will feel.

I pulled Lillian inside then and closed the door and brought her over to the bed, and she laid the baby beside us and looked at me with those eyes, which for some reason in the darkest corner of that sorry flat suddenly looked as blue as endless sky over a placid midday ocean.

"We will not be in this trap forever." I loosened the buttons on her dress. She pulled at my shirt. The telegram was on the floor.

"I've been waiting all day to tell you," she said sadly.

I kicked my clothes off and kissed up and down her face and neck, then her beautiful swollen nipples.

"Careful. That's for Michael."

The boy was sleeping like an angel. We all rocked together

on the same bed. "I dreamed about doing this," I murmured. "For years. For most of my life."

It felt as if we were huddled in a lifeboat in the gentle rocking seas, in the high sun and the soft breeze of an innocent-looking world after some disaster has capsized and swallowed our ship.

"Ramsay. Ramsay, dear."

As if we probably would not make it to shore but were safe now in this particular hour.

"Please, dear. Pull out! We can't have —"

I stopped, still inside her. She was pushing against my hips as if I'd forced my way in.

"I can't have another child right now."

I slid off her and stared up at the naked bulb above us. When I looked across the room Margaret had seated herself as she sometimes did. She looked completely sympathetic to Lillian's cause.

"I'm sorry," Lillian said. "I knew you'd understand."

There was a long, awkward silence while I held Margaret's gaze. She seemed ready to laugh at some story she couldn't tell me while Lillian was in the room.

I blinked and blinked. But she wouldn't go away.

"I'm so sorry about your father," Lillian said, holding me because she did not want me to go. And when I did not answer — Margaret was just sitting and watching us, waiting — she said, "What did the gallery owner say?"

Ten

The door was large but smooth to open, well oiled. I walked into a plain-looking meeting room with a square of tables, a stenographer, some assistants, and a lumpy man sitting in a wooden chair surrounded by papers. I suppose I had expected something on a grander scale, more judicial perhaps, with oak panelling and the weight and feel of old leather.

"Ramsay Crome? Private, Seventh Pioneers Battalion? 403776?" The commissioner stared at my submission through reading glasses.

"Yes," I replied, and took a seat opposite him, though at a fair distance, the hollow space at the centre of the square of tables between us.

"Mr. Crome, as you are aware, this is a hearing to determine the possibility and extent of reparations due to you as a result of alleged maltreatment during your incarceration as a prisoner of war in Germany. I have here your statement of fact. I also have your service record, including your medical statement upon leaving military service March twenty-second, 1919. We will get to a full review of your claim. But first, do you have any further documentary evidence to submit at this juncture?"

He spoke like a clattering typewriter.

"No, sir."

"You have no recent medical records, doctors' certificates? Nothing to substantiate your claim to disability?"

"No, sir."

He sighed, a marginal movement that told me all I needed to know about my chances. But in a moment he was back to business.

"All right, Mr. Crome. Let's review your background material. You enlisted in Victoria, March twenty-fifth, 1915, were captured at Mont Sorrel June twenty-second, 1916. Is that correct?"

"I was captured June third, after some time separated from my unit," I said. "At first I was reported dead and my pay was stopped. The twenty-second of June is the day my pay started again, when the Germans reported me captured. I was taken to the camp at Raumen, later transferred to Münster."

"Released at Dover, November fourteenth, 1918," he read.

"Yes, sir."

"Prior to enlistment you were a machinist? What was your rate of pay?"

"Seventeen dollars and sixty cents per week."

"And now you are an artist? What is your present rate of pay?"

"I am unemployed at the moment."

"When you *are* employed, Mr. Crome, what sort of wage do you usually command, as an artist?"

His pen was poised to write down whatever I said.

"I have earned as much as two thousand dollars a year. I'm an illustrator, a graphic designer. I've worked for a few different companies. You just tell me what you want the picture to look like and I can —"

"Yes," he said abruptly, cutting me off. "Are you married, Mr. Crome? You've left this section blank."

"Did I?" I said and half-rose as if about to head over and see if it was indeed blank.

"Sit down," he said. "Just answer the questions. Are you married?"

"Yes, sir. I was married in 1929."

"Children?"

"One boy."

"Right. Now, Mr. Crome, what is the nature of your claim of maltreatment?"

I hesitated. By then it seemed to me complete foolishness to be there at all, so many years after the fact, explaining such miseries to a man who'd probably never missed a meal in his life.

"My complaint is of nothing more brutal than what I'm sure you've already heard from hundreds of others, Mr. Commissioner," I said. It had somehow stuck in my head that he liked being addressed that way. "During my time in the camps I was near-starved. Most days we received only a slice or two of the most worm-eaten, disgusting bread —"

"Yes," he said impatiently. "Were you beaten in any way?"

"Sometimes."

"Can you recall a specific occurrence? You've mentioned something here . . ." And he looked at my statement again.

"I was involved in an altercation in camp that included a beating by guards —two of them. That was followed by three days of solitary confinement."

"Three days, yes," he said dismissively. "What caused the altercation?"

"It was a fight involving gambling."

"With other prisoners?"

I nodded.

"Were you punished for gambling or for fighting?" he asked, as if there might be some important distinction to be drawn between the two.

"We were starved men," I said. "And we were made to work long hours at labour that would have been exhausting even if we had been fed beef and roast potatoes. And they stood us in the rain and the wind and snow for ages until men collapsed and then they stood us longer. They beat men for failing to salute their non-commissioned officers. They beat men for not working hard enough. They beat us when our tools broke and withheld our food parcels even though we were starving. Sometimes they broke the parcels apart and trod on them right in front of us. The three days I was in solitary I stood in a hole in the ground. It was February, and snow fell on top of my head. They lowered a pail of cold, soapy soup once every afternoon."

He was listening. But his pen had stopped moving, and the words halted in my throat. I felt nearly angry enough to pitch the table across the room and stalk out.

"What *lasting* injuries, if any, did you sustain from this ill-treatment, Mr. Crome?"

"I have weak lungs, sir, and get sick most years with bronchitis."

"How long does it last?"

"Several weeks, sometimes."

"Have you lost wages as a result of this illness?"

"I do my best to work through it, sir. When I have work."

"And what is this you've mentioned in your form about your left arm?"

"In the episode of the fight, sir, I was smashed on the elbow with a rifle butt, and the arm has been weaker than normal since then."

"Are you left-handed, Mr. Crome?"

"Right-handed, sir."

"So has the elbow injury restricted at all your ability to earn wages as an artist?"

"No, sir. I suppose not."

"Many of the men have complained of neurasthenia. But you haven't mentioned anything," he said, hunting again through my papers.

"I have weak nerves sometimes, Mr. Commissioner, and sleep poorly. And I get agitated."

In silence he made notes and read through parts of my file again.

"Could you give me more detail, Mr. Crome, about the circumstances of the fight that led to your being placed in solitary confinement? I need to ascertain whether the guards' actions were justified. You've stated that you were gambling. What was it, poker or pontoon or some other —"

"It was a local ... contest, sir."

"Of what nature was the contest?" he pressed. When I failed to answer right away he said, "I take into account the frankness of your replies, Mr. Crome, and your willingness to be open and truthful with this commission."

"We bet about almost anything," I said at last.

"What was the name of the man with whom you quarrelled, Mr. Crome?"

"I can't remember, sir."

"It might help me immeasurably to cross-reference cases before this commission and find corroboration."

"I'm afraid I can't remember, sir," I repeated, and stared him down. He looked away.

"Are there any other injuries or disabilities resulting from your time as a prisoner of war, Mr. Crome?" He looked at his watch discretely, a flick of the eyes downward as his fingers pulled the timepiece out of his vest.

"No, sir."

"As to the malnourishment and degraded living circumstances of your confinement, Mr. Crome, I have heard ample testimony from over two hundred former prisoners now and am quite familiar with the extent and nature of the situation. I am finding that all the prisoners suffered similar difficulties and treatment, at least those not from the officer ranks. As you know, Germany itself was desperately short of food, especially in the waning years of the war, and it would be too much to expect a nation to feed its prisoners of war better than, or even, perhaps, equal to its own general population. In my findings, then, I'm afraid I must focus on the question of extraordinary maltreatment beyond the issue of nourishment. I can tell you now that your case would be more compelling to this commission if you had supplied a statement of medical health from your doctor. I note that upon leaving service the military physician who examined you found you 'completely fit and sound.' That's your signature below, is it not?" He leaned forward to show me the damned form I had signed in a rush to free myself from military clutches years ago.

Then he began writing intensely, barely pausing to look at me. "As in all cases, I am reserving my recommendations at this time. I will be reporting later in the year, I hope, or next year at the latest, and you can wait to hear our final judgement from the commission. But I can tell you, Mr. Crome, that in the absence of medical proof of disability and maltreatment beyond that which was generalized for nearly all prisoners of war in Germany, it will be difficult to find in your favour. But thank you for your candour and for bringing your case forward to my attention."

"Thank you, sir," I managed to say before leaving.

Eleven

"*Drei Tage*," the German duty officer says: three days. He seems to take it personally, this trouble we have caused, although it is my elbow that has been smashed, and Witherspoon and I will have to serve the time in solitary, not him.

Perhaps the Germans have their own method of accounting and punish their officers whenever prisoners fall out of line.

One last time the duty officer eyes us like criminally insane children. Then he stamps out, and the guard shouts us down the hall and outside into winter's darkness.

"Three days isn't bad," I mutter to Witherspoon. "A little peace and quiet, eh?"

But we don't take the usual route to the holding cells. We go right, then left again, and the spotlights of three watchtowers blind us as we walk. Why didn't I find a way to bring my greatcoat against the cold?

"Where the fuck are we going?" Witherspoon asks.

To a different compound beyond a bleak stretch of barbed wire fencing. I get turned around in my fatigue and the disorienting lights. And our guard detachment grows — from one scared guard to perhaps five, now surrounding us, their boots kicking up clouds of dusty snow.

We enter an open courtyard. Beyond the bright lights the darkness is impenetrable — anything might be out there.

Two of the guards pull up from the ground an iron grate lightly covered in snow.

"Oh, Jesus," Witherspoon says weakly.

Suddenly a guard butts him across the shoulders with the stock of his rifle. Witherspoon stumbles to his knees. As he is rising they hit him again and he disappears down the hole.

They shove me in a different direction and someone buckles my knees from behind. My legs fold. I reach out and hold on until they kick my fingers off the frozen edge. My injured elbow smashes something on the way down — everything spins and thrashes in pain.

The earth grabs me and I collapse onto the wet mud that stops my descent. I shriek like a half-slaughtered animal. When the panic subsides I look up at the tiny square of blackness with four pinholes of light — unimaginably distant stars.

Then I shake until it seems my limbs are intent on battering themselves against the rock and frozen muck that surrounds me.

Feet and hands, blowing breath, this hard cramp in my leg, my shoulders knotting, elbow still ablaze with pain. One step and, glancing into the wall, one step and turn, this tired little space.

The square above me turns from black to cold grey to

colder light, and snow begins to fall, a few flakes making it all the way down to my cracked lips. Sometime in the day a pair of hands pulls off the grate and a little pot of slightly warmed liquid is lowered down. I reach out with a freezing urgency, nearly upend it with the tremors in my hands, but manage to unhook the handle and then glory just to stand and warm myself, however meagrely, against the pot.

There is no spoon. I have to tilt the pot to my hard lips, somehow steady it despite my shivering, and drink without spilling the greasy bitterness. I stand waiting for the bread but there is none, though the soup has mushy parts near the bottom that I slobber down — peelings, perhaps — and then a sharp bone that cuts the roof of my mouth so that I spit in the darkness and yell up to no one.

I count the seconds leaning against the cold wall, then force myself erect, perform my little drunken shuffle-dance, anything for movement, for something to keep the blood from congealing in my veins.

Just for a moment I close my eyes in a clever way, so I can sleep on my feet and not freeze to the wall or floor. Sleep while shuffling, the empty soup pot now at my boots, tripping me up at every step.

I could sit on it, it occurs to me. I could turn it over with my foot and slowly, slowly squat down like this, make myself smaller and smaller ...

"Ramsay?"

I open my eyes and look around for the owner of the voice. My shoulder is strangely numb. I hit it and feel nothing. Everything is dark again; even the little square in the sky above has been erased.

"Ramsay, get up now!"

I can barely move my head. But it's better this way, I think. Warmer, somehow. All that foolish stumbling about was only mixing up the air currents, making me colder and colder.

"I'm going to lift you from behind, but you'll have to push with your legs. Do you understand me?"

I nod my head although she couldn't possibly see me — it's too damn dark.

Her hands are surprisingly strong under my armpits, and I try to push, but most of my left side has gone dead. I thank her sincerely for all her efforts but tell her it's no use.

"This won't do, Ramsay. You're going to have to wake up!"

"But if I do you won't be here then, will you?" I say cleverly. It's Margaret, of course, come to help me die.

"Yes, I will."

"How can you? Did they capture you as well?"

She has me again under the armpits and braces herself better this time. I feel it in the strength of her frame.

"None of your backchat," she says sternly and heaves up again, but it's no use, I've already told her. My limbs fold under, and she stands holding me awkwardly against the wall.

"Ramsay — try please!"

"Let me go."

"I won't!"

She leans me into the soil face and rubs her warm hands up and down my back and sides, my shoulders, legs, my damaged arm, even my ice-cold feet. "Don't you fall on me while I'm down here," she snaps. "Stay awake. Concentrate!"

145

It's a terrible thing to have life burning back into your limbs. They crackle with fire, will roast any moment and smoulder black with smoke.

"You're a stupid man, sometimes."

"I know."

"I can't think of a more foolish way to die."

"I'm sorry."

"Don't be sorry. Keep your feet moving, unless you want to be buried here."

I try, though it seems useless. The meat in my limbs is half frozen already. But for her I try.

Miracles begin falling through the grate. Crusts of cheese, bits of biscuit and then an entire greatcoat whumping down. It covers my head, and I stagger, uncertain what is happening. But within moments I've wrapped myself with it, and for a time I feel as if I've fallen frozen into a fireplace and am happily thawing.

I rub the mud off the crust of cheese and biscuit, gorge myself, then stare up at the square of light. No drunken snowflakes are dancing through the grate now. But I see feet sometimes, passing directly overhead, and I glimpse a black bird. For endless long, gnawing stretches my heart wheezes in a yearning ache to catch sight of the soup pot, which does not come however much I stare.

"You said you wouldn't go. Not if I stayed awake!" I turn in case my voice could somehow spiral out and get to her.

No reply.

I close my eyes to summon her, stamp my feet like an angry child.

"Margaret! Where the hell have you gone?" I strike out at where she might be hiding. But she is safely behind the wall and hits back at me with the force of stubborn earth.

"Ramsay," she says finally behind me. I turn and try to make her out. "Look what I've brought!"

Bread, for God's sake — familiar, black, rock-hard German bread that she has to break for me and guide the pieces with her warm fingers between my lips, I am shivering so badly. I turn my cheek to lean against her hand, the way a dog will.

"That's all right, Ramsay." She holds my head with both her hands. They feel heavenly, like a scarf that has been left drying by the stove.

"Remember I said —"

"Shh."

"I said that after the war I would come back as a —"

"This is not yet after the war, Ramsay."

Her voice is very calm, tucked with humour, as if she will begin to openly poke fun at me any moment.

I suck slowly on the black bread pieces while she holds my head. "Where did you get these bits of food?"

"Some of the men have agreed to throw down a few things when they can. But you weren't looking, were you? You just wanted to go to sleep."

We do a little shuffling dance together, one step and then turn, and one step and turn. As long as I can keep some strength in my arms to hold her, she will warm things.

"If you want to sleep now, Ramsay, I'll hold you up."

"I can't sleep *and* dance."

"Of course you can, dear."

"But I'll pull you over. We'll both —"

"Everyone is doing their bit except for me," she says. "But feel those legs, Ramsay. Feel them!"

I reach down, grip through the fabric of her dress.

"Aren't they strong, for a woman? So you sleep and I'll dance for us both."

It is like that, a long, slow, somnolent dance. For ages we are silent, Margaret and I, as if we've been married for decades, have known each other's thoughts so long we do not need to speak. And then, as if to break the gloom, she rattles on with funny stories and tidbits of news — *Chu Chin Chow* and her father and the redcap guards pulling him over to check his papers.

"If the King would only call," I mumble.

"Yes, darling, that's exactly what he said. But sleep now, would you?" and I feel her grip tightening, my feet dragging upon the floor.

I wait, wait for the soup pot to be lowered. It comes down in a dream, hazy, like a dark bit of boulder, wobbling as it descends. When it reaches me I can hardly lift my arms, so Margaret has to receive it. She remembers to hook on the old pot, and I stand stupidly watching as it floats back up the shaft of dimming light.

"Ramsay, dear, stay still please, or I'll spill it on you."

I try to keep from shaking.

"I can't hold and feed you at the same time. Rest against the wall, dear. It will be all right. This will warm you, I promise, it will."

She pours the soup in a slow trickle between my quivering lips. The warmth dribbles down my cheek and chin.

"There you are. Slowly. We have no shortage of time."

I manage to hold the bowl in my own hands.

"Look, a bit of onion! This is something of a picnic!" And I finish it, chew slowly on the mushy bits — even some meat in the end. It must be a mistake, I mean to say to her. To be jocular in the right way.

"I'm going to die here," I say instead.

"Nonsense. You may sleep for a while, but I'll hold you. Doesn't it feel better with a bit of soup inside you?"

I concentrate all my will to straighten up, to look at the darkening square above. "I'm going to die here," I say.

"Did I tell you about the price of bread, dear?" she says. I am leaning back against her, which she allows, though only as a rest, because she hasn't had enough of my dancing.

"Don't talk about bread," I whisper.

"It's been going through the roof! You were right to get out of London when you did, I'll tell you. All the households have been restricted as to where they can shop. You register with a butcher, for instance, and must go there with your ration book, and if the shipment did not come that particular day or you missed out in line, well, fortunes of war, m'lady, it's quite simply too bad. Are you listening to me?"

I try to look at her in the dizzy murk of the hole.

"Because I don't think I can marry a man who isn't able to listen to me. It would be an awful sort of existence, wouldn't it? To be married to some taciturn, withdrawn sort of man who didn't care about the daily joys. You would bring me flowers, wouldn't you? Any man who brings me flowers has halfway won my heart. There's a hint, Ramsay. A clue!"

"Boulton brings you flowers."

"Let's not talk about Henry," she says quickly. "But he does, you're right, he can't cross Covent Garden without picking out something for me. I would hate to be married to a man who was so self-absorbed or so wilfully neglectful of the beauties of — Ramsay, wake up! You've slept all day, and you're getting heavy."

"Sorry." I try to shift my weight.

"I'm giving you clues, darling. You really must pay attention."

"Yes."

"It would break my heart if you didn't."

I lose track of the square up above, can't say anymore how often it has been dark or light. It seems to change whenever I look or be something else, somehow, an ugly eye peering down at us, blinking sometimes and staring others.

The shivering worsens, settles in for good, and even Margaret with the warm blood catches it. "It's no good," I say, holding her, trying to get her to lie down with me against the wall.

"But we're not married!" she says, only half joking. Her voice has grown faint and her face seems dangerously pale.

"You shouldn't be here," I whisper.

"I can't lie down with you if we aren't married," she says again.

So I say, "Margaret Crome, marry me."

"But we're cousins, dear Ramsay." She kisses my face — so coldly. I feel the weight of enormous sadness, knowing what I've done in bringing her here.

"Marry me anyway."

"It wouldn't be right," she replies, but in a teasing, falsely argumentative way. She is already leaning towards the wall, is almost slumping beneath me. "Your father would be furious."

"My father —" I start to say.

"He'd blow his top — his son marrying a cousin."

"My father," I say slowly, trying hard to form the words, "would approve. If he knew all the facts ... and circumstances."

I am pressing, trying to get her to bend, but she is stronger than me.

"Would we have children, do you think?" she asks.

"Let's not get lost ... in the details."

"I would want to have children. I would think that a life without children —"

And then she straightens me, despite my waning strength, and in a moment has me shuffle-dancing again. "You see," she says, "whenever you believe you can't possibly take another step — if you stop to think about it at all, you've taken it already."

"Margaret Crome!" I say suddenly. "Marry me, and I will carry you out of this pit on my shoulders and all the way back to England!"

"There," she says, and I catch a silvery glint in her eye. "Now you're sounding like someone I might want to consider."

"Ramsay. Ramsay, wake up," she says. It is so warm down in the mud I am certain for a moment that we've been lying together. The shivering has stopped. She picks up my greatcoat, rearranges it around my shoulders. "You'll get cold."

"I'm not at all," I reply. Even the buttons of my shirt have been ripped off. I am strangely steaming with heat.

"Wake up. Dance with me, Ramsay. Come on!"

"That's all you want to do," I slur. My legs feel stumbly, I have a hard time working my arms to keep the coat away.

"Yes, dear, I'm a dancing idiot."

"You never want to —"

But she has me, and the pain of it is awful.

"I didn't tell you," she says.

"What?"

"Come on, darling," she says, hoisting me — pushing my arms up where they don't want to go, twisting my poor body this way and that.

"What didn't you —"

She has a hard time with the rope. It won't go though, she tries again and again, and I am useless, my legs and arms are dull as sandbags.

"There you are, darling," she says at last, and I am jerked up in the air. I thud against the walls, torqued like a dummy being hoisted onto a truck. Then I am even again with the ground, and snow bites the bare skin of my chest, and the brightness blinds me for a time. I collapse, get hauled up, collapse again, stumble finally, clutching the shoulders of two other cursing fannigans.

On the ground, as we wobble past, I make out the body of poor Witherspoon, frozen solid blue in the winter wind.

Twelve

"Excuse me," I said after I'd pushed open the office door. I had my portfolio under my arm, my hat in my hand. I'd been wandering for some minutes along a warren of dull offices scattered on the third floor of an old stone building on Peel Street. "Is this the Barnesworth Agency?"

There was no sign on the door, but the number, 317, matched the one I'd copied from Gil Jenkins's folded note.

The small, dark-panelled waiting room was dominated by a hulking desk on which perched a monstrous black typewriter. The little woman behind it in glasses and severe suit seemed dwarfed by the desk and typewriter both. She looked at me in silence too long.

"And you are?" she said eventually.

"Ramsay Crome," I said, and stepped towards her. I put down my portfolio and thrust out my hand. "I'm a commercial artist, and I heard that you might have a position. I can do oils, watercolours, pen and ink, any kind of sketching. I'm very good with lettering, even drafting —"

She had not moved from behind the safety of her desk, and my hand stayed absurdly in mid-air until I let it drop.

"I've brought some samples of my work," I said, and started untying my large case.

"We're terrifically busy at the moment," she said. The office looked completely deserted except for the two of us. But doors to the right and left might have led to busy though silent inner workings, I supposed. The one low couch along the far wall was empty.

"Perhaps if I could just speak to Mr. Barnesworth," I said. "Or I'd be happy to make an appointment. My work has appeared in catalogues, in magazines, in newspapers." I pulled out a colour drawing I'd done before the crash: *The Way Ahead Is Unlimited*. It showed a handsome and hard-muscled prospector kneeling by a river to inspect the bedrock exposed by the current. *Canada's mining industry grew 10.5% in 1928 over 1927, with greater years bound to come for those with the courage to invest!* it said.

The little woman pushed up her glasses and scanned the figure of the miner.

"I've also done some architectural sketches, some portraits of children and dogs."

"What about women?"

"Yes, I've done some fashion things." I sorted through my materials to find a series of pen and ink sketches of women in hats. She flipped through them as if gazing at a particularly uninspiring hand of cards.

"I'm afraid Mr. Barnesworth is not in," she said abruptly. She handed back my sketches and readjusted her glasses. "Perhaps if you left your card."

I had no such thing, but made a motion to check through my pockets anyway. "I'm afraid I seem to have left the house without —"

"That's fine. If anything comes up I can certainly contact you," she said, and started clattering away on her typewriter as if I'd already left the room.

"But how could you contact me —"

Her eyes stayed on the carbon-copied form that she was typing up at a noisy and prodigious rate.

"I see then," I said, and slammed the door behind me. I steamed out of the building and got several blocks away when it started to rain. Then I turned and sprinted back to the building and up the stairs again.

"Listen here," I said when I burst back into the office. "You've treated me very badly and —"

The woman was gone from her desk, the typewriter sat abandoned, and another woman, a nurse, was sitting with her legs crossed on the couch that had been empty. Both other doors remained closed. The nurse had lustrous black hair, blood red lips and skin that looked softer than brushed silk. She glanced up at me, faintly amused. Her uniform was terribly tight, and her legs, even to her stocking tops, were clearly visible.

"You're not the same fellow as last time," she said.

"And you're not the same girl," I quipped in confusion. "A woman was here just a few minutes ago behind this desk —"

"Miss Dorsett?" the nurse said. "She'll be back shortly, I'm sure."

How quickly my anger drained into renewed awkwardness. I shook the rainwater off my hat and remained standing, my portfolio in hand, although I could have sat beside the young woman on the couch. After a minute or so I doubled over into a terrible coughing fit.

"Are you a new artist?" she asked when I finally recovered enough to look at her again.

"I'm an artist. I don't know how new I am."

She shifted in her seat and recrossed her legs, then cut me a dazzling smile like something out of the movies.

Miss Dorsett came through the door on the right then, a stack of papers pressed to her trim chest. "You're back," she said to me, without emotion. And then, to the young nurse she said, "David's not here. I don't know where he's gone. This is the third day he's done this to me."

"You could check the bottom of a bottle," the nurse said.

"Listen here!" I said. "You were terribly rude to me just now. You said that you would let me know when Mr. Barnesworth got back and yet you didn't even take my particulars —"

The nurse started laughing, her raised leg jiggling prettily with the effort. Even Miss Dorsett's face lightened.

"What are you laughing at?"

"There is no Mr. Barnesworth," the nurse said.

I looked from her to Miss Dorsett, who put down the stack of papers on her desk.

"There's a reason why you're here," Miss Dorsett said, pointing at me.

I stood dripping on the floor, trying to figure out what I'd landed in.

"You're here," she said, "because David is not." She kept pointing her finger.

"I like him better than David," the nurse said.

"Yes, but David is *very* good," Miss Dorsett said. "Are you *very* good?" she asked me.

"Is this an audition?"

I followed the two of them through the door on the left into a dark studio space. A roughly constructed frame for what looked like an elevator door stood absurdly on a small platform. Against the wall was a workbench, crammed with tubes of paint and jars of brushes, with an easel leaning against it. A row of pre-stretched empty canvasses stood in shadows against the wall.

"You can see the set-up that David has been working on," Miss Dorsett said. "We pay the models by the hour, so don't take forever. Elizabeth, is there anything you need? I can bring some coffee, if you like."

I glanced around again at the elevator frame, the workbench, the small platform.

"No, thank you," Elizabeth said.

Miss Dorsett left us alone. I turned my gaze to the beautiful Elizabeth — except for a poutiness that would take over her face sometimes, she was ravishing — and leaned my portfolio against the workbench.

"You would like . . . a portrait, is that it?" I asked doubtfully.

"It's whatever you want to do," Elizabeth said. She could see my confusion and seemed in no hurry to clarify the assignment.

"Is it an advertisement for nursing?"

"I never know what it's for, exactly," Elizabeth said. "Nobody tells me anything."

"But you're not a nurse."

"No. Sometimes I'm a secretary, sometimes I'm in my swimsuit and we make a little beach." She batted her eyes at me, enjoying my predicament. Finally, and mercifully, she said, "It's for calendars, of course. And knowing David, he would probably want the hem of my dress caught in the elevator doors, and the caption would read something like, 'On your way up, Nurse Jones?'"

"Ah," I said, finally starting to imagine it.

"Of course you could do anything you wanted."

"Let's see what that would look like." I positioned her by the flimsy fake elevator doors. I tried several times but they wouldn't stay shut firmly enough to keep a grip on her hem.

"David usually has some broken coat hangers," Elizabeth said. And sure enough on the workbench I found an old tobacco tin holding various lengths and shapes of coat hanger wire. I picked out a couple and went back to where I'd left her standing by the elevator doors. Then for the next while I fumbled with the wire to hitch up her hem. But nothing would stay.

"You could run a long one from the top of the door frame," Elizabeth said.

"Yes," I said, and thought about it some more.

My bunk. Collins and the others rub my nearly frozen hands and feet and ply me with warm tea, soup and biscuit gathered from private stocks.

"No *Kranke*!" I say, almost delirious. I can't let *Herr Doktor* at me again.

I can't stand to pee. Collins brings the bucket close to my bunk, and I lean on him and Napier when the deed must be done.

"At least that part didn't freeze off," Napier quips.

Muster is called, and if I'm not on *Kranke* I must be on

my feet. So they carry me out, shivering wildly still, lungs torn from coughing. I link arms with Napier and Richardson and hang somehow between them, my feet nominally on the ground. The wind rattles me like a sheet of roofing tin, set to fall the moment someone lets go.

Agony blathers on. I look around desperately for Margaret. She could stand behind me and heat the whole earth, and I could fall into her arms.

"Anyone who won't work for the Fatherland," Collins translates, "will not get any more cream or pumpkin pie. And don't laugh, or I might be next after Crome!"

Poor Collins looks bent as an old stick. And there's no Margaret. My heart races as if I'm sprinting up a hill, but nothing is warm. My blood feels like ice water.

I'm not going to survive. The certainty of it slowly takes away everything — fear, worry, sense, nonsense. Only a few things are real: these arms holding me up, the cold earth underfoot, the blackness coming on. Hurry, I think.

But it won't. Everything takes forever, even this.

Then I am in my bunk again. At last Margaret is stroking my forehead. She is older somehow. She looks as if everything has been taken from her as well. When she speaks she has Collins's voice.

"I might be able to arrange a transfer," she says. "But you'll have to be able to walk on your own. It's either that or *Kranke*."

"No *Kranke*," I whisper.

No *Kranke*, but I can barely work. My shovel tip bounces off the frozen ground and dislodges mere chips at a time. Mostly I lean on the shovel, trying to angle myself out of the killing wind. I have woollen socks on my hands, and they have found me an old scarf of Witherspoon's to wind around my face.

"It'll be better in Münster," Collins says to me.

He hunches like an ancient woman, wrapped in Witherspoon's blanket. Our shovels come upon a rock too big to move. We slide the tips along the edges and tilt, slide and tilt. Termites could make more progress.

"It's pretty cushy there," Collins says. "Two wood stoves in every barracks. Latrines that work."

The *scrape, scrape* of metal on rock.

"And it's not just for you. Napier, Fines, Wilkens — I'm arranging it for a bunch of us. Before we die here in this jolly field."

Even in the socks my fingers feel as dead as the wooden handle they're gripping. No — death wouldn't ache like this. Death would be a glorious shroud of nothing.

"But we need to sweeten the pot for Agony and Blasphemy. Fines has those marks his sister sent him wrapped in the fruit bread, and we've pooled all the bully beef, razor blades, soap and chocolate we can find. Anything you have, Crome, will be helpful. Are you following me?"

Scrape, scrape, but the rock is welded into the hard-brick soil. Termites would be sleeping now, down in the ground. They'd be eggs waiting for spring.

"Two blankets for every bed in Münster. And soft work. Captain Fielding was telling me. But we have to be smart about it. Are you listening?"

The rock moves a little bit. So we pull back our shovels,

then dig in harder. It's impossible not to. Just human nature. If the rock will move, then we must move it.

"I can do them both a drawing," I say, my teeth clattering.

"It's not what David would have done," Miss Dorsett said in a critical tone. She was looking at my painting of Elizabeth. In the end I'd forgotten the elevator completely and just rendered her leaning back against the high stool, her long legs crossed at the ankles, the nurse's uniform straining at the chest.

"I'm not David," I said.

"No, clearly you're not."

Elizabeth had gone by this time. Miss Dorsett and I were standing in the deserted studio looking at my work, still wet on the easel. I'd lost track of the time and felt quite hungry and weak all of a sudden. I'd had no lunch. I was aware too that my throat was burning and I'd soon be coughing if I didn't get something warm to drink.

Miss Dorsett didn't take her eyes off the painting. "What is she about to say?"

"Does there have to be a caption?"

"Usually. She looks either as though she's about to slap you or invite you to bed. Or maybe one after the other?" Miss Dorsett took her eyes off the painting then and looked at me. "You didn't find that expression on Elizabeth's face, did you?" Miss Dorsett looked back at the work. "And that isn't quite her face. Which is fine. You've done more with it. You do love women." She turned her glasses on me again. So many men don't. They think they do, but they haven't the slightest idea."

The statement hung in the air between us. Obviously a reply was expected. But the wrong word might ruin everything. For a moment I felt as if I wouldn't be able to breathe if I didn't get this job.

I stayed quiet and returned her gaze.

"I can pay you ninety-five dollars a month, Mr. Crome," she said. "I'm sorry it's not more. All the paintings become the property of the agency. There is a little more studio space here in the office. You aren't a drinker, are you? I'd hate to think I'd brought in another David. One is all I can handle. There is one other thing."

"Yes?" The air felt pushed out of the room, but I didn't want to let on.

"The models come through me, and if you touch one of them, if you behave in any way that is ungentlemanly or unprofessional — "

"I'm a married man, Miss Dorsett!"

"Many married men have fallen from grace, Mr. Crome. How is your wife going to react when you tell her you're working for a pin-up agency?"

A cough threatened to take me over. I turned away and gave into it for a time before willing my body back under control.

"Ninety-five dollars a month is a little low," I managed to say.

"We'll see how your work sells." Her eyes narrowed. "You don't look like the kind of man who has dozens of other options at the moment."

I stiffened at the remark and she caught it. "I'm sorry," she said without hesitation, and her face softened. "I can't pay you more for now, but you're very skilled and it really would be an honour if you could join us. May I call you Ramsay?"

"Certainly," I said. "And you are —?"

"Miss Dorsett," she said, then her smile returned. "Dorothy, to you."

Alone in the crowded barracks, trying to live off the meager body heat of thirty-three of us packed together, I open Margaret's letter. According to Napier's faulty wristwatch it's three minutes to nine, which means three minutes till the one pitiful electric light is shut off for the night.

And this is her first letter in ages. My eyes begin to leak even before I can extract the page.

Dearest Ramsay,

I hope and trust that this letter finds you well. I am sorry I have been such an inconstant correspondent. I have no excuses — I was not ill or suddenly pressed into consuming war work. What I can say I suppose is that I lost my way for a time and blundered about in a sort of self-induced darkness, as many people have I suspect in this war. It's the unrelenting nature of it: we are pressed in on all sides by the poverty of our food and the awful jingoism of our news — framed forever in the appalling lists of the dead which assault us daily — and the dreadfully frantic way the young men strut and career about the town like fruit flies set to expire within the hour. I'm sorry, but years of this, and perhaps of paying too particular attention, smothered me like a black curtain. It is nothing, I know, compared to the gas and

bombs and bullets and the hard cruelty of capture, all of
which you have faced.

Yet it very nearly defeated me. I feel so dreadfully
ashamed and unworthy.

But I can tell you that I have been comforted and am
more myself, like the old self you knew (back when you
knew me). One might even say I have been brought back
to life. And of course it was Boulton — my dear Henry
— who knows me better than any man and whose gentle
nature and steadfastness have buoyed me no end.

There is no easy way to say this now, but to simply
write it: Henry and I were married last month. It was
a small and sober affair, in keeping with wartime. But
joyful — so very joyful for me and for Henry — and
I know you will wish us well. We are living here with
Mother and Father until Henry has secured a promotion
in his office.

Thank you, dearest Ramsay, for your understanding
and friendship, I dare say for your love. If you had seen
me in my darkest days you would be happy for me now,
for I really was in a kind of prison (and how unworthy
I feel writing such words to you, of all people), a strange
melancholy that pressed me until I could hardly catch a
solid breath.

Be well, Ramsay, and come home safe. Please know
that you are in our constant thoughts and prayers.

> *Deepest regards,*
> *Margaret*

I look up just as the light goes out. I hear the barking of dogs
in the distance, the hard wind of winter. Someone shits in the
pail by the door. I cannot even tear the paper. The words are
from Margaret. Evidence of life beyond this purgatory.

Sometime later the door swings open, and a wind riffles the pages in my hands. Agony stands in his frozen greatcoat, like some dark snowman who has blundered in. Among the jangle of his harangue I understand just two words: *Crome* and *Münster.*

Then he is dragging me out. I leave clutching my coat and my letters wrapped in a small bundle, including these words from Margaret I'd trade the world for her not to have written.

No one else is being shipped out. I look around at Napier, Wilkens, Fines, at the shocked face of Collins. He straightens up by the pail, it seems to me to look Agony in the eye. There is only time for the briefest grasp of hands. He is an old man trying to look away from the grave.

"Keep your nut low!" he calls out just as the door is closing.

Thirteen

"Delores," I said, "if you could ease this way a little. Yes, and raise your knee — left knee, there, is that comfortable? I'll make a quick sketch like that. I'm just roughing out ideas. Are you from Montreal, Delores?"

I liked to repeat the girls' names a couple of times at the beginning so I could remember them later on. Delores had full, bouncy auburn hair and a more pointy chin than I was going to give her on canvas, and her teeth were a little grey, which I could certainly fix. Her legs were the prizewinners, and standing the way she was, stretching to reach something on a top shelf — I wasn't sure what it was going to be yet — her bottom was perfectly formed.

"Yes, I grew up in Westmount," she said.

"That's a nice neighbourhood. Now could you turn towards me? Just a bit. Very good. You have a lovely neck, Delores."

A fine blush coloured her face. She was perhaps twenty and unconsciously beautiful, if that can be said of anyone posing in such a way in a studio like ours.

"We were hit pretty hard," she said, "in the crash and

everything," and I began to realize that Delores was not one of those Westmount girls who keeps everything to herself. "My dad has had to find work at Morgan's. He was lucky to get anything, actually. He's in the shoe department. And we're taking in boarders, who've been very nice so far. None of the servants could stay, of course. So I help out any way I can. I just heard about this because of Nancy —"

"Oh, you're Nancy's friend."

"We used to summer together at Georgeville. You've heard of what her family has gone through. They lost *everything*. The house wasn't sold so much as taken, and Nancy's father used to work at the bank. You'd think they would've shown some leniency, but the men who are left would jail their grandmothers if a payment was missed. What's the world coming to?"

"Just a little more stretch with the right hand. It's awkward, I know."

The serious topic was bringing out the beauty in her face.

"The banks are showing their true colours," she said. "A few years ago they'd loan money for any hare-brained scheme, and now if you don't already have money of your own then you certainly can't expect a bank to loan you any. Another friend of mine actually works in a bank. One day her till was short — twenty-five cents perhaps — and they nearly fired her on the spot. Twenty-five cents!"

"You can rest now, thank you. Just have a seat on the stool. I'll probably ask you to take the position again in a while. Have you a young man, Delores?"

A much deeper blush spread down her neck as she told me about him — Jimmy or Teddy or something like that. "A lot of my friends who still have money," she said suddenly, "seem completely oblivious of what's happening. I was with some of them last week, wandering back home after the theatre — one of them had extra tickets — and we came upon some homeless men begging for nickels. And Janet, whose father practically runs Sun Life, almost spat on them. She said to us — and she was wearing a fur coat as she said it, and the one man could still hear us, he had an open sore running down the side of his face — she said, 'They just don't want to work.' I was furious with her. The others had no idea why I got upset."

"It's not been a bad depression for those who still have money."

"That's it! If you have any money at all these days the world's your oyster."

I paused to just look at her — her kind eyes, the roundness of her shoulders, the clean femininity of her face, the unspoiled completeness of her youth and beauty. I thought: I am getting paid to do this work. For ninety-five dollars a month I sit and chat with Delores and her attractive friend Nancy, and Elizabeth and the other models that Miss Dorsett finds. I gaze at them and sketch, and some of these old wounds of mine, which they cannot even see — a girl like Delores was barely born when the war broke out — heal slightly, without fuss, a little at a time.

Something about her reminded me of Lillian. Or perhaps what I wanted Lillian to be. As far as my wife knew, I was doing the same sort of advertising work as with Frame. I hadn't lied directly but had simply failed to correct her mistaken impression in the small moment of triumph when I told her the news. But how would she ever understand or approve? I would have to find the right time, the right way to tell her.

"If I could just get you to stretch again the way you were before — yes, good! A little higher," I said, and watched as Delores turned back to her duties.

At the new camp in Münster many of the men have boils and burns on their skin from working in the salt mines. In the bleak barracks at night they rest their bodies and stare blankly at nothing. Their hands, especially, are lacerated with running sores from handling the hard, sharp salt that burns into the skin.

But my luck holds. I am too weak to work in the mines and instead am assigned to a shoe factory, where I sweep the floor, clean up piles of cuttings and other garbage, and shuffle about looking busy. The instant someone takes notice of me I might be returned to Raumen or sent to the salt mines.

How to stay invisible? For hours each day I think of Margaret in her dark moods and how Boulton is comforting her. And how this change of camps means several more months before any mail makes its way to me. And anyway she is married. Hope was slim and now is gone, and yet thoughts churn away regardless.

And I am not invisible to everyone. A young, wan, wraithlike girl runs messages up and down the winding wrought-iron staircase between the shop floor and the manager's office perched above us like a watchtower. It's my own fault, I suppose. But anything female is a rarity, and so I gape at her. She has lank brown hair, matchstick arms and grey eyes that pop out as if being pressed from behind.

As I am brushing scrap and dust from one little corner of

the factory to another she passes close by on her way somewhere else and whispers, "You are English, yes?"

I am too startled to respond right away, and then she is already several steps past me. As far as I know she didn't look directly at me.

Some minutes later, on the return route, she passes by quite close again, so I whisper, "Canadian."

She doesn't acknowledge me. The next morning, however, I am wiping dirt off a window ledge when she drops some papers close to my feet. As she kneels to deal with them she says, "My family took me to Cornwall one summer before all this."

"Yes?"

"Padstow," she says, and goes on her way.

A few days later she manages to say, "Do you fight . . . black bears?"

"Black bears?" She is pretending to be looking at an account book as if she has suddenly discovered something there while walking.

"In Canada!"

"There are black bears," I whisper, "but we don't fight them very often."

It goes on like this, halting and strange, for several weeks. I learn that she loves English gardens, that she thinks the sea is very beautiful, that Canada is full of red Indians and wild beasts. Every fitful bit of conversation is *verboten* — if caught we both might face severe punishment — and so we keep up the charade.

Finally she asks, "Do you have any . . . extra food?"

Just for a moment she looks directly at me, then she is past. She immediately says something harsh to one of the older factory workers. His neck and face go stiff and he bows slightly. I have no idea what it is about. But I think: she could have me sent off. She could make up almost anything and I would be beaten and made to work in the mines.

So the next day I bring a small packet of dark chocolate from a Red Cross parcel. As she descends the iron stairs I push my broom away from her, and when I know she is looking I leave the packet on a ledge where she can pick it up.

I bring tea bags another day, and dried fruit. I start doing sketches in the barracks, though I have no access to officers this time to pay me and the men are as poor as I am. But packages are getting through, and I make enough to keep this girl from turning on me.

Then one day I am in the storeroom loading boxes by myself when she comes in, apparently looking for something. The door closes and I catch her eyes on me in the first naked gaze she has allowed herself.

"My name is Henrike," she says.

We stand for a time just breathing, staring at one another. Then she says, "The food is keeping my mother and father alive. *Danke.*" She stares some more, then remembers herself and leaves in a great hurry, and I continue to look dumbly at the back of the door.

Lunch at DeVrie's was thirty-five cents and included pork baked to within an inch of eternity but sliced thin enough to fall apart on your tongue, and brown gravy hardly more than greasy water that pooled in a lump of mashed potatoes big enough to see you through the rest of the day, with a few lonely, jaundiced strings of cabbage — it must have been cabbage — to round out the plate. We hardly ever ate out, but now it was Dorothy's birthday, the twenty-third of June, and two others were with us: David, with his big, leathery face and wild, thinning white hair, and Elizabeth, with her large eyes and glamorous skin. Slight Dorothy somehow remained dominant, the centre of the conversation. We had a table near the big street-side window, and the rain lashed sideways like the spray from a firehose turned against us. David had had Elizabeth posing with a little dog that Dorothy had found for the day — a bad-tempered terrier who was supposed to pull cutely at her hem but chewed it instead and bit David on the ankle.

"I will not return to work with that hound unless management guarantees removal of his incisors!" David declared. He pounded a fat fist onto the table; the jolt spilled some water from my glass. All the seats in the place were filled and the room smelled of smoke and wet clothing. Loudly as the rain roared against the window, we were louder, like drunken sailors ignoring the storm.

"He'll bite me next!" Elizabeth said. "And he's ruining my skirt."

"At this very moment he's probably eating most of my brushes," David said. The dog had been left in David's studio, leashed to a table leg.

"Well, he seemed gentle enough this morning," Dorothy explained. "I was just walking over to the office when a very elderly man — you know the type, he walks as if he's had a yardstick stuck in the back of his trousers since his school days —" She straightened up and pursed her lips. "He looked at me as if he wanted either to propose or turn me over his knee and give me a good whack for the dissolute life he thinks I'm leading. He had one of those moustaches that certain men will trim, you know" — she made a funny motion with her fingers in front of her upper lip — "like they're trimming a hedge. I knew whatever he was about to say was going to be awful. So I stepped closer to him, the way a fighter will step inside to avoid a punch." She looked at me now. "My father was an amateur boxer."

"Really?"

"Three knockouts, one serious concussion" — she paused, then flashed a disarming smile — "and he won a fight too, I believe, which gave him bragging rights for the rest of his life. At any rate, I cut in on this old man. 'Would you mind terribly if I borrowed your dog for the day?' If I *had* counterpunched him, his face wouldn't have looked more screwball. 'I'm with an art agency, and we're looking for talent, real talent, and I think your dog has ... a certain quality. Look at him!' I bent down, of course, and the dog started to shake and whine as if he'd never been this excited in his life, poor thing."

David finished scraping his plate clean and turned his considerable body fully towards Dorothy. "He thinks his dog is going to become famous?"

"I never *said* Rin Tin Tin, but from the look in his eye I think the gentleman is now counting on Hollywood millions. Perhaps you should get back and finish with the mutt."

David glanced outside in alarm. "In this typhoon?"

"It's hardly raining now," Dorothy said. "And I promised to have him back by four."

"Eye of the storm!" David said, but he was standing now and fumbling through his trouser pockets, which were not jingling. Dorothy watched him for a good long time — while Elizabeth was sorting through her raincoat and arranging a scarf and fussing with her umbrella — until finally Dorothy said, "It's all right, David. I'll get the cheque. Elizabeth too. Now hurry!"

"Thank you, good lady," David blustered. "I know I had money this morning. It must be some capitalist conspiracy. Workers of the world!" He looked around at the tables of men and women chattering though their lunch hour.

Dorothy finished the thought for him. "Get back to your labours. Ramsay and I will follow shortly."

We watched as David held the door for Elizabeth, then Elizabeth raised her umbrella for David, who huddled himself under its slight span, and the two hurried along, Elizabeth catching most of the rain.

"Such a gentleman, our David," Dorothy said. "If I can just keep his wages low enough, he might refrain from drinking himself to death." She smiled and looked at me, then sipped at the tea left in her cup. "Now what about you, Ramsay? What are you so unhappy about?"

"Unhappy?"

"Perhaps you aren't unhappy," she continued, and what had been a light conversation suddenly turned serious. "But you have a certain … look. You've always had it, ever since you first stepped into the agency."

She sipped her tea. Both our mugs were nearly empty, but it would have cost beyond the special to order more. She looked out at the miserable weather. "I suppose it rained dreadfully in the war?"

I had never told her I'd been a soldier.

"Famously," I said. I waited for her to comment further,

but she seemed content to nurse her tea. I finished mine and made ready to stand.

"My brother was in it," she said. "Charlie. He was the kind of boy who would walk into a room and make everybody feel better. He must have had seven different young women desperately in love with him, and even when he told them he couldn't possibly marry, they still thought he was the grandest fellow."

"And he was killed," I said, to cut the story short. But I had subsided back into my seat and instantly regretted the tone of my voice, the hard mask I could feel forming on my face, because hers looked suddenly vulnerable.

"No," she said softly. "He came home. But there was barely anything in him that I recognized any more. He'd had several teeth smashed out. That was the worst of it — from some brawl in a canteen. An army dentist fitted him with a bad set of dentures that Charlie refused to replace. He didn't care anymore. He killed himself in 1925." Now her tea was finished as well, and she was carefully studying the tablecloth.

"I'm so sorry," I said.

"I saw parts of Charlie in you that very first day. Not just the sad parts, either. He would never talk about anything to do with the war. I'd sit him down and even ply him with booze, but he couldn't seem to say a word about it. Not to me, not to my parents. He kept it all inside. He said it was too ... no, he didn't even say that much. He said we would never understand."

The rain began to pick up again and pelted the window in a cold fury.

"Do *you* talk about it?" Dorothy asked.

"Not much to talk about," I said curtly. "Unless you want to wallow in the depravity of it. I'm happy to have it behind me."

"Is it really behind you?"

I smiled uncomfortably. The waitress came by with the pot of tea and Dorothy ordered more for both of us.

"Shouldn't we be getting back?" I asked.

But Dorothy sat where she was, looking at me until I felt my face burning.

"How did you end up running your own agency?" I asked. "Who was Barnesworth?"

"My uncle on my mother's side. He gave the business to me. He thought I might have a good head for it. My uncle somehow believed Charlie's death was all his fault, because he'd encouraged him to join up with everyone else. For the Empire!"

She was looking at me too closely, as if she felt she had the right to peel back my skin.

"You probably lost some good friends," she said.

"We all did," I said vaguely. She kept looking, looking, in the most unsettling way.

"Perhaps we should head back," I said.

Once or twice a week we meet in the storeroom for a few stolen moments. I continue to leave small packets in convenient places for Henrike to pick up and take home to her parents. She slips inside the room and closes the door, always with either her clipboard in hand or other papers to press across her chest, as if they are needed for protection. Sometimes she is at my side before I manage to turn around.

Her eyes stay open. After the first few times words are irrelevant. We breathe, sweat, yearn, gasp like animals. I feel her hard ribs beneath her clothes, the boniness of her back and hips, smell the smoke of her hair. She kisses frantically at my scrawny chest and inserts her cold, searching hands in the folds and crevices of my prison uniform.

There is only time for famished kissing. I send my hands beneath her skirts only to have them slapped down even as her own are tugging at my seams and buttons. Her groans are noises of frustration. She circles me for a while, then rushes off clutching her papers again. My brain, my limbs are faint with fatigue and hunger, but this too is a hunger demanding to be fed.

Our longest stretch together could not be more than seven or eight minutes. If we are seen I might be shot, Henrike disgraced. But months pass in quiet safety.

She always leaves first. Sometimes, at night, I stare at the rough and darkened planks of the barracks ceiling and hold my fingertips to my face to try to smell the aching want from her skin.

"Get up!" Margaret steams, and I look at her, startled. The air is hotter than a boiled bath, and I can feel the sweat rotting my joints. I try to see up, up where I know the little space should be — the window to stars or snow or night or day. But the window isn't there.

"You're sleeping your life away!" Margaret says. She is all in black, in mourning. For Witherspoon?

"He'll still be dead no matter what I do," I say. I feel as if I'm breathing through sopping canvas. Even Margaret is sweating. She takes a lace handkerchief from her sleeve and mops her brow and cheeks.

An alarm clangs and Collins rushes past us in a German uniform except for his boots — he still has on his fannigan wooden clogs. They make a horrible clacking on the floor. Margaret pulls at my arm.

"If it wasn't for you, he would have been all right!" she says. "Now get out of bed!"

I am waiting for Agony to follow after Collins, for the dogs and the guards. Suddenly I can hear them, a mob smashing at the barracks door.

"Jesus!"

I sat up and looked around. Awake now, blinking, breathing like a sprinter.

I saw Lillian's slumped form beside me. She'd kicked all the covers onto the far corner of our sagging bed. It was stifling hot, even with the one miserable bedroom window thrown wide open. The air smelled of rot and sweating bodies. On the ceiling ghostly little clusters of loose paint flakes were waiting to snow on us in the middle of summer. Time and time again we'd scraped them off, only to find them replaced within a few days by more moulting flakes. The landlord would not paint, and I couldn't spare the money — not for decoration, when there was barely enough for food and the rent for this horrible flat.

Lillian turned over uneasily. She was in her lightest summer nightdress. I thought of nudging her awake, of trying to stir up the night air.

But I didn't move. I closed my eyes to picture Margaret again. Margaret without Collins, without Witherspoon and Agony and the rest. Just Margaret on her own, in the skin, if I could manage it. But all I saw was Dorothy's face, her large eyes, the slim taper of her fingers.

What was that joke she had come up with this morning? She was bursting to tell it: how the police raided a brothel last night not far from where she lives and found a Catholic priest, the fire chief and the attorney general. "The police ask the men, 'What have you got to say for yourselves?' She put on her deepest voice.

"And the priest says to the police, 'Several of these women have sinned and I have been taking their confessions.'

"And the fire chief says to the police, 'The room in the back is poorly ventilated and poses a significant risk.'

"And the attorney general says to the police, 'I thought you guys weren't booked in here till Wednesday!'"

Her laughter sounded across the building. I thought about how she blew smoke out the side of her mouth and looked away so often when she was talking, only to turn back with those grappling eyes. I thought about how a woman will build up in your mind and body, settle in like an illness you want to have.

The baby started to cry. I got up quickly, relieved for the distraction. The air was even worse by the baby's bed. He was glistening with sweat in the silvery light, tossing and moaning in his sleep.

"Michael." As I carried him onto the fire escape for fresher air he nuzzled his tiny face against my chest and moved his lips in a semi-conscious search for his mother's breast. It must have been two or three in the morning. The street below was deathly still. A yellow dog ran across it, sniffing at something I couldn't see, and the breeze blew a few paper bits this way and that without conviction. The whole city had settled into silence. But the air was fresh and almost cool compared to what was trapped inside our tenement rooms.

Michael stayed cuddled in my arms, and in our own ways we studied the middle of the night. I found myself singing a silly old marching song.

> *Wash me in the water*
> *That you washed your dirty daughter*
> *And I shall be whiter*
> *Than the whitewash on the wall.*

Lillian came out then. She'd wrapped her robe tightly around her and looked at me suspiciously.

"What are you doing?"

"Trying to breathe," I said.

"Were you singing? It's the middle of the night."

She turned around then and disappeared into the gloom.

I stayed where I was and looked again at the street. A few dusty-leaved trees waved ghostly fingers in the desultory gusts of wind, and the yellow dog was making his way back towards us with something dark in his mouth, pulled from the garbage no doubt.

"Some nights like this," I whispered to my boy, "I looked out at eternity. Some nights in battle everything would fall still, and the birds would sing — nightingales — their beautiful, gentle, high-pitched little love songs. And starlings would swoop underneath the moon, and it seemed that if anything could last forever, this would. This peace."

The baby buried his warm face in my shoulder.

"Are you coming?" Lillian called. She sounded fed up. How could I blame her? This was no way to live, packed in a squalid little box, afraid of every little expense, of every sniffle. I stood and adjusted Michael on my shoulder, then stepped back into the stuffy air. When I eased the child into his crib he yawned and balled his fists and rolled over, his face pushed into the pillow.

In the bedroom I settled myself as lightly as possible beside Lillian's still, tight body. For some minutes I listened to her breathing, which was slow and deep but mostly an act. When I brushed my hand against her backside she tensed.

I know how you feel, I thought, but I could not say the words.

I withdrew my hand and lay as still as possible, trying not to look at the murky paint flakes on the ceiling.

"Ramsay, do you think you could carry a box of files to my apartment for me? It's only a couple of blocks away, on Stanley," Dorothy said to me.

We were well into August now and I'd finished for the day, a very nice portrait, I thought, of a young woman in the act of taking off a swimsuit in front of a mirror and surveying the red damage of sunburn on her lovely shoulders and arms. The box in question was covering most of Dorothy's desk. She was getting ready to close the office when David came stumbling through the door of his studio. He wiped a rag over his sweating face.

He always seemed to sweat when he painted.

"I can certainly take a box for you, my dear!" David said. "I'm just heading your way, I believe."

Paint smears decorated his red, puffy cheek. He turned to me. "Have you seen the young one, Ramsay? What's her name?"

"You mean Rebecca Childes," Dorothy said.

"Rebecca Childes! Rebecca Childes!" David sang. "Her body is the closest approximation to heaven I have ever seen. And you can quote me, my dear!"

"You say that nearly every day, David," Dorothy replied.

Then the size of the box registered with him, and suddenly his back was feeling unreliable, and he announced that he was not finished with Rebecca Childes after all. To me in a stage whisper he said, "She should pay you for this box-hauling time. She'll have you scrubbing her kitchen floor next, and fixing her windows."

"David, you go fix your own windows!" she said.

I lifted the box. It was heavy enough that I wondered if my elbow could manage it.

"Can I trust you to lock up, David?" Dorothy asked.

"Of course. Just let me steal the profits first!" He disappeared again behind the door. I caught a glimpse of his Miss Childes, a statuesque redhead sitting in a black slip, sipping from a coffee cup that she rested on her lap.

I carried the box along the hall and down the stairs, then out onto the busy sidewalk. The city had been baking for weeks. I was in shirt sleeves, and I had loosened my tie and wore my hat pushed high on my head. It was not as muggy as many late afternoons in a Montreal summer, but the sidewalks radiated heat and the traffic on the street moved sluggishly, like camels in the desert.

Dorothy was a fast walker, her tiny legs scissoring in high-heeled shoes. Under my load I had to push to keep up with her, and I began to regret the assignment. Within a few minutes sweat was stinging my eyes. Up the hill we marched, then we turned into her building and climbed five hard flights. When we finally reached her door my chest was heaving and my arms screamed for release.

"I am so grateful to you. You're wonderfully strong," she said, and before she slid her key in the door she touched my shoulder with her hand.

I carried the box into the apartment and willed myself to let it down slowly onto the table, rather than drop it. When it was down I rubbed my arms and flexed my fingers to revive the circulation.

"I hope that wasn't too awful?" she said, in her slightly mocking way. "Can I pour you a drink?"

"Some water would be fine, thank you."

"How about a real drink?"

I stayed with the water and watched her pour out two fingers of scotch for herself, which she downed with a quick, convulsive tip of the glass. Her face was newly flushed and her eyes shone.

"I wonder, while you're here, if you could look at a shelf for me in the other room?" She pointed to what I could plainly see was her bedroom. She looked as if she was trying to fight off waves of embarrassment.

"What's wrong with it?"

"Something's loose," she said nervously. She didn't move

towards the bedroom but remained with the glass in her hand, staring at me.

It's an extraordinary thing when a woman shows her desire. I felt as though, without moving, she'd taken several steps towards me. My breathing was still ragged from the lifting.

"Is it . . . fastened properly?"

"I'm not sure that it is." Her eyes did not flicker away.

I'm a married man, I imagined myself reminding her, though the words didn't emerge. I moved towards her and she stayed exactly where she was: wary, open, holding her breath.

I didn't know what I was going to do. She tilted her head as I got closer. I ducked mine and stepped past her into the bedroom, then scanned the walls idiotically, looking for a loose shelf. She did not follow me right away, but paused to pour herself another drink. I wished I'd taken one as well.

The bed was in a far corner, single, with a plain white cover. The drapes were beige, masculine. But a pretty writing desk under the window looked delicate and finely wrought. The only bookshelf ran along the wall to the left of the desk. I strode over to it, happy to have some sort of purpose, and tried rattling it, but the wall fasteners were solid.

When I turned around she was sitting behind me on the bed, her legs swinging gently. She leaned back on her right arm and sipped more of her drink. Her hair was loose on her shoulders.

"I'm afraid I can't," I said without looking at her.

For several seconds those were the only words that hung between us.

"It's all right," she said finally. She pulled at my hand until

I looked at her. "I don't make a habit of this, if that's what you think."

"No, I —"

"Shut up a second. I know you're married. But you've kind of snuck up on me, Ramsay Crome. These are such sad times. Now you know where I live."

She let go of my hand and downed her drink.

"The lady has just told you how she feels. You should thank her and leave it at that, and I will see you at work tomorrow."

I could hardly move towards the door.

But — "Thank you," I managed.

I walked home almost drunkenly, the heat of the early evening oiling my limbs. It seemed the earth itself had tilted. But cars chugged down the streets in their same old oblivious way, and men and women continued to walk the lanes, and the stores that still remained open advertised their wares at rock-bottom prices.

I was dizzy with the nearness of so many sharp edges.

I mounted the rickety iron stairs to our old flat, newly disgusted with the poverty and grime of the neighbourhood, with the stench of rotting garbage from the bins behind the building, with the shabby windows and the grubby door that stuck in the heat, and with the dark gloom within those walls which was the best that a middle-aged fannigan could afford.

"Long day?" Lillian said when she saw me. She was clutching Michael to her chest, and the tiny kitchen smelled of boiling potatoes. I kissed them both quickly.

"I need to wash up. I'm afraid I'm filthy. I walked in the heat."

"Was something wrong with the trolley car?"

"Everything was so slow," I said vaguely, then splashed water on my face from the basin. I imagined guilt reeking from my pores. But all I could see in her face was what had been there for a long time already: the slow, grey fatigue of living poor in the city, the shadows lining her eyes as if it were forever December.

"What are you working on?" she asked.

"Nothing special. An advert for shoes."

I walked into the other cursedly tiny room, happy to escape for a moment any further conversation. The newspaper lay folded on the rickety excuse for a side table. As I opened it the mail fell out and on the floor.

A manila envelope, addressed to me, had a fancy seal on it. I looked at it without curiosity, then my eye fell on the newspaper again. Six "workless men" had been arrested and hundreds more tear-gassed for protesting the shutdown of their plant. Communists were believed to be behind the agitation...

I opened the envelope in irritation and then had to concentrate fully to process the words. *Dear Mr. Crome,* it said. *Further to your application for war reparations due to alleged mistreatment by Germany during your incarceration there 3 June 1916 to your release at Dover 18 November 1918...*

A cheque fluttered to the floor. I picked it up and looked at it in amazement.

You have been awarded the sum of $500 in compensa-

186

tion towards your claim, plus 5% p.a. dated from 10 January, 1920, the date upon which, under the Treaty of Versailles, Germany undertook to pay and assume a contractual obligation to make good the damage caused during the war.

The cheque was for almost nine hundred dollars.

"Ramsay, are you all right?"

When I looked at Lillian — she was holding a plate of cabbage and potatoes for me, with one tiny sausage — the room swam in tears.

"We're getting out of these damn rooms," was all I could say.

Fourteen

Old McGillis's farm in Mireille had long since been sold, and he was living now with Maisie Campbell down the way, tending her cows, straightening her fence posts, and trying to stay out of range of her preaching. But another property opened up not too far from the former family land. It was mostly woodlot and there was no house, but it came with a meadow and a promise of being a place on this earth for a man to stretch his arms. And it came too with the sight of old childhood hills to bring the blood back to my young wife's cheeks and plenty of country air to fill my baby's lungs.

I broke the ground myself. With a team of lads from the local farms we dug the shallow foundation and framed out the walls and roof of the house. I knew nothing about construction except what made sense. Most of the men had built barns. While the roughest of the work was being completed, Lillian, Michael and I lived in a big canvas tent down in the meadow. It was on the soft grass of the meadow that the boy learned to walk and where his incessant runny nose cleared up.

We started to build in late August. By October I had to return to work in the city, and for the next few months I logged full days in the office and then worked into the night on the property, setting down the roof shingles, framing in the rooms, laying in the plumbing and wiring, finishing the walls, fashioning and hanging doors. Young Michael would quietly root and play beside me and had to be watched, of course, among the stray nails and boards, the sharp tools lying around.

For days on end it rained. The tent was cold and smelled of must and did little against the chilly wind, but Michael only grew stronger, and Lillian too began to revive. She was like a plant kept too long in a dark corner but now returned to fresh soil and air and light. Her face shone in a way it hadn't in the dust and grime of Montreal, and she brought her own strong will and farm sense to fashioning a good life out of disruption and chaos. She chose the plot and broke the soil for what would be the garden and fed us with soups and stews and bread and turned us out in clean clothes, ironed dry despite the rain.

And at night in our cots her embrace was warmer than it had ever been before. Often we would sleep together on one cot, entwined in a single bed roll, our legs interlaced as we snuggled warm against the deepening cold of the night. I would wake up in the darkness with my limbs stiff and numb but not daring to move, wishing only to prolong the feeling of breathing together, of having our hearts beat out the same drum song.

"I'll be a little sad when we're finished," Lillian said to me. We were on our knees fitting boards. Sawdust covered her hair and lit on her eyelashes like a butterfly's wing dust.

"Aren't you looking forward to having our own room and waking up not chilled to the bone every morning?"

"Of course!" she said. "And having a garden, and decorating all the rooms, and getting some decent furniture. I know we can't afford it all right away —" She saw the warning look in my eye. She stopped and put her warm hand on the back of my neck. "But this has been good too."

There is great comfort when things are getting better, when you can see the structures rising around you and the materials smell of new hope, and your efforts seem to stand plumb and straight against the rains and winds of the world, the drunken, reeling decisions of the gods.

"He has deigned to appear!" Dorothy said, as I stepped through the office door. She had moved the coat stand for some reason, and I stood in dumb silence looking for it as the rainwater drained from my coat and umbrella.

"I'm sorry," I said. "Yesterday I was working on the wiring. I just couldn't get away. I should have sent a message that I wouldn't be in."

I spotted the coat stand then — behind her desk, hidden under clothing, of course.

"I'll stay late tonight," I said. "I'm sorry if it's extra for the models, but I really couldn't —"

"Mr. Crome," she said, looking down now at her papers. Her face was white and hard. "I'm not sure I can afford an artist as preoccupied as you've become with this country house of yours. You've missed days and been late on other occasions."

"It won't happen again," I said quickly.

"You're looking unnaturally happy as well," she said then,

and without tilting her head she let her clear grey eyes roam upwards to catch my gaze. "The country air seems to be good for you." The slightest edge of a grin was beginning to appear.

"Yes."

"And the wife and child, are they well planted?"

"I've put them in the back meadow between the old cornstalks. They get full morning sun and shade in the afternoon. They should come up like blazes in the warm weather."

David wandered into the office then. His coat was hanging open and the buttons of his cardigan were done up in the wrong order. He had his hat in his hand and his grey mess of hair was flattened on one side, as if he'd been sleeping against it on a soaked park bench until three minutes ago.

"My Lord. It's an apparition!" David said, looking at me.

"Ramsay has left his family with the chickens," Dorothy said. "And he promises we're going to see more of him."

"Thank God for that. I'm getting tired of holding up this business single-handedly. Perhaps I should just go home and let Ramsay do *my* work for several weeks while I recuperate?"

I wedged myself behind Dorothy's chair and set to hanging up my coat and umbrella. She scooted her chair back so that my legs were jammed against the file cabinet. "There now! You're trapped. No more escaping to Arcadia. You will stay here and do my bidding, do you understand?"

Featherweight though she was, she was pushing with some force against me, and it would have taken an effort to move her. She was grinning at me too, like a girl racing around the playground.

David shuffled his feet, his own soaked coat in his hand.

"If I didn't know better," he said, "I'd swear you two were married."

"How have you been, Ramsay?" Margaret asks. It is late at night and the cold wind is seething through the barracks walls. I'm shivering in my clothes beneath a single hard, threadbare blanket, straining to make her out in the gloom.

"I didn't expect to see you," I say.

Her neck is so white. She has wrapped herself in a shawl but her throat is exposed. Her eyes are dark and thoughtful.

"I haven't forgotten you."

"But you've married Boulton!"

"Would you shut up?" someone says in the darkness, and several others groan. A few men smoke in the corner, the dull light of their cigarettes poking the gloom. But I'm not the only one making noise. There are the usual assorted sobs and snores and angry whispered conversations with the devils in men's own head.

She kneels close to me and puts a hand on my cheek. "I had to see how you were."

"A bloody mess," I whisper back. Her fingers are cold, as if she's been walking miles in the frigid wind to get here.

"I don't want you to forget me," she says.

Someone laughs out loud, a harsh, breathless, lunatic noise.

I stare at her. I can't move, can't take her face in my hands or kiss her lips or push her away. Her hair is coming undone at the back. One good pull from me and it will cascade all over.

"Margaret, you are a dark poison in my brain. I couldn't

root you out if I wanted to. Why in God's name did you marry him?"

She is quiet for the longest time, and her glistening eyes hold mine no matter where I turn. I feel myself slowly crumbling into just another sobbing wretch.

"You come back to London," she says gently. "I need to see you safe."

A thousand blasphemies rise and die in my throat.

"You come back to London," she says.

Now the paint was dry. We'd been moving furniture most of the day. We'd even somehow managed a Christmas tree with homemade ornaments and a few trifling gifts for ourselves. But we were in our castle and the boy was asleep in his own room and the walls smelled of paint, not wet canvas tenting. We had running water, wooden doors, glass windows and a new electric icebox that vibrated the whole house when it hummed.

Here was my new studio surrounded by windows that, in the light of day, would look out on blue mountains and rolling fields. And here was the storage room where I could keep my paintings under proper conditions, safe and private and free from dusty, crowded corners. And here was my tired but blossoming wife, and here was our bed, and everything was new and built and in order.

"I can't believe it," she said, and let herself fall backwards onto the mattress. Her body bounced once and again, then she lay giggling. "It's ours."

"Mainly the bank's." I followed her onto the bed. Our

beautiful new coal furnace was heating the house prodigiously against the cold of Christmas Eve.

"But we own this bedroom."

"Yes. This part is ours." I rolled on top of her and we kissed and she settled herself beneath my weight.

"I hope we never have to move."

"Never. They'll bury us out back!" I said, and I kissed her again. She smelled of the sweet bread she'd been baking all afternoon. I was waiting for her to tell me she was exhausted or to remember one more thing to do for Christmas. But she stayed where she was.

"It *will* be better here," she whispered.

We left the lights blazing. I'd done all the wiring myself, all the plumbing, had raised the walls and seen it through, and we deserved this night of love. I yearned to lie in the soft, strong luxury of her flesh and feel her waters rise. I wanted to keep my eyes open and have it last eternally. She was gaining a taste for it. It had been a long time coming, but the exit from Montreal was what started it, the months under canvas added to the momentum, and now she moved to my touch and bound herself to me, and our bed jumped and clanged on the new, unfinished floor.

I fell asleep against her as she stroked my hair and held my head.

That night I dreamt I was walking in the woods, although the mountains in the distance were not English, and Margaret was wearing a long gown I'd never seen her in. I was looking for a spot in the bushes, some dry clearing out of sight where I could take her hand and pull her next to me. But nothing seemed to be quite right.

She said, "You really do deserve this, Ramsay."

I kept looking.

"After everything."

She didn't seem jealous at all. I could picture myself peeling off her dress. But we would need to get into the shadows, away from the sun. It was hot, not wintertime at all. Even the leaves on the trees were warm, and her skin was so fair she'd redden easily, even blister.

"It's silly to think of a man loving just one woman for all his life," she said. "You could love two quite easily. Or more, perhaps. If only society weren't so stuck."

She was inviting me — clearly she was. I hadn't known before, but now I did. All I needed was the right spot. I looked and looked, but the wall of the forest grew thicker.

I looked.

And Lillian said, "Ramsay!"

I bolted upright. The room was filling with smoke.

"Michael!" Lillian screamed and left me in a moment. Most of the bedding either followed her onto the floor or, wrapped round her, went down the stairs, where I could see licks of flame in the blackness. "Michael!" she screamed again and again. A moment later I heard her cry, "There you are!"

I still hadn't moved from the bed.

The heat of the fire sprang through the walls. I ran to the closet that still had no door and pulled something off the rack and around my body. Then I stumbled into my studio and opened the storeroom and began to throw the paintings out the window in pairs, in threes, in singles. I could see first Michael on the ground — he was tiny, in bare feet, scrambling on the snow — then Lillian in her nightdress gathering him up.

"Ramsay! Come down!" she screamed to me.

"I've got time!" I yelled back and continued tossing. I tried to send them flat into the night so that they would land as softly as possible.

"Ramsay!"

Even in the shadows and the smoke I could see the paint on the walls bubbling and blackening. *But this is not it*, I thought. *I am not going to die tonight.*

I got the last of the paintings out. Lillian was screaming at me from below, but at least she had sense enough to stay a good distance away with the child. I flung myself into mid-air and fell flat upon landing, the thin snow barely cushioning my fall.

But nothing broken.

"Get away! Away from the damn thing!" I yelled. We sprinted down to the meadow. I was in sock feet but somehow didn't feel the cold, not immediately. We hadn't struck the tent yet and thankfully some blankets had been left out. I was sick at the sight of the house — a crackling burst of light in the cold darkness. Then we heard alarms in the distance, and neighbours ran to help now, voices shouted for us. Even down in the meadow the heat of the blaze drew sweat to my face.

I saw in Lillian's face a register of the shock of it, and baby Michael looked on in wonder as timbers started to fall.

"Your paintings!" Lillian said suddenly.

The south wall folded like a man suddenly driven to his knees, and a burst of flame and chaos spread over the ground where most of the canvasses had fallen.

"Let them burn," I said quietly.

"But you saved them!"

"I was stupid to even waste a thought." And then, when I saw the look on her face, I said, "We're all safe."

"But what are we going to do?" Lillian wailed. "Everything's gone!"

"Do?" I said as lightly as I could. I felt oddly happy, as if my sails were unexpectedly full of wind. "In the morning we'll have breakfast and then start again from scratch."

Soon the neighbours found us with their flashlights. Their voices were full of excitement and concern. "We're over here!" I called. "We're all right!" and I stepped forward. I had Michael in my arms now, and young as he was, I wanted him to see it. I wanted him to know what to do when the world has come crashing down.

"I need your help." The words slip out almost carelessly, although I've been rehearsing them for days. I am pushing my broom with feigned industry while Henrike stands behind me, apparently watching a pair of birds that have slipped inside the factory.

"Yes?"

"I need clothes."

"For winter?"

"To leave."

She turns around as the birds swoop low past long, whirring machinery belts and then wheel higher into the rafters of the old place. We are all watching them. Her face betrays nothing.

The cracked windows and leaky walls of the factory keep out none of the gathering winter. We are defenceless against it — all of us, Germans, British, Belgians, Russians. For months it seems we've been hearing the news of the great Fatherland's victories, but the German faces on the street are as pale and gaunt and joyless as ever, and the soup in camp has not thickened. But the packages from home have stopped coming. Either the Germans are stealing them outright, or the war is grinding out its victories by devouring both sides.

I wait for a sign from Henrike. She is preoccupied the rest of the day, then absent the next, which is not unusual — the leather shortages are so acute that our production some days falls to nothing. The next day is idle too, and I spend much of it sitting in a spot of sun behind the shelter of the least grimy window in the place. I allow myself three cigarettes and smoke them as slowly as possible.

When she comes back at last she pays me no mind until near the end of the day. Then she gives me a slight nod, a signal that usually means for us to meet later in the storeroom. But the door is locked, and I cannot contrive to wander by it more than twice without arousing suspicions.

I begin to wonder if I spoke to her in the first place or have imagined it all.

Finally, about a half-hour before the end of the day I see her talking with some of the men who work the machines. Once she points directly at me, and they all look. They continue their discussion. I die slowly on my feet, my heart breaking. If they come for me I will seize the first and shove his body into one of the leather cutters. I'll grab the next and fling him into a whirring belt, and then I'll run like a rat until they catch and kill me.

She leaves the men. She is walking towards the storage area, and it seems the workmen are still staring at me, but when I look at them they appear preoccupied with other things.

It's a trap, but I have no choice. I leave my broom standing up against an old locker and walk directly to the storeroom even before Henrike is out of sight. No sense hiding it anymore. She is betraying me. It's not her fault. It's the fault of the war, which is stronger than nations, than empires, than history itself. The war is calling me, and I have no choice.

I leave the door to the storeroom open so the men can come in and catch me. When Henrike enters her eyes are wild with alarm. She stands shaking, feverish in the face despite the awful chill.

"Change quickly," she says, and thrusts a bundle of clothing into my hands. "Then out through there." She barely indicates the broken window high up the wall behind her.

She lowers her head and leaves, closing the door behind her.

The clothes are a fit for a German giant, not for me. Yet there seems nothing else to do but to carry on with the charade. In a moment men will burst through the door and beat me to death right here.

But they don't come. I have time to bundle my prisoner rags in the corner, to take the rope belt from my old trousers and bind it round the new ones to keep them from falling, then to climb on an old table and up some shelves. The door does not open. I reach the window and hear some men coming. I imagine them with heavy spanners and huge iron wrenches, clubbing me senseless in just a few minutes.

But the door stays shut and all becomes quiet.

I struggle out the window and peer down from a dizzying height at an empty, filthy cobblestoned back alley I've never seen before. On the way down I have almost nothing to cling to — a bit of ledging, some faults in the brickwork where the mortar has fallen out. I jump the last several feet and land with the grace of a bag of rocks falling to the ground.

When I regain my feet and look at the opened window perhaps fifteen feet above me, it seems impossible that I was up there myself just moments before.

What to do? I have no extra food. I can't even think of what side of the factory I'm on or how I might best hide myself until dark. The alley is walled on three sides and leads, apparently, out to the large street that fronts the building. The doors on the left will only bring me back into the factory. I don't know what's on the right.

I stand in shock and indecision until a wagon comes clopping up the alley towards me. The horse is tired and slack, her ribs standing out and her head drooping almost to the cobblestones. An old man is driving. He nods just the once as if we were introduced long ago and he knows all about me.

When he gestures towards the back I stand rooted for a moment, stupidly uncomprehending, until I force myself to move. The bed of the cart is made of wood so old and worn I think it must have been fashioned in medieval times. I burrow under a pile of canvas sacking that smells of earth and rotten potatoes, and then the wagon starts backing up. All the way down the alley we ride. Between the sacking I can just see a strip of sky, segments of the grim and crumbling walls of the factory. I can hear the horse's hooves slipping on the cobblestones as she awkwardly manoeuvres backwards. Then we must be emerging onto the street, wagon first, with me cowering, trying to stay still.

At last we change direction and I watch the roofs of the

buildings scrape the edge of the sky and hear other vehicles — many horse-drawn, but some with engines. I stay as still as possible. Gradually the old town of Münster gives way, and I can smell the countryside and feel the difference in the ride and noise of the wheels from paved road to dirt and rocky lanes.

Finally the wagon stops. I smell mud and manure and hear the honking of a goose. Cautiously I look up. The farmer is standing on the ground now, motioning to me. I crawl down stiffly and he hurries me into a low rock barn, which is packed with hay in one corner. He doesn't say a word but points, and so I climb into the damp, smelly mess and cover myself. Then he leaves. The wooden door bangs shut and I wait. When it gets dark I'll head west. Münster is close to the Dutch border. But I didn't get a good look around and will be lost if I can't glimpse the sun before it goes down.

Cautiously I stand up and approach the door. Silence. I creep out and survey the area quickly: a shabby old farmhouse, a series of low walls, pastures down a hillside, trees in the distance where the sun appears to be heading. I steal past the edge of the barn, trying to seal the sight into my mind. Then I am seized by an overwhelming need to pee. I fumble with the new trousers.

When I am finished I turn to fix myself up. The farmer's wife is staring at me, her fat arms full of a tray laden with bread and cheese and a mug of milk so warm from the cow it shimmers in the cold air. She says something to me in German and I nod at her dumbly. She motions to the door of the barn, then backs up to let me pass. I enter once again and sit on a wooden rail. It takes all my will to not throw myself at the glorious food.

"Are you friends of Henrike's?" I ask slowly, hoping she will comprehend. She says something back in German and I struggle to find words. Two years in the country and what can I produce?

"Danke," I say.

Fifteen

I shook his hand, making sure not to cripple him, but his chin wagged a little so I let go immediately and sank into the solid oak chair on the customer side of his desk.

"I was so sorry to hear," he said. "What a tragedy. What an awful, awful thing." He straightened his tie and so I straightened mine. And he started shuffling through the file dispiritedly.

"It was the wiring," I blabbered. He'd see it all in his file anyway. "I did everything myself on that house, but I'd no experience with wiring and must have crossed something somewhere. I'll get someone qualified next time, of course. And no one was hurt. That's the wonder. It's only money." I smiled at him and he looked up from the papers finally, his pale eyes reflecting dull disbelief at the naivety of such a statement.

"The fire was entirely your own fault, and you had no insurance," he said.

"No, unfortunately I hadn't gotten around to that."

He stared bleakly at me, then returned to the file.

"I'm good for it," I said. "The full amount. I'm gainfully

employed, this is only a small setback. It means I'll be a few more years repaying you. Which is a good thing in your business, isn't it?"

He tapped his pencil on the blotter pad and with his left hand massaged his eyes behind his glasses.

"The only collateral you have, Mr. Crome, is the deed to the land."

"Oh yes, that, and I have a wife and child. I'll gladly give them up to you and the bank trustees if I ever miss a payment!"

His gaze was withering.

"Listen," I said, leaning in, trying to burn my eyes right back into his. "You know I'm good for it. I fought, killed and starved for my country. I built that house with my own hands, and by God I will rebuild it better than it was. And I will work to my dying day to fatten your bloody profits. There's nothing for you to decide here. Sign the form right down there." I pointed to the box where I knew his name was supposed to go.

A minute of hard silence passed. I kept leaning in. He stayed looking at his papers.

"Mr. Crome, you're asking for an extension of your loan for an extra fourteen hundred dollars when the original deed values the land at seven hundred and eighty-five dollars. I doubt we would even get that if we tried to sell. Property prices have been so depressed in the area in recent years —"

I slammed my fist on his solid, respectable desk. "What kind of man are you?"

He was hardly rattled. He took off his glasses, ran a hand through his thinning hair and, with a quiet anger, studied the rest of my file. "I did take note of your war record, Mr.

Crome. It seems to me you were barely in it for a few months before you were captured. So you were safe behind the lines most of the time. I was at Passchendaele, you see, while you were probably engaged in amateur theatricals with other hapless sorts."

I'm not sure what kept my fist from smashing his fleshy face.

"Anyway," he went on, the words maddeningly clipped and careful, "that has no relevance now. There is a science of financial investment, and your fundamentals are poor at the moment. This can hardly surprise you. The original mortgage, of course, remains in effect, and I trust that you do not anticipate any difficulties in continuing to meet the conditions of that agreement?"

I waited for some sort of divinely inspired wind to hammer him out of his comfortable seat, but he remained untouched and unperturbed, his ink-stained fingers flexing slightly as I stared at his hard hands.

"What did he say?" Lillian asked.

She was in the spare room at Maisie Campbell's house, where we were all staying now. The farmhouse was a lot like all the others in the area — rundown and snow-covered at the porch, with thick-furred dogs lying silently outside until the approach of a stranger sent them into barking fits. The farmhouse roof sagged in the middle, and it leaked in the summer rains, I imagined. Our room, in the back by the kitchen, looked as if it had last been papered in the previous century, but we were warm at least and eating regular meals.

I sat myself down on the corner of the bed and tried to shake the cold out of my hands.

"He said — no."

Lillian crumpled in front of me, her face set in a wince of pain as if quick-frozen and about to break.

Michael was holding himself upright against the bed, setting an empty can on the edge and then knocking it off and tottering after it.

Lillian looked at me with fearful eyes. She had barely slept in the days since the fire but lay awake or else got up and kept perpetual watch over the child.

I stood to take her in my arms. "It'll be all right." She remained clenched and wooden and pushed me away, breathing heavily now.

"But what are we going to do, Ramsay?" she cried — almost a moan of despair. She turned to the wall. "We have no money. The house is gone! They're going to take the land just like they got all of Papa's, and what if you lose your job again? Where will we go? Maisie has no money either. We're eating what she put aside for the winter for herself. It's too much for her even to be looking after my father."

Michael burst into tears at his mother's tone and the can fell again.

"Shut up! Shut up!" she screamed at him, and he wailed louder.

"Lillian — calm down," I said and reached for her. She rushed past me in a fury, then picked up Michael and shook him till his head wobbled like a blur. I struck her arm then and grabbed the child and held him still into the flat of my shoulder. Then Maisie Campbell appeared in the bedroom doorway and looked at us all with large, alarmed eyes.

"Things might seem bad now, but —"

"*I can't live like this!*" Lillian pounded her fists against the bed frame as if determined to cripple herself. "You won't take church charity and you won't take any of your brother's money and —"

"Stop it! Stop it!" I said, and reached to try to restrain one arm at least without letting go of the boy. She whirled on us both then and pushed us back until we thudded into the wall and a small, framed picture fell onto the floor.

"Oh dear!" Maisie Campbell said. She stepped one small stride into the room but then halted, her right hand quivering in front of her face.

The dogs started barking outside.

Lillian shrank to the floor, her hands over her head as if expecting to be beaten by the world. She was sobbing now, her breathing half choked, and she seemed to be trying to wedge herself under the bed as if to hide. Michael said, "Mummy! Mummy!" and reached his hands out towards her.

I didn't know whether to approach her or keep the child away.

Lillian's father appeared now at the door, useless and silent.

"We can't just fold at the first breath of bad luck," I said.

What followed then was not words so much as a howl of pain, a scream from within that seemed terrible enough to tremble the walls and set the air to bleeding.

I went out later that evening with the child wrapped in thick clothing. Maisie and Mr. McGillis saw Lillian to bed. It had snowed in the last few hours, and the first job was taking an old broom and brushing off the section of the south wall and roof that had collapsed. The footing was unsafe and I didn't want the boy to get hurt, so he tottered off to the side to play with scraps of wood. It was too cold, really, but I didn't want to leave him with Lillian for the moment, either. I was afraid of what she might do in her despair.

When I had a good section dusted off and had tested and trod about, I took out the hammer and screwdriver I'd stuffed inside my coat. Then I brought the boy over and set him up to watch what I was doing.

"We're going to be doctors, all right? Brain surgeons. We insert our scalpels like this, see" — I put the blade of the screwdriver under the frozen shingle closest to hand. "Then we take a surgical mallet like so and tap gently. We don't want to kill the patient, understand?" I knocked the screwdriver under the shingle and lifted slightly on the left side, then the right, until the whole thing started to come up.

"How many nails did we put in each shingle?" I asked him.

He seemed to be trying to remember.

"That's right, just one, centered near the top, and we want it back. We want the nail, we want the shingle unbroken, so we lift like this." I continued easing the screwdriver under first one side and then the other. "How long is the nail, do you recall?"

Again he seemed to be trying to remember.

"That's right. It's short and stubby. There it is." I pulled out the shingle and held it up for him. It hadn't torn at all. I extracted the nail and dropped it in a glass jar. "We'll pile the shingles right here on the ground. Do you remember how neat they were when they first arrived on the big truck? That's how we want them now."

The boy nodded seriously.

The moon was a dull, cold smudge of light in the purple sky, and the hills were lost in shadows. My cheeks and eyes were smarting at the cold. Michael wouldn't last long, even happy and bundled as he was.

I moved more quickly now, prying up the shingles one by one, saving the squat little nails, taking apart these remnants of the house as deliberately as I'd originally put them together. I worked at it for some time until Michael started to fidget and tremble in the cold, so I picked him up and rubbed him vigorously.

"Let's make a quick tour of inspection."

I carried him high on my shoulders around to the north side of the wreck. More than half the house was still upright, but most of the timbers were blackened to some extent. The furniture that was reachable and still good had been moved down the road to Maisie Campbell's house. What remained looked ghostly in the gloom.

We returned to the south section and I started in again. The glass jar tinkled with the sound of nails, and the pile of reclaimed shingles grew steadily behind us as the bald patch on the downed section of former roof began to spread. Cold as my fingers were, with the work and movement I began to feel the warm spread of sweat under my clothes.

It was a relief to give my body to mechanical movement, to throw myself into labour without an ounce of extra thought.

Michael started playing with the jar. "Don't spill that now," I said. He tipped it over anyway and I had to keep myself from yelling at him. He started crying for his mother, so I picked him up and held him close against my warm neck and face.

"Don't mind your mother," I said. "She's going to weep and rail and run off to church. That's her way through this. We'll just remove these shingles, for a start, and every one will be a little victory. Every board we save, every nail we straighten and use again, that's another victory. That's how you win the war. You refuse to yield no matter what loss you've sustained. Are you stumbling like a fool? Then stumble forward, at least. If she wants to cry all night that's her affair. I'm going to work on the house."

"Boom!" Michael said and pushed the jar over again. He fell backwards at the same time and began to laugh.

"Don't stick yourself in the bum, little boy!" I said as he rolled around on the stubby nails. I picked him up and brushed several off his coat and padded pants while he gurgled uproariously. "That's the last thing I want — to bring you home all bleeding and full of tetanus!"

"Tit-mouse!" he exclaimed and kicked at me until I had to put him down. Then he tottered to the jar again and righted it and pushed it over even though it was empty. "Tit-mouse! Tit-mouse!" he said again and again.

I wait until the darkness deepens. If I were a decent man of any description, I think, I would leave a note for Henrike — just a simple thanks. But I have no pencil or paper, not even Margaret's letters, which I carry only in my head.

I step out alone. I've managed to keep from devouring all

the cheese, a hunk of which now rides in the pocket of my German clothing. My boots slip and slurp in the mud. The way westward is over a wall and across a pasture and then across a dirt road and more field. Soon enough I reach some woods. It's a relief to be under cover, but very quickly I lose my certainty about direction. The night is not black so much as thousands of shades of grey, from sombre trunks and cavernous shadows to silvery rocks and pale, dying leaves.

I nearly stumble into a creek, but I recover and drink from water so cold my stomach convulses in shock before finally settling down. The border is within a few days' journey, I'm certain, even for a weakling like me, but if I stumble about in circles I'll never make it. Yet if I remain still and exposed at night I might freeze, I'm so thin and underfed. I have to keep walking even if it's in the wrong direction.

I expect to hear hounds at any moment, soldiers beating the bushes to flush me out. But the woods are as still as they would have been eons ago, before any men, any war, could disturb the silence.

By morning I reach the forest edge and am too tired and fearful to go further. I lie in a depression, cover myself with branches and dead leaves and look out at a sleepy roadside that borders more fields. I allow myself to slowly suck on a small morsel of cheese.

And the hours pass.

The cold is not extraordinary, just relentless — the slow, inevitable draining of heat and strength. My body feels close to subsiding into the rotted leaves and sticks and clods of earth surrounding me. I curl myself in a ball, tight as in a womb. If I stay this way till dark then I might well remain here forever.

Painfully I crack the stiffness from my limbs and creep along the edge of the road. My brain is working so badly it takes ages to realize that the sun has risen far behind my back and that somehow, through the night, I've been heading in the right direction after all.

Hardly anyone has come along that road, but I am too afraid to expose myself, so I follow the edge until I reach a small bridge and then I duck under it and along the extension of the wood. Even that small bit of walking helps my blood and limbs, and for much of the afternoon I sleep under cover by the creek — it must have been the one I stumbled upon in the night in the woods. The water is brown and sluggish, so I drink again only sparingly. By nightfall the last of the cheese has been sucked away.

I must be close. In darkness I brazenly cross fields and scramble along roadways. Suddenly a convoy of four trucks rumbles past and I barely have time to duck under a fence. The border must be close. But my chances of being caught are rising.

If I am hauled back to solitary, I will not survive.

Morning takes me by surprise. I've made such good progress, but where is the border? I leave the wood behind and pick my way warily along the road for at least half an hour. Then I stumble onto a farm and am immediately driven off the property by a barking dog. Further along I slip into a storage shed, but all the farm dogs for twenty miles, it seems, are baying now. In the shed is a sack of not-so-badly rotting turnips and potatoes. I use a stick to scrape off what skin I can and then suck quietly in the shadows, wedged behind an old carriage and a rusted plough, with an oily tarp pulled over me. Perhaps I have a good chance of remaining hidden.

But I am so tired it doesn't seem to matter. I sleep sound as any baby wrapped warm in soft blankets.

Late afternoon, it must be, I am startled awake and see an old man standing in the doorway. At first I think he too is an escaped fannigan. His face is speckled with grey whiskers and his eyes appear hollowed in the sunken caverns of his skull. I don't know if he can see me in the gloom. But he doesn't look anywhere else. He starts to move away from the door, but his eyes stay on me. His right hand finds a rusted pitchfork hanging from a nail on the wall. He doesn't brandish it at me, but simply holds it as if he is going off to do some work.

He says something in German and spits on the ground, then leaves.

When I burst through the door a group is watching — the old man, some women, a pair of boys standing glumly. I run to a crumbling stone fence and then over and huddle low as I scramble along the opposite side. I'm looking for anywhere to hide — a hole, a hedge. There are other fences and then fields so open. They must see me! So I run hard and surprise myself with the leather of my lungs, the strength still left in my legs.

No dogs are chasing, no bullets sing past my head.

At last more woods! I allow myself to stop and gasp against the trunk of a tree that is hollowed to the world but still standing. It's an extraordinary thing to touch the iron in the depth of your own bones, to feel the last, hard fires fighting to stay lit. I ache in every pore but know without a doubt I will continue. Like a beast in a trap I will chew my own leg off and bleed a dozen miles rather than give in.

But they do not come for me.

In a few more hours darkness falls again, and I walk in a fit of resolution. They do not come and they will not get me. I stand straight and hard and almost wish for them to try — to bring on the dogs and guards. So this is what it feels like to be invulnerable: the blood sings through my veins, I can unearth trees and stride the rivers of the globe.

And Margaret will have me despite Boulton, despite convention, despite the world. It is almost a certainty.

Yet by morning very little of that giant remains. A thick fog shrouds the land, and I am delirious. I can't stop but won't last another day. I can hardly see twenty feet in front of me and so have no idea of direction. I might well be bumbling back to Münster. But stilling my feet would mean death.

When the fog lifts I find myself alone in a frozen field looking at barbed wire in the distance, perhaps a mile off. I fall to the ground and begin to crawl. I push and slither with my feet and arms. I feel as if I am leaving half my skin on the hardened German mud. I scan the distance for guards and patrols. How many escaped men have been picked up this close? I have no cover at all, and yet there is no point in turning back, in trying to wait through another day and make the crossing at night. I won't last that long.

No one comes for me.

There are no guards. It doesn't seem possible. For a time I am certain again that I've gone the wrong direction, that I've made it round in a horrible circle back to Münster after all. I am not in my right mind.

I see a group of men near the roadway on the other side of the wire. They have no guns and are not wearing German uniforms. I get up and walk towards them. It is well past dawn by now and still cold enough to see our breath. They look like a huddle of steaming cows, these men: shivering and still, all facing the same direction, out of the wind, by the hut at the gate. Some of them are fannigans, I can tell by the raggedness of their clothes, their eyes.

When I approach they tell me that the war is over, has been for two days. I am not the only one who didn't know. We look back at the cold dawn and someone says, "Has anyone got some food?" and one man has a tin of biscuits that we share round. They are thin, flimsy things that crumble into pieces in our fingers, and the white sugar crusts on our hardened, swollen lips, then disappears to nothing on our tongues.

Sixteen

I was so tired from the strain and effort of the last weeks and months that on the climb up the office stairs I felt like a fannigan again, famished for the ease of a normal life. When I entered the office my face must have broadcast my weariness, for Dorothy turned and stared. She was watering a pair of geraniums that she kept in the window, and as she looked at me the jug stayed in mid-air, halfway set to pour.

"Are you all right?"

"Fine," I said, and started to explain the most recent progress. "The walls are pretty well roughed in. Some of the farm boys are helping me out, even though I won't be able to pay them right away. But I'm going to need —"

I hadn't even got my coat off and certainly hadn't planned on launching into my plea right away. But she caught my meaning anyway.

"More time?"

I noticed, through the opened studio door, that the model had already arrived. She was sitting on a stool reading a book, and I immediately liked the way her black hair fell off her shoulder. Dorothy must have followed my gaze. She said,

"Isn't she terrific? Her name is Eleanor and you're going to fall in love with her. I bought a pan from her at Eaton's. And I just want a graduation theme. Think spring, youth, beauty. I asked her to bring a dress, and what else have I got for you?" She rooted through her bag, then handed me a white carnation corsage. "You really look as if you need to sleep for about two weeks."

I shed my coat then and entered the studio, carrying the corsage. When I introduced myself to Eleanor, who stood taller than me even in her low-heeled pumps, she didn't know where to put her book. She was wearing a cream long-sleeved blouse with a brown cardigan and a loose pleated skirt. She looked perhaps twenty years old, and her face was luminous.

"Dorothy mentioned that you'd brought a dress?"

"My mother's evening gown." She pointed shyly to the screen behind which, I supposed, the dress had been hung.

"Perhaps you could change into it, and we'll see how things look from there."

She dipped her head modestly and walked behind the screen, placing her book on the workbench as she passed by.

I didn't like to look at models while they were changing. It made them self-conscious, and I was uncomfortable with the way it affected me sometimes. I didn't like to get emotionally involved in my work. I wanted to be concerned with light and line, with shade and nuance and colour, with shadow and shape. It is an old artist's trick to turn an object upside down and paint it as if it were an abstract. The eye looks for detail and proportion then; it sees the actual line, not the one that force of habit has blurred or skewed.

But I couldn't turn Eleanor upside down. Now she stepped

217

out from behind the screen wearing an evening gown to heal the world. The sight of her hit me with a near-physical wallop. Her bare white shoulders were strong and perfectly rounded. She had pinned her long hair high exposing her exquisite neck. She picked up the corsage and held it in front of the fullness of her chest, and I must have gaped because she stopped and smiled and we stood eyeing one another.

"That's some dress of your mother's," I said.

Dorothy looked in on us later in the day. I had Eleanor posing very simply, as if the door had just been opened and she was standing waiting to go out for the evening. Dorothy stood very close behind me and whispered, "You do have a way with the female form, Mr. Crome. What is it you're doing with her skin? "

I continued with the work.

"It looks almost warm to the touch." And she reached out her hand as if ready to plunge her fingers into the wet paint. I didn't move and she stopped the barest distance from the canvas. "Eleanor, you're going to love yourself when you see this. You're just going to want to stand like that all day and have men swooning over you."

I was painting very quickly. I felt at one point like a rabbit who will bound over a fence too high to contemplate, change directions four times in a heartbeat and then stop, still as a piece of moss. The world shrank to me and the canvas. It seemed that the light and the paint and the tools and the day were all conspiring.

And the more I stared at Eleanor, the more I felt her beauty seeping into crevices within me. She was more than medicine, and she too seemed to glow even more intensely in the avidity of my gaze. Dorothy too was conscious of something unusual happening and stayed by my shoulder longer than she needed. I could feel the heat of her, the soft touch of her breath on my back, and I remember wanting time to freeze. I spent too long filling in the door frame, working on the edges of an image that was going to be cropped by the camera anyway.

I don't remember Eleanor leaving. Somehow she was gone and Dorothy and I were left alone in the studio, looking at the painting and breathing rather deeply. I don't know how long we stood there, still quite close together, without touching. Finally, though, it seemed she was holding something out to me, a thickish envelope.

"What's this?" I asked.

"Just take it."

I could see there were bills and I backed away, nearly knocking down the easel.

"It's not a gift," Dorothy said. "It's a loan or an advance. I'm not even thinking of you, I'm thinking of your boy and your poor, suffering wife and of my own business interests. For once in your life would you accept a bit of human kindness?"

She waved it in front of me again. I snatched it from her hand and threw it towards the door. Bills scattered everywhere and she slapped hard at my face. Then I smiled so madly at her that she suddenly hit me in the chest and I fell backwards away from the painting. She followed me down in a heap and we began kissing. She kept her eyes on me, and the small silver chain round her neck leapt and bounced with her movements.

We were both ravenous. I remember the storm of it taking us over and how wild we seemed to be and how the grit of the floor impressed itself on my skin wherever I'd lost my clothes. But the mounting sweetness stunned me, and the cold winter rain seemed worlds distant.

"Not inside me, sir!" she gasped, keeping her wits when I was losing mine. She pulled herself away and I sent my seed arcing off. "I'm sorry, but I can't risk —"

"Shh!" I said, catching my breath.

Afterwards we lay outside of time, her cheek against my chest, my big hands resting on the hard bones of her slight body.

"Now I absolutely cannot take that money from you," I said.

How she laughed.

Later — and how much later I have no idea — when we had both blown hot with a new storm, then subsided again, lost in thought, I felt almost as if I were in a dream and could say anything.

"I have known you before," I said.

"Yes?"

"It was long time ago, but it was you. You in a different life."

"Oh yes?" All the practical edges of the office had fallen off her. Her hair was loose and wild now over the small shoulder straps of her slip. She looked so thin and pale, waif-like yet full of fire.

"I was in a different life, too. We saw each other across an unusual space."

Very slowly the world started to intrude. What was I doing? Lillian and my young Michael were waiting at home. I had to rouse my body, get myself to the train station, at least, before it was too late. I had just moved my marriage like a house to the edge of a cliff.

But I was feeling too blissful, too relieved to stir.

"Why me?" I asked instead. "Is there no appropriate young man?"

"Oh, listen to you," she said, a hard edge suddenly in her voice. But then she smiled and gently kissed my eyes and cheeks. "You have no idea. You have the hungriest eyes." She laced her slim white fingers in mine. "They've seen things. They know what they want. And look how long and strong and dark your fingers are. But you hold a brush like a wand of life." She kissed my fingers, slowly, as if we had all the time in the world. "Either one without the other wouldn't work. The hunger without the hands, the hands without the desire ..." The thought trailed off. "Were we lovers?" she asked. "That time before?"

"Lovers in a way," I said.

After dark the Montreal train pulled into the little station at Mireille. I was thrilled still, flushed with the heat of Dorothy. I left the station on foot and alone, legged it along Mill Road, down the hill and across the bridge and then up again. In town everything was quiet for the night except the pool hall, in front of which a few trucks were parked. The door and windows, closed against the cold, were still leaking light and smoke and muffled conversation. If I wasn't so late I might have slipped inside.

Instead I continued out of town. On the way to Maisie Campbell's I detoured up the lane and looked again at the shell of my house. If I'd come home straightaway I might have been able to start work on the floors, I thought.

Instead I cleared some scrap from the doorway out to the edge of the meadow, where a pile of frozen rubbish was growing. I hadn't eaten since my sandwich at lunch. The hunger now felt somehow just, as if a part of me believed it could not be right to feel such electric passion for life — not now. Not in these circumstances.

I suppose it was nearly ten o'clock when I stepped onto Maisie Campbell's lane and sent her sleeping dogs into paroxysms of barking. I let them circle and sniff at me, but they growled and challenged longer than usual, and I imagined they could smell the guilt on my skin.

I stepped through the door as quietly as I could. Maisie was knitting in the front parlour, a large long-haired cat snuggled warmly on her lap.

"Good evening, Mr. Crome," she said. "You're a long time getting here." Her eyes stayed steady on mine.

"I had to stay late at work," I mumbled. "And I'm still getting used to the trains. I was too slow getting to the station for the 7:15 . . ." The more I said the less credible I sounded. "I'll just . . . have a look in at Michael."

"Yes. *I* put him down hours ago," Maisie said.

"Is Mrs. Crome . . . asleep?"

"Mrs. Crome did not get out of bed all day." Maisie's words were curt and clear. "And her father has been no help."

"You've been awfully kind."

Her chin quavered and her stare was so relentless that I believed she could see every falsehood hidden in my bones. "Christ's mission is to help the less fortunate," she said finally, and focused again on her knitting.

I stepped down the hall and blew out a bitter breath. Then I passed through the kitchen and into the room where Michael, on his little cot, was clutching his blankets to his throat. His face looked peaceful, his fine brown bangs drooping lower than his eyes. He had Lillian's fair skin, but there was some of Father too in the sharpness of his chin.

Lillian was lying in the big bed, silently watching me.

"You're awake," I said. "I'm sorry I'm late." I launched into a stumbling explanation about the trains and the house.

"Yes," she said in a lost little voice.

"Are you feeling all right?" She didn't answer. "You should have a look at the house," I said finally. "It's coming together." I sat on the edge of the bed and took her hand, which was so warm I wondered if she had a fever. The movement seemed to perk her out of her gloom for a moment. She reached up with her other hand and felt my cheek and smiled in her old way. "It won't be as large as we'd originally planned, of course. We'll leave the upstairs for later and concentrate on the main floor. If I can put in some good weekends of work, and if the others keep helping the way they have..."

She was staring off at the shadows in the room. Finally she said, "We did go over to the house. Yesterday. And Michael was playing in one of the piles. In the rubbish. And we saw ... parts of the paintings that you had piled there. Some parts ... Michael saw." She turned her gaze on me now. "I saw new paintings there! New paintings of *her*!"

"Lillian."

"*God is punishing us for your sick thoughts!*"

Michael groaned in his cot, and I could hear Maisie Campbell's footsteps in the kitchen.

"Please keep your voice down."

223

"*I won't!*" Tears now streaked her face.

"Don't be jealous of Margaret. For God's sake!"

"Your language, Ramsay!" she said bitterly.

I got up and opened the door. Maisie Campbell stepped back.

"It's all right, Mrs. Campbell. Everything is fine. Good night now."

I kept the door open until her feet were disappearing down the hallway, then I closed it again softly. Michael yawned and rolled partway on his side, then settled back into sleep. I sat down again on the edge of the bed.

"You said you would not hurt me." Lillian looked hard at the wall. "Yet you paint that woman again and again. Do you do them at work? After your advertising pieces? Are they going to fire you, Ramsay? What about Michael and me?"

I hardly knew where to begin, what lies to tell to counter which nightmare concoctions of her overworked imagination.

"You still love her," she said, before I could begin.

Mrs. Campbell's footsteps were in the kitchen again, soft but unmistakable.

"Let's ... just get through the next months," I said. "The paintings are gone. We have a house to rebuild. Margaret is ... larger in your imagination now than she is in mine."

I could hear Maisie Campbell breathing again outside the door.

"But why do you keep painting her when you know how much it hurts me?" she whispered finally.

I tried to keep my voice steady. "Beauty is like ... food and air to me. If I paint a woman's beauty I am breathing, I am

224

having dinner." The tears came harder. Of course I could not tell her anything more.

"The past died in the fire," I said. "I won't be painting her again."

She could see it in my face and did not press for answers. I was sitting in the studio trying to render a girl in a bathing suit. The girl was long gone, and the bathing suit would not shape properly. I'd returned to sketches and fiddled with colours, and the closer I seemed to get to a version of reality the less right it all looked.

"I gather you are regretting your misdeeds," Dorothy said.

She stood away from me with her jaw set and her eyebrows knit together with the hardness of the moment. I looked away and stared at the floor, as if some message might be there telling how to keep from blowing us all apart.

"Does your wife know? I'm afraid I don't even know her name."

"Lillian doesn't know. But if she finds out —"

"Come for a walk with me."

We climbed the hill from the office, walking all the way to the forest trails on Mount Royal. The winds were particularly cold, the skies impenetrably grey. Her body was crushed to my side, with no words passing between us. Parts of the trail were slippery. An old man looked up at us from a bench and then returned to his bottle, which was almost empty. Otherwise there was no one: we seemed alone in a wilderness.

Yet through the leafless branches we could also see the

tops of the towering buildings down below us. I did not have a sense of the time except for the oppressively general feeling that the hour was late, that doors were closing and bridges burning all around me.

"I do love you," she said finally. Her large grey eyes were impressively clear. "I would never have thrown myself at you otherwise. You must understand that. But I will not compete with your wife and child."

We were stopped and looking at a frozen log that had rolled somehow onto part of the trail.

On we walked until the darkness began to gather and I felt an unspoken question: train or city? For a moment the privacy of her apartment beckoned enormously. I could see myself in her bedroom. I could see the two of us wrapped in the luxury of endless stretches of time.

"I have to make my way home," I said.

"Of course you do."

I kissed her neck and throat and then her mouth. She closed her eyes then, and I lifted her a few steps off the trail and leaned her against an oak that must have stood five hundred years. Even in her winter coat she felt lighter than leaves. She wrapped her legs round me and we embraced and an airplane roared above us, but I did not open my eyes. Then a horse trotted by pulling something and after that a dog, and later I heard children's voices on the trail just steps away.

If we close our eyes, I thought, they will not see us. If no words are spoken then it is not so. Time will slide us through this moment and there will be no need to choose.

London. Stokebridge Street. Once upon a time I stood as a young soldier gazing at this lovely semicircle of row houses. Battle mud was still on my puttees. I carried a pack and rifle, for God's sake. I'd travelled all day and slept out in the park like a barbarian, full of the juice of life, then walked the King's Road all morning to get here.

Now I am hardly standing. No bag to carry. A half-dead fannigan in someone else's ill-fitting uniform, rustled up to replace my German rags. Standing at the gate of number thirty, the perfect middle of the arc. My hand is on the black metal gate. I am pushing at the latch. Inside will be Margaret and her sister Emily and my aunt and uncle. Their warm fire. I will see them and my sentence will be over.

I am pushing at the latch but it will not budge. It's frozen hard. I hit it with my hand but it will not move. And I am seized with the absurdity: I walked out of Germany but I can't unlatch Margaret's gate. My strength is gone.

The door opens and I stumble back some terrible steps. A woman emerges, dressed in black. Even in the veil I know her as my Aunt Harriet. With her is Henry Boulton, the weedy man in a mourning suit. He is putting on his top hat and holding Harriet's elbow as if she cannot walk. I know immediately that Margaret is dead. I have come too late.

She has died in the Spanish flu that is taking so many of the healthy and the young.

I stare, stunned, as Uncle Manfred emerges from the door, struggling with his own top hat. And Emily, the sister — my cousin Emily, whose portrait I painted, who has written me throughout the nightmare — walks out veiled as well and shuts the door behind her. Boulton gets to the gate and unlatches it with a smallish nudge of his left hand. That's how weak I have become, I think — even Boulton can dislodge what I could not move.

He holds the gate open for Harriet, who steps as if not far from the grave herself. And Uncle Manfred grips Emily's arm — I can't decide who is supporting whom.

They are going to Margaret's funeral. The realization burns inside me. For there is the taxicab waiting, its engine puffing. I didn't even notice it before. Boulton holds open the black door and helps Harriet in.

They've not seen me. I'm standing only steps away, but I'm a fannigan ghost.

Now Boulton is helping Emily up the vehicle's step.

"Emily," I say softly.

She turns and looks at me, confused. "Did you know her?"

It's Margaret. Not Emily at all. She looks deep into my face, my eyes, in that way she has that breathes life into everything.

But not this time.

"Did you know my sister Emily?" she asks again.

Not the least spark of recognition, even when she lifts her veil and looks full bore into my soul.

I hurry off blindly. God knows where. If I ran my frame would shatter into a thousand shards. I can barely shuffle my feet. But no one comes after me. I do not hear my name.

Seventeen

We could not stay with Mrs. Campbell forever, of course, and eventually the prospect of having her own home again spurred Lillian on. She did much of the inside finishing during those days while I was off in the city. If there was no paint she cleaned; if there were no tiles she found old rugs and beat them into newer ones; if the furniture was incomplete she banged together crates and odd ends of scrap to make a dresser, a table, something for a child to sit on. And if she was not happy then at least she was not immobile in bed, staring off at nothing. I moved myself into the spare bedroom on the main floor, ostensibly because she slept so poorly now and I had to rise so early to catch the train. I remember my father telling me that separate bedrooms were the salvation of many a marriage — a truth I had not understood until now. Lillian had the farm, the garden and Michael at home, and I had my studio, where I confined my ghosts behind a door that locked, with cornering windows overlooking hills and fields, trees and sky. It was a truce of sorts, a truce that held as days played out and years stole by in a house of sorts, cobbled together from the remnants of past errors.

If you do not choose, that itself is a choice, and sometimes love, like a wild weed you fail to keep from your forgotten garden, roots itself and grows as fast as a child and for a time seems to lend its beauty to everything else, even though you'd meant to kill it in the beginning. Which is to say that what I should have put an end to in the city I didn't. For Dorothy came alive then too. It was as if she'd been waiting for me for ages, and now that the terrible effort of patience was done she couldn't contain all that she'd been holding back. She burned in her glances and I did not shy from them. A man too waits a whole life for a partner whose gaze sets the sky alight. There were days when I worked in a kind of fever, when the lovely feminine flesh that life had conspired to lay before my eyes fed me, fired me for hours. And I would look across and really begin to see, to know my Dorothy.

Her face was smaller than my hand, unremarkable except for narrow-set, wary grey eyes that looked as if they knew everything, or at least everything they wanted to know. Her skin was pale. It reminded me of mushroom flesh from the darkest, wettest corner of the forest. When she smoked, which was most hours of most days, her wrist would bend as if under the weight of the cigarette. I would hold her hand sometimes just to look at the enormous difference: mine so thickly ribbed with work veins, my skin brown and ill-used, every nail cracked and beaten up. Her hands were as delicate as paper.

Sometimes when I was with her I was nearly overcome with the feeling that I could crush her in a moment, like crumpling a leaf, and she would simply watch with her large eyes and let the rain blow hard against the window.

For it always seemed to be raining: cold, harsh, bitter

Montreal rain that was likely to freeze against the glass, to turn her street into a ruinous obstacle course. So often cars furiously spun their wheels halfway up the hill, angled sideways like horses helpless in mud. The tires whined as bystanders hopelessly pushed, trying to get any sort of grip on the pavement with shoes or galoshes.

I would fight my way up Stanley like a hardened, desperate salmon, then through the doors and up those five flights. The initial staircase was wide and well lit, an inviting boulevard, but after the second and especially third floors, the stairs narrowed and the light cheapened. Like everything in those hard days it was strained through a lens of absolute necessity. Even the handrails narrowed, and the broad, generous oak of the first floor turned into mean, skinny iron painted black, cold on fingers already chilled in the freezing rain.

Dorothy hated cold fingers. I would beat my hands against my thighs as I approached her door, down the gloomy hall- way and around to the right. I imagined myself some sort of native warrior enacting an elaborate, perplexing ritual, a shivering, hand-slapping dance after climbing such slopes, the rivals — those whirring, feckless cars on the streets — left far below.

She ate almost nothing — bits of toast with coffee, a meagre half-sandwich at her desk for lunch. Her bones felt hollow, the outline of her ribs showed through her skin. And yet her appetite for other things . . .

It was the heat of her that was so impressive.

I would be shivering like a child even after those five, hard-pulling flights of stairs. But there were days when she would fly straight at me, she wouldn't even let me get the door closed. And if she wasn't much for the eyes across a room, a desk even, she was overwhelming and radiant from close range.

Sometimes she would order me straight into the bath, I was so cold. And those fragile hands would start to unbutton, to pull me free of my chilly clothes and soothe down my battered body.

Once, that was all we had time for. She filled the tub and submerged me in the heat — her building had a good boiler, and you could usually count on hot water, at least — and we kissed and kissed until her face and hair and blouse were soaked.

"My train," I said. "I have to —"

"Yes."

"Michael is in a show after school . . . I have to, really —"

"Yes," she said, and, still clothed, climbed in on top of me, the water flooding onto the floor like something biblical.

From a few inches she was incandescent. I've never known anyone else who could change that way, absorb in an instant so much of the wattage around her. Her eyes crimped half-shut and she smiled as if these were the moments of a lifetime, right now, *this instant*.

I did know love.

Love had a way with clocks, of burning through stolen hours like a gambler spending found cash. I remember fighting my way out of that bath and sloshing on the cold tiles, my feet suddenly pointed at the ceiling — those were high, shadowed ceilings — and my head slamming down. For a moment I thought that God Himself — Lillian's God — had reached out to smash my brains for such behaviour.

"*Froggie Went a-Courtin'*," I blabbered. "I said I'd be there. Michael is playing the cornbread."

I scrambled up, towelled and dressed myself in a panic.

I'd lost a sock. I searched on my knees, underneath the chesterfield, by the umbrella stand near the door, while Dorothy laughed, her clothes soaked and her face still flushed with desire and heat.

"You're never going to make it!"

Under the coffee table and through her closet and behind the radiator upon which she kept an ancient row of African violets. I upset one with my sleeve and caught it awkwardly, spilling half the earth onto my wet trouser leg.

"Get going!"

"I can't go with just one sock!" I yelled at her, as if determined the entire building should know what we were up to. She was normally obsessed with secrecy, but the madness of the moment had taken us both over.

"Why not?"

As I ran out I glanced back to see her framed in the doorway, her blouse half-torn from her shoulder, bathwater dripping down her hair and face and legs. Her skirt was plastered to her slight frame but her expression was Amazonian, as if she could take on all the storms of the world and blow them off in a dozen directions.

I sat on the train with my chest heaving from the exertion of making it to the platform, and crossing and then uncrossing my legs, ashamed of my one bare ankle. I was convinced that everyone on that crowded, smoky car knew every black mark smudged and etched on my soul.

Seconds after I got home Lillian asked, "Where's your sock?" She saw my bare ankle all the way across the house from the kitchen.

"It was soaked and I took it off," I said, too quickly. "I put it in my pocket but it must have fallen out."

She pressed her lips into a flat, unimpressed line. When I'd left early in the morning she'd been at the dishes, and here she was still, with her hands plunged in suds as if she hadn't moved the entire day.

"I put your dinner aside," she said. "Was the train late again?"

She looked steadily a few feet to my right at some invisible thing of interest on the floor.

"Work was piled up, so I took a later train. Where's Michael?"

She motioned over her shoulder. The upstairs had been finished for some time and I knew she had given him permission to range around my studio. I pulled off my hat, shook the rain from my overcoat, fought down the rising anger. Lillian's face was headache-pale. The right thing would have been to embrace her in the middle of the kitchen, to take her hair in my hands.

Instead I walked up the stairs, terribly conscious of my sockless foot. She took a step towards me and I lengthened my stride, ascended two stairs at a time.

I entered the studio. "What are you doing?" My voice was harsher than I wanted. In the north corner, where there was a little floor space, a train set I'd bought for the boy was partially assembled. But he was on the south side and half the canvasses I'd done since the fire were ranged out on the floor.

"*Stand up!*" I said as I stamped towards him.

"I'm sorry. Papa, I'm sorry!" Already Michael was in tears.

He was playing among landscapes, nothing he shouldn't have seen — a frozen field in late fall, the furrows raggedly ploughed; a skier cutting through the bush in winter. But I was mad with the tension of the moment, with what he might have dragged into plain view.

I pulled him several feet away from the paintings. He was six years old, small for his age but getting stronger.

"*I told you!*"

"I'm sorry. I'm sorry, Papa!" he blubbered.

"He didn't hurt anything!" Lillian said.

My hand was raised above him and I felt my whole body shaking.

"Ramsay, let him go!"

I dropped my arm and staggered off a few steps. *It's all right*, I thought. *Walk softly, and maybe this house will not explode.*

"I'm sorry, Michael," I said. "I'm sorry."

He ran to his mother, of course, and buried his face in her apron.

Later I sat alone and quietly read the newspaper, close to boiling. Lillian was fiercely mending by the fire, the silence welding our jaws shut. Eventually I rose and slipped into the boy's room and ran my hand through his soft, soft hair. He opened his eyes and gazed at me the way I wanted him to — with the gentle trust of half-sleep.

"Forgive me, Michael. How was it? Were you a terrific cornbread?"

He nodded his head sleepily.

"Was there a big crowd? Can you say your line for me now just the way you did in front of everyone?"

He sat up and thrust out his chest importantly. "*If you want any more you can sing it yourself!*"

"Excellent!"

"Everyone laughed!" he said. Then he got very thoughtful.

"Do you think, one day, when we all have our own planes, there will be runways everywhere instead of roads?"

"I don't know. I haven't thought about it."

"And would there have to be flags flying in the air to show us where to go?"

"Maybe."

He closed his eyes and I thought he was going to drift back into sleep. Then he opened them again. "They would have to be suspended from balloons."

"What would?"

"The flags," he said. "Did Mummy tell you about the letter? Three cousins are coming. But I can't remember their names. Except for Alexander. That was the boy."

"Cousins?"

"And two girls. Mummy was reading it. I read some words too. They're coming for a visit."

He finally drifted back to sleep, and I found Lillian staring hard at a pair of Michael's trousers worn through the knee. I asked her about the letter.

"It's from Rufus," she said curtly. "He wants to bring her here."

"Who?" I stayed standing where I was, the blood now pounding to my brain.

Lillian got up abruptly and walked to the desk at the other end of the room where we kept the family papers. She picked up the letter, returned and threw it at me.

"It was addressed to both of us. That's why I opened it. I'm going to bed!" Then she marched off to her room. I glanced at Rufus's writing.

3 March 1937

Dear Ramsay and Lillian,

How we used to regret Father's lack of letters when he was off draining the swamps of Nicaragua, and yet here I am pursuing some interesting travels of my own and can hardly find time to write. Well, to remedy that, I can say that Vanessa and I are just back from London, where besides a spot of business now and again I managed to hook up with some of the English relatives. Uncle Manfred and Aunt Harriet both send their love, Ramsay — they remember you so clearly as a young private. Though frail, of course, they are both in fine form although Manfred has lost most of his hearing and rails at top voice about the communists and the government and of course about this pipsqueak Hitler who thinks he has become so important in the world. Harriet does her best to reign him in. Manfred that is, although I imagine she could do a fine job on Hitler too if given the chance!.

I also met the Boultons, who came for a rollicking luncheon that stretched on for hours and then turned into a walking tour of Chelsea with Henry Boulton giving a running commentary of amazing depth and perspicacity (he did go on somewhat). His wife Margaret is our cousin, Ramsay, whom you met when you stayed with the family during the war. I suppose you must have told me at some point about all this but I'd quite lost track and so was surprised (and somewhat embarrassed) when Margaret plied me with so many questions about you and seemed to assume that you must have told me all about her.

Perhaps you know this already, but her health I'm

*afraid is not all that it should be, but she soldiers on
with remarkable fortitude. They have three children
—Alexander, Martha and Abigail—and by the time we
needed to take our leave she seemed quite convinced that
they would all be making a family trek to North America
this summer to visit. She was particularly adamant
about stopping in to see you. I suppose in the course
of several conversations I had described somewhat the
beauty of your surroundings, with those lovely hills and
fields and such, and she became smitten with the idea of
a visit.*

*I assured her it was a splendid plan and that you
would all be thrilled to meet the English side of the family and renew old acquaintances. Dates and so forth
have not been set, but is there a time in the season when
it would be most convenient? I told her that your rooms
are not large—she was fascinated by my account of the
fire and your extraordinary rebuilding—and she said
they are quite happy to sleep on floors and have a truly
wilderness experience.*

*Well, what a quaint idea of Canadian life the British
can have sometimes.*

I will write again with more details as they emerge.

Yours as always,
Rufus

"What a luxury a cup of tea is," Dorothy said, and she looked
into hers. She was in her light gown, which was not quite pulled
around her, and it was afternoon — the sun was streaming
through her window and through the smoke of her cigarette,

and her legs were crossed and her hair was free and we were both flushed still. There was a sense of the day having sunk into resin, that it would remain a quarter to five for hours if not weeks, and the steam from her tea would fill her eyes, and if we willed it we might even retract some minutes and again be joyfully skin to skin.

But the world was crowding her little kitchen. The news of the massacre at Guernica in Spain had been out for only a few days and was still fresh in our minds.

"How can the Germans sit in good conscience on the Non-Intervention Committee and commit acts like that? And those poor people in Bilbao just waiting to be slaughtered," Dorothy said. Mola and his insurgents were narrowing in on the Basque town by then, and the newspaper was full of the British and French effort to ship out the civilians in time.

"It's the largest refugee evacuation since the Belgians in 1914," I said.

She stubbed out her cigarette and gazed at me, some of the memory of what we'd just been up to still in her eyes. "I don't want your wife cursing me for you being late again." I suppose I appeared in no hurry to move off. "Is there something else you need to tell me?" She looked at me in her way, her eyes like the flat head of a screwdriver prying up a lid. "You are very silent these days, Mr. Crome."

I took a sip of my tea and avoided her gaze. "I, uh... I will need to take a few days off next week. My cousin is coming to visit with her family. From London."

"You have a cousin in London?"

I nodded, and felt the warmth of the cup — a delicate, feminine thing that did not fit my hand. She blew smoke across at me. I lit a cigarette of my own, and the heat of the afternoon — unusual for late spring — began to drain a little more quickly.

"She's, uh — I visited with them in the war," I said, trying to keep the hesitation out of my voice. "Just for a week. And now . . . she's visiting back."

"Does she have a name?"

"Margaret. And she has three children now, and an insufferable husband."

"And just this slight mention of her turns Mr. Crome's face into a radish," Dorothy said. When I did not smile, her own face paled. "Oh," she said then. "Should I be worried about this cousin Margaret?"

My silence stretched unbearably.

"I see," she said, and sat back and examined the edge of the table.

"It isn't what you think," I said finally. "I love you, and I'm sorry for never saying it. I'm sorry for this skulking and hiding and sneaking around. I want to make it right. I did have feelings for Margaret — I do have them — rooted like old teeth. But it was a long time ago. And now my brother Rufus is dragging her to my house to visit and I will need to take a couple of days."

"What did she do to hurt you?"

I stubbed out my cigarette then, stood and carried my teacup to the sink. Dorothy rose too, hesitated, then held me from behind, her thin arms strong as binding wire.

We simply stood together for the longest time, and then I had to go.

Eighteen

I borrowed a hay wagon and a draught horse, Charles, from my neighbour Mr. Bretton, a crusty old farmer. Together Michael and I drove slowly along Mill Road, the great beast's hooves slapping the gravel and his occasional snorts punctuating the afternoon air. It was an indecisive sky, cloudy to the east and grey, with some blue promised from the west. The hills were hunkered down in shadows, keeping their own secrets, and it was a bit cool for the end of May.

Michael maintained a running commentary. "There are three cousins," he said. "Alexander and Martha and ... who is the third cousin?"

"Abigail, I think."

"Do I have any other cousins?"

"These are cousins once removed from you."

"Why are they removed?"

I did my best to explain it, and he frowned until I stopped talking.

"But do I have any other cousins?"

"No. Your Uncle Rufus and Aunt Vanessa have no children yet."

"Well, when are they *going* to have children?"

"I don't know."

"Have they been married a long time?"

"Ages."

"They should have children by now!"

"Don't ask them about it," I said. "It's private."

Instead he asked to drive so I stood him up in front of me. "Gee up!" he called and snapped the reins. Charles maintained his plodding pace as he pulled us up the hill towards the station.

"What time is the train coming?"

"Ten minutes after two."

"And what time is it now?"

I showed Michael my watch. A belching truck rattled past us, shaking so much I expected pieces to fly off. Even Charles raised his head.

"Where's the little hand?" I asked, looking back at the watch. Michael pointed to it. "What's that number?" Michael frowned. Charles crested the hill and we could see the train station — completely deserted — below us in the distance.

"Almost one o'clock!" Michael announced after much prodding and discussion.

"We'll park Charles in the shade here. Look, there's some grass for him to nibble on."

After we got down Michael spent some time walking around Charles's enormous legs and patting the huge muscles, while Charles sniffed the scraggly grass at the edge of the lot.

"Is Alexander the oldest?" Michael asked.

"I don't know."

"Why were you and Mummy fighting?"

Michael was on the other side of Charles and I couldn't see his face.

"We weren't fighting."

"Yes you were. All last night."

"No. Just for a little bit."

"Mummy was crying."

"Let's sit on the bench by the track and see if we can see the train coming."

Michael petted Charles some more, but when he saw I'd left he ran after me. We walked through the quiet little station, then sat on the bench on the platform. Michael looked north up the line, the direction from which my Montreal train always appeared.

"They'll actually be coming up this way," I said, pointing south. "From the United States."

Michael gazed down the tracks, then asked again why his mother and I had been fighting.

"Parents do, sometimes. It's nothing to worry about."

"But I can't sleep when Mummy cries."

As I was grasping for what to say to him, he got up and ran the length of the platform, threw a rock across the line and into the woods, then ran back.

"Are we going to have a war?" he asked. "The man on the radio said so."

"Nobody knows for sure."

"What if the Americans attack us?"

I laughed. "The Americans haven't attacked us in a long time." I ruffled his hair. "It's the Spanish fighting each other, across the ocean. There are all kinds of different groups —factions they're called: monarchists, communists, fascists, anarchists. But there are also Italians, Germans, French, Russians, Moroccans, people from all over the world. Even some Canadians are fighting there. It's like a little world war all on its own. What most of us are worried about is how to keep the fighting just in Spain. Because Spain is in Europe, and it won't take too many more sparks to make the whole thing go up."

"Like the fire in our house?"

"Think of everybody's house on fire. Think of fire falling from the sky and burning all the roads and fields and houses and barns and buildings. All the cities, everywhere people might live and work. You think of Mummy crying last night. Think of everybody's Mummy crying most of the time. It's the very worst thing, and we're just waiting for it to start again."

I thought I heard the train then and looked down the line, but it was still too early. Michael asked how much more time, and so we looked at my watch and figured it out. Then he ran back to Charles and grabbed handfuls of grass and fed them to the great horse, calling back to me every so often.

I looked down the line again. I remembered the first time I'd arrived at this station, years ago, with a rucksack and fishing gear, set for a weekend lark away from the big city. My train rounded the corner and blasted straight through the little station and on past by a quarter mile or more before finally stopping, then backing up sheepishly. Surely that's how Margaret would arrive, I thought. But her train wouldn't stop at all — not for this little town, not for me. She would sail on by and up the line.

Even now I couldn't really believe she was on her way.

Yet then there she was, a distant figure of a woman in a long beige skirt, short jacket and blouse, her hair well-hidden beneath her sensible travelling hat. The children crowding around her were her size or larger. The boy, Alexander, looked stretched and awkward, already taller than his parents — and me for that matter — and the girls were in flowered hats and white dresses. Her husband Henry, in a bowler hat, struggled with two large suitcases. He looked noticeably older than the stringy youth I'd met twenty — no, twenty-one — years ago. His face was puffy and slack, his shoulders rounded nearly into a stoop, and even with his hat on I could see that most of his hair had gone the way of his youth. Rufus appeared from behind in a black coat and took one of the suitcases, and Vanessa towered beside Margaret and said something that set them both laughing.

I could hardly make my feet move towards them.

"Is that them?" Michael asked. He had come running with the first train whistle, but now was sidled against my leg, clenching my thigh.

"No need to be nervous," I said, and hoisted the boy onto my shoulders. Margaret had seen me by now and stood staring in my direction.

She held herself erect but seemed hollowed out, her eyes even larger than I remembered, her face quite white, her shoulders thin as a cabin door.

"Which one is Martha and which one is Abigail?"

"Let's find out."

Rufus intercepted us before we could reach the main party. "Michael, what a huge man you're becoming!" he said and he reached up to shake the boy's hand. I started to lift Michael off my shoulders, but he resisted so he stayed there as the others were introduced. Alexander's cheeks blushed pink as a girl's, and his handshake was soft. The two girls stared openly up at Michael, and then the older one, Martha, said, "I *told* you he was very small!"

Henry put down the suitcases and clasped my hand and said something about the air being extraordinarily fresh.

My eyes were on Margaret and hers were on me. She extended a gloved hand, not to me but to Michael. "Cousin Ramsay," she said. "My, how you've grown. And you have two heads now!"

"*You're the lady in Dad's paintings!*" Michael blurted.

We all were silent through a cavernous moment.

"Well, thank God!" Margaret said, finally looking me in the eye. "I was worried you might have forgotten me."

I left Rufus to organize the baggage while Michael and I went to get Charles and the hay wagon. As soon as Martha and Abigail saw the means of transportation they raced over to greet Charles, broadcasting their excitement. Even Alexander got over his embarrassment and came down off the platform to pat Charles's hard-muscled flanks. I told them to be careful far more often than was necessary — Charles could have trod through a maternity ward without harming anything — and found myself focused on getting the luggage aboard. I felt as nervous and clamp-jawed as any adolescent. When Margaret's trunk appeared I insisted on lifting it myself, without help from Rufus, and shushed him over comments about my arm, and then nearly whacked young Abigail on the side of the head turning the blasted thing around.

It weighed enough to be full of water.

On the way back to the house Rufus sat beside me and talked on and on about his trip to London, which had been months ago. Everyone else sat in the back or stood by the wooden rails. Martha and Abigail exclaimed over every fascinating inch of the journey — the flies buzzing around Charles's ears, the sparkle of river water as we rode over the bridge, the boarded windows of the dusty stores along Mill Road and beyond. Every few moments I could hear Margaret affirming, questioning, answering them in a practiced, motherly way.

I concentrated on the driving, as if Charles might bolt at any moment and start leaping fences to our doom.

"How has your work been?" Rufus asked. "Have the advertising contracts started to come back?"

"A little bit," I said vaguely. It had been years since we'd seen one another. He looked unaffected by passing time.

"Any magazine work? Book covers?"

"Calendar stuff," I said. "It pays the bills."

When we reached the house I unloaded quickly and then insisted on returning Charles and the wagon right away. Lillian appeared at the door in her apron. My heart slipped when I saw the fatigue in her face and the strange colour in her cheeks. She'd put on some sort of rouge, I realized, which she never used and which made her look like a fading, out-of-costume stage actress. I hurried Charles and the wagon down the lane and did not hear Rufus's introductions or what kind words Margaret had for my wife. At Bretton's farm I insisted on towelling off and brushing down the huge horse myself. He had raised something of a sweat, and I needed to compose myself before facing these English guests.

The walk back was about a mile, and I didn't know if it was hunger or nerves that so unsettled my stomach.

When I reached the house they were all seated in the meadow, at a long table of cedar planks I'd slapped together the summer before for outdoor meals. The edges of a white tablecloth waved in the breeze and the table was overflowing with bowls of food: boiled beef and cabbage, carrots, mashed potatoes, fresh bread, rhubarb preserve, plates of butter and pitchers of lemonade. There were even flowers at both ends of the table: daisies and lilies and dried Queen Anne's lace. When Margaret turned at my approach I became intensely aware of the smell of Charles on my clothes and hands.

Lillian was intent on serving the children, who all sat around her.

"I'm afraid I'll have to wash up," I said, and retreated into the house. From the kitchen window I watched them. Margaret, in the middle, seemed to be orchestrating the conversation, turning now to Rufus and Vanessa, now to Lillian, to the children, laughing sometimes so gaily I could hear her voice all the way up at the house.

I cleaned myself, changed my shirt and trousers, and finally returned to them.

The chair that had been left for me was opposite Margaret. Almost everyone else had finished a full plate of food, although Margaret had taken only a small amount and it was barely touched. Alexander was chomping through what must have been seconds. Just as I was seating myself Margaret said to him, "Please, dear, this is not a wolf feast!" He looked up guiltily but could not manage to slow down.

"What a marvellous lunch, Lillian!" Margaret enthused, and then she turned her gaze on me. "Married to a cook like this, I'm surprised you haven't ballooned in your middle age, Ramsay."

I smiled lamely. Lillian seemed not to have heard the compliment. Margaret turned her considerable wattage towards her. "I understand you're from this area, Lillian? And your father lives nearby?"

Lillian stiffened. "My father died two years ago."

"Oh. I'm so sorry." Margaret looked around at Rufus, evidently the source of the bad information. He appeared sheepish, as if just now remembering that he'd been unable to attend the funeral.

Lillian passed around a bowl of sliced beets. An awkward silence settled over the table while Rufus threw apologetic looks in every direction and Lillian stared hard at her hands.

I chewed my food. "Mr. McGillis lost his health after the bank took his land. We all miss him." Lillian still would not look up. "How is your health, Margaret?"

"Oh, let's not speak of it," Margaret said quickly. "The doctors are panicking a bit about my heart. The less said about it the better, as far as I'm concerned. I *so* wanted to go on this trip before Alexander is completely grown and the family begins splitting apart. It happens so quickly. We have very little time, any of us really, when you think of it."

Henry passed the bread to her. "Darling, you should *eat*."

"Look at what I've got on my plate already!"

"Mummy almost made us miss the coronation!" Martha said. At Margaret's reproving glance she said, "You did. The first passage tickets you bought were for four days before the coronation. And then you said we couldn't change them. We had to *beg* you!"

"Yes, and for all that what did you see?" Margaret asked. "The backs of most of the crowd."

"We saw the horses and the guards and the big parade and all the flowers. And we heard the King on the radio!"

"We heard him too!" Michael burst in. "Remember," he said to his mother, "he was all the way across the ocean. And he said so too. It was the first time!"

"I read the most transfixing account of the ceremony," Rufus offered. "The shafts of sunlight streaming through the ancient windows at Westminster Abbey just as the King was being crowned!"

Margaret was now eating something. She gazed at me and for a moment we might have been miles away, quite alone. I wondered if she remembered — that touch of her hand in Westminster Abbey on my first day in London, when I'd gone so suddenly cold and dizzy wandering in that great tomb.

It was like hot water cutting through ice, that touch.

Now Vanessa was speaking. "I'm afraid I really don't understand this British and Canadian fascination with royalty. It's a symbolic function anyway. Poor Edward has run from it into the arms of his Mrs. Simpson. He couldn't seem to get away quickly enough. Why all this gushing over an outdated and expensive institution? Of course I'm only an American, and we overthrew the monarchy over a century and a half ago."

It was Henry's turn then, and as he talked — about Cromwell, and poor beheaded Charles I, and how important pageantry and pomp were to the British psyche and the strained bonds of the Empire itself — I couldn't keep my gaze from settling on Margaret. She seemed not to be listening to her husband at all, but had her eyes fixed on the butter dish beside my plate — or perhaps on my hands near it. She looked thinner and more pale than I remembered, leeched of some layers of vitality. Yet in that light she seemed an entrancing counterfeit, at least, of the woman she had been.

And I was terribly conscious of looking lifetimes older than the young soldier she had known.

"Think of that one historic moment," Henry said. "Our new king, George VI, is able to speak into a microphone and be heard directly by millions of subjects, thousands of miles away, in the sweltering cities of India, of Singapore and Hong Kong, here in Canada —"

"And he didn't say anything important or memorable," Margaret cut in. "What he actually said was so bland it was hardly worth listening to. But the fact of the matter is that he will be revered and his brother will be reviled, and why? Because Edward chose love over duty, and he did it at a time when we all know we're going to war again. And it's going to be soon, and we'll need someone willing to wear royal garb and to tell young men and their families — over the radio, no less — to sacrifice everything for the good of the nation, for king and God and whatever else we can think of. Edward just wants to hole up in a rented Austrian castle and be with his American divorcée. And what's wrong with that?"

She spoke with such sudden force that everyone else fell into a shocked silence.

Finally Henry spoke. "Certainly, darling, we don't know at all that we are going to war."

"No, no, you're right," Margaret said. "Just because Chamberlain's new budget includes seven and a half *billion* pounds for rearmament, and Germany, Russia and Italy are happily fuelling the war in Spain, and the Japanese are running around

China, and Mussolini is parading into Africa, and the Nazis are imprisoning more and more Jews and now are rounding up Catholics, for God's sake —" She stopped herself. Lillian, especially, looked shocked. "Excuse my language, children," she said. Then she looked at everyone. "Excuse me."

She picked at her food while Henry eyed her with a sort of tolerant patience that, I imagined, could drive its object to murder.

"I wanted us to take this trip while it's still possible," she said. She raised her glass of lemonade. "Here's to family. To love, and peace, and children, and to all of us. To the simple pleasure of ordinary days."

I drained my glass and she looked back at me as if memorizing my features.

"What do you think of the new divorce bill, cousin Ramsay?"

"Well, I —" I stammered. "It's not being proposed for Canada, is it?"

"But surely there has been debate here? Should adultery remain the only allowable grounds for divorce? What about cruelty, or insanity, or if one's spouse has been thrown in jail for life? What about habitual drunkenness or, what's the phrase — 'inveterate drug addiction'?"

Henry cut in. "Everyone in London is talking about this. Because of Edward, no doubt. Certainly there should be no grounds for divorce at all in the first five years. How many young couples would stay together through the early storms of getting used to one another?" Henry and Margaret exchanged a particularly married-looking glance. "Well, it's no secret," Henry stumbled on, addressing Margaret directly.

"You had some unhappy periods in the early years, before the children, and I was learning the ropes, so to speak, as a young husband. These things take endurance. It's not all the dance and stuff of fairy tales."

The meal was done, and flies were beginning to buzz about the mostly empty plates, but nobody moved while this topic sat among us.

"Of course we hardly make marriage any easier with our tax laws," Henry said. "And I should know. A couple of modest means, say two hundred and thirty-five pounds a year, would pay about twenty-two pounds in taxes if their income were split between them, but as a married couple the bill is over twice that. And the wealthier you get, the worse it is. A man making forty thousand pounds would be far better off to split his income and live in sin with his mistress —"

"Money aside," Margaret cut in, "how many friends do we know who are clearly mismatched, and have been for years now, and who struggle on unhappily, because that is the way it has always been done? They are in love with someone else, and everyone knows it, and yet it must be tiptoed around because adultery and divorce itself are considered so disgraceful —"

Lillian got up and started scraping and stacking the dishes closest to her.

"It all goes back to choosing a spouse with utmost care in the first place!" Henry exclaimed. "So many of our friends married during the war, you'll remember, when people were throwing caution to the wind. Frances had no idea whether she would see William again. But when he came back he was a different William. We all recognized that. He was a *returned* man." Henry took a sip of lemonade and thanked Lillian for collecting his plate. "We *are* talking about Frances and William, are we not?" he said to Margaret.

"*We* married during the war, dear husband," Margaret said, smiling. "And we are talking *in general*. Surely there is no need to drag names into the conversation. But now that you have, I should say that William works with Henry at Inland Revenue. Or at least nominally he does, though he's drunk much of the time, and we happen to know that Frances, who has become a friend of mine, has taken a lover for the last four years perhaps, whom she met through some volunteer work she was doing with the East End poor. He is not a poor man, but a doctor, and a young one at that. Now, if she were to get a divorce, would she have to endure the stigma of confessing to adultery in court? Would the doctor's family agree to allow him to marry a divorcée? Or should she just continue to plod through a sham marriage until William drinks himself to death in an honourable and publicly accept-able manner? What if he takes forever?" She turned to Lillian. "Let me help you with those," she said, rising.

"No, please," Lillian insisted. But Vanessa got up then as well, and with some prodding both Martha and Abigail joined them, and soon the women and children were off cleaning up and the men were left to smoke in the garden.

"Your wife is magnificent!" Rufus enthused to Henry. He turned to me. "Isn't she? She's beautiful, she's brilliant, she's full of unusual and challenging ideas." He turned back to Henry with a smile. "She must be hard to handle sometimes at home, though?"

Henry shook his head ruefully. "There is no handling

Margaret. My main challenge is in trying to understand clearly what she wants. Once I've attained that, then I just do whatever it is, and we're all happy." He did not look like a man who was kidding. "For a time," he added.

Rufus laughed. "Now there's a sane man's prescription for a happy marriage!" he said. "How are things in Inland Revenue these days?"

Henry eyed him wearily. "I am looking forward to my retirement," he said. "But at present rate of savings, that will be in about a hundred years. Once Alexander is settled in a good position, and the girls have been well and safely-married—" The thought trailed off into nothing. "Of course it's hard to plan these things with the world as it is." He looked at me sadly. "I suppose you know more than any of us what things can come to."

We were silent for a time, and then the talk swirled with the issues of the day, about Bolshevik trade unions in particular—how harmful they were for business, Rufus said, and how they were pulling us all towards civil war. "You'll see, in a few years every industrialized nation will be headed by strongmen who will get us back on track. Most sensible people will yearn for it, as opposed to this chaos. Can you believe it—even the busmen in London went on strike for the coronation. It must have been pandemonium in the streets, Henry."

"And yet we managed somehow," Henry said meekly.

Sometime later the women came out again and saved Rufus and me from fisticuffs. He'd done so well by his wife's money, and was now moving entirely in such well-shod circles, he seemed to have lost track of the surrounding desperation.

"I hope you men have been solving the world's problems," Vanessa said cheerfully. Then, without waiting for a reply, she added, "Of course if it were up to women we wouldn't have problems. Except what to wear. That's always a problem. What do you think — if men worried more about what they wore, would we still be bombing each other and erecting huge trade tariffs?"

"If women were in charge of the world," Rufus said, standing now, evidently relieved to be onto a lighter topic, "then university courses would focus on flower arranging and hat design, and international trade talks would founder for months as the negotiators gossiped about their children and sweethearts."

"And the world would be a better place," Margaret said pleasantly, as if in apology for the heat of her earlier words. "How about a walk in the fresh country air?"

We were all standing now. Henry said, "Darling, I should think a nap would do you better. We've had a long train journey and you don't want to overstrain —"

"I feel perfectly fine!" Margaret said. "Why don't *you* have a nap, dear, and I'll go for a walk with these handsome young men?" She linked arms with both Rufus and me. "And their beautiful wives, of course."

"But you haven't slept the last several nights —"

"Because you kept talking to me about the importance of sleep! Honestly, we're here, finally. I don't want to sleep through it. That's not what I've crossed the ocean for."

"Why did you cross the ocean?" I asked.

"To go on this walk, of course," she replied.

I found Lillian in the kitchen, wiping the counter with furious concentration.

"Everyone seems to want to go for a hike. I thought perhaps down to the river."

She didn't seem to have heard.

"Does that sound all right?"

"Are you asking permission?" She stopped and glared at me. She had taken the rouge off her cheeks and donned the tight blue kerchief she often wore around her head for performing housework.

"I think we should all go," I said.

"And who's going to make supper?" She started to wipe again, some stain she looked ready to start chiselling.

"Lillian, we just ate." I was trying to keep my voice soft. "Come with us for a nice afternoon walk in the country." I stepped behind her and put a hand on her shoulder. She stiffened until I pulled away.

"Where is everyone supposed to sleep?" she asked suddenly. "Didn't you tell them our house is too small? I don't have enough sheets or beds. And I don't want to ask them to sleep on the floor."

"We talked about this. Margaret and Henry will take your bedroom, Vanessa and Rufus will have my spare room, the girls can take Michael's room, and I can set up the tents outside, one for the boys and one for us. It's what Alexander wanted, as far as I know — a wilderness experience."

Lillian threw down her rag. "Your cousin just asked me if she and Henry could have separate bedrooms, because he snores and she can't sleep and gets headaches. What are we, a hotel?"

"Henry can sleep in the tent with Michael and Alexander!" I said. "He can sleep with us for all I care! What does it matter?"

"Yes. What does it matter?" she snapped.

Nineteen

Michael led the way. He had latched onto Alexander like a burr and the two ran down the trail together through the woods, Michael's little legs churning beside his teenaged cousin's loping strides. Martha and Abigail chattered together and waved their hands wildly at the odd mosquito or deer fly.

"The more you fuss, the worse it gets!" Henry said to them. "Try to stay relaxed. It's only nature."

"But nature is eating *us*, Father!" Abigail said.

Soon the girls were running after the boys, Henry not far behind. Rufus and Vanessa had linked arms, and Margaret, who talked with them for a time, drifted back to walk with me. In the shadows it was cool, the ground muddy from recent rains.

"I'm sorry, you're going to soil your good shoes," I said. "I'm sure Lillian has an extra pair for working in the yard. I should have got you those." She was wearing black oxfords with heels that sank into the mud and left her unsteady.

"I'll just have to cling to you," she said, and took my arm

even before I offered it. Walking together like this we slowed, picking our way past the wetter bits.

"The ground gets a little firmer up here a ways."

"I was hoping it would," Margaret said immediately. "It has felt quite sticky ever since I arrived." Before I could comment she hurried on. "I'm afraid I've upset your wife. Is that why she didn't come on the walk?"

"No, no," I said quickly. "She has things she needs to do. She wants to impress you all, of course. She'll be fine once she gets to know you better."

The children started clattering about something in the distance, but they were around a bend and I couldn't see what was going on.

"I guess we all get better at it as we get older," Margaret said.

"At what?"

"Lying, of course."

That nearly stopped me short, but she continued pulling me along. As we rounded the bend I could see the whole group of them hunched around a low spread of plants, touch-me-nots, which they were trying to pop. Margaret rushed into the middle of them and let Abigail drag her from plant to plant.

"They're called jewelweed," Henry said — he was on his knees, the most animated he'd been since his arrival — "because of the way the leaves hold in moisture. And look how they're crowding out all the other plants. They're very aggressive that way. But I fear it might be too shy in the season for them."

Michael was able to find one or two early performers and laughed gleefully as the seed pods exploded. But most were disappointing, and the mosquitoes punished us for lingering. The boys tore ahead again, the girls right after them. Rufus started to go on and on about our rough childhood days when we would race around the woods, nearly naked and three-fourths wild, as he recalled it. "Do you remember Mother's enormous dinner bell? As long as we were within range of that, everything was in bounds. We could have been a hundred feet up a red pine, shooting arrows at one another, but as long as we came home on the dinner bell, there'd be no questions asked."

At the river the sun hit our faces, and the trail broadened out to show the dance of the water, the folds of the current over and around the myriad rocks and fallen logs, the slightly deeper pools that were still fine for wading. Michael had already led his cousins to one of them, and shoes were off, dresses hiked, trouser legs rolled to the knees. Henry was right in the middle of them, his bowler hat tilted back on his balding head. They were all bent over something of interest, which Michael was poking authoritatively. Rufus and Vanessa sat on the rocks close to the children, and Margaret and I stayed a little way off, our faces turned to the sun that was high over the trees.

"What have I been lying about?" I asked her.

"You are a good host and husband pretending I have not terribly upset your wife, but I'm afraid I have."

I insisted again that Lillian was not upset, but Margaret turned her head away in a gesture of dismissal.

"And I suppose you are going to claim that I have not upset you," she said. "When I have forgiven you."

"For what?"

Rufus got up then and approached us. "It's rather extraordinary the way you are monopolizing Margaret," he said to me, only half joking. "Do you still fish in this river?" Without waiting for an answer he sat down between us. "Ramsay suddenly disappeared one summer," he said to her. "We were living together in Montreal. We both had office jobs. And then Ramsay was gone almost every weekend, fishing! And I kept asking him — where are you going that the fishing is so good? And he would become very vague. But every weekend he would come back ... without any fish!"

Margaret laughed so he kept on, regaling her with this old story.

"One weekend I was determined to get him in with the right crowd. Do you remember Elizabeth Dillingham, Ramsay? She was an artist, too, from an excellent family — very well off. I remember asking you to give up your fishing for one tiny weekend so you could come to the Dillinghams' dance party. I was even willing to lend you a proper coat and shoes. Elizabeth had bent my ear for ages to make sure you came. Do you remember her at all?"

I nodded my head slightly. "A bit of a horsey face."

"She was so stuck on you. But you were riding the train every weekend to court this mysterious farm girl, all under the guise of fishing!"

Margaret smiled at my embarrassment, a fine bit of sunlight in her eyes.

"So the fisherman got caught!" she exclaimed. "Was it a wonderful romance?"

"Whirlwind."

"So that's why I never heard from you," she said lightly. "You were here, probably right at this spot, courting your Lillian and forgetting all about me."

"You were married at the time, I believe," I said to her.

"Yes, and every Guinevere wants a Lancelot to be pining for her, at least a little bit, somewhere far away." She touched Rufus on the leg. "You're very bad to be listening to all this. It's none of it serious, you know."

Rufus didn't seem to know what to make of it. He looked from Margaret to me and back again. Finally he said, "Ramsay fell in love with the land too. I was so glad when you were able to buy your property down here, Ramsay. I'm glad I made those calls."

"What calls?"

"To Father's connections! He knew you weren't going to get that reparations money any other way." Rufus glanced at Margaret as if this too was all a joke, then back at me. "Didn't I tell you? Father was on his deathbed and made me promise to make those calls. I don't think he would have allowed himself to go otherwise. He was so concerned about you."

"What are you talking about?" Margaret asked.

"Ramsay applied for war reparations money, but the commission was so stingy he wasn't going to get anything unless someone made a special appeal." He turned to me with only the faintest shade of embarrassment on his face. "Of course you know this is how it works, don't you?"

I ground my teeth in silence.

"The world owed you, Ramsay. You suffered, but then you got your land out of it. Everything balances out."

There was a ruckus then, and we all turned to watch Henry holding a small turtle by the shell while the children splashed and jostled to get a better look. Abigail called out to her mother to come have a look.

"Yes dear, I can see!" Margaret called back. "He's beautiful!"

"But come here, Mummy!" Abigail said. So Margaret got up and walked to the edge of the water, and Henry brought the turtle over to show to her and Vanessa.

Rufus was staring at my face, watching me look at Margaret.

"Sometimes you are an absolute surprise," he said.

After Henry had handed round the turtle for all the children to handle and let it go its merry way, Michael pointed out minnows in the shallows, and there were butterflies to watch and talk about and a course of stepping stones to build. Eventually I was enticed into the water to help shift some of the larger rocks, and Henry lectured us on beavers — he had a particular fascination and was hoping to see some. Michael was nearly ecstatic to show him and all the others three beaver-chewed birch stumps on the opposite shore, and he made certain that his cousins learned that the beaver must continue chewing wood or else his teeth will grow through the bottom of his mouth. Margaret, especially, listened with rapt fascination, not to her husband but to Michael.

The sun moved higher, and Margaret pulled her hair free from its coils beneath her hat and let it fall about her shoulders. Of all the times I'd seen her — the phantom of her in my mind — now it seemed both impossible and absolutely normal that she should be before me.

"Perhaps we should go back," I said as the afternoon burned on.

"But is there something further up this trail?" Margaret asked immediately. "It doesn't end at the river, does it?"

I explained that the trail indeed went on for some miles,

all the way up to a scenic spot that looked out over the town and several lakes. "But it's a good two hours' hike up there. Maybe tomorrow, if we have the energy."

"Our train leaves tomorrow afternoon, doesn't it?" Margaret said.

"I thought you were staying the week!" I glared over at Rufus, who had written me with all the details.

"There are a few things to do in Montreal, before our cousins sail for home," Rufus said in his feather-smoothing tone. "And we thought . . . well, I knew —"

"We didn't want to put a strain on your household," Margaret said brightly. "Short visits are best, aren't they, dear?" At her glance Henry chipped in that even on a short visit she mustn't strain herself. His hat was on the ground beside him, but he had tied a white handkerchief on his head into which he was sweating profusely. "You tend to push too hard on very little food or rest, and then —"

"Oh, poof!" Margaret said to him. "I feel perfectly fine. We just had an enormous meal —"

"That was ages ago, darling," Henry said. "And it is tea time now. I'm beginning to feel nearly faint myself."

"Then you go back and have some tea! I'm perfectly fine!"

I told Margaret it was absurd to come all this way then rush off.

"The tickets are bought, I'm afraid," Henry said. There was more discussion but I didn't press further. At least Lillian would be happy, I thought. I glanced at the children, who were lolling like lizards on the smooth rocks.

"Now what about this walk?" Margaret said. "Ramsay, will you accompany me? Just a little further up the trail?"

"But, dear —" Henry said.

"I will be *fine*."

"*I* could show you!" Michael announced, suddenly full of vigour again.

"But your mother will need help with the tea," Margaret said, too quickly and with too much strained cheeriness. We all looked at her in awkward silence. Vanessa, especially, was glancing from Margaret to me to her husband, whose expression seemed to be keeping her quiet.

Then I said, "Michael, you make sure everyone knows the way home. We won't be long. We'll probably catch you up on the way back."

Without waiting for another word Margaret started across the river, her shoes and hat in her hand. Henry protested again, but she simply waved at him as if he were talking nonsense. She was halfway across before I headed after her.

"We won't go far," I said to Henry and the others.

At the crossing the river was less than fifty yards wide and shallow most of the way, but the stones were slippery and the passage slow. When she reached the other side Margaret did not wait for me to catch up to her but continued along the trail without even putting on her shoes. By now the afternoon was waning and the shadows in the woods were deep and cool. I gained the other side and shoved my wet feet into socks and shoes, then hurried along. In the low areas by the riverbank the soil was wet and black and smelled of rot and swampy gas.

"It's perhaps not the best trail right here," I said when I

reached her. "But you'll want to put your shoes on soon. It's going to get rocky."

"The mud feels so good between the toes," she said. Then she stopped and faced me. "That was clumsy, I'm sorry. But I am only here a day. Why have you never written? Why did you not come see me at the end of the war?"

"*Of course I came to see you!*" I blurted. "*You did not see me!*" I could barely look at her, I was so flabbergasted.

"I beg your pardon?"

I explained it as clearly as I possibly could. Her face fell further into bewilderment.

"What are you talking about?"

"I was standing at your gate. You looked straight at me. You didn't recognize me. You could have planted me in the soil right there, I was so devastated."

"Ramsay, stop this!" She raised her hand as if about to slap my face. "I did no such thing!"

I stepped to her, pulled her arm and moved her some paces up the trail. "Not in this bloody swamp." I sat her by a mossy tree trunk, out of the mud, and wiped her feet clean with my handkerchief, then struggled them into her shoes. I pulled her up and held her hand and we walked faster and faster, a cloud of mosquitoes and blackflies now on us. We climbed rapidly until we reached a boulder jutting out into the sun. I hoisted her up and joined her, and lit a cigarette and blew smoke to clear the bugs.

"Do you want one?" I asked her.

She shook her head. "It's a filthy habit."

I laughed rudely. "You used to smoke."

"I never did."

"You begged me for a cigarette once. When we were in clear view, walking on the street."

"I swear you are hallucinating!"

"No, I'm not." I blew more smoke and tried to contain my anger.

"I have smoked one or two cigarettes in my life, and that has been it. You know almost nothing about me." She reached across then and took the cigarette from my fingers, stuck it in her mouth and inhaled deeply. Then she blew out in the direction of a few lingering bugs, and handed the cigarette back to me. "It's still a filthy habit." She coughed slightly. "Now you must tell me. What in God's name are you talking about?"

I explained it again. "It must have been the day of Emily's funeral. I was standing on Stokebridge Street when you walked out to the cab. You looked straight at me, but I was a shadow. A starved man, Margaret. Skin and bone. I know it's not your fault."

"Did I say *nothing* to you?"

"When I stepped onto the pier in Victoria my mother broke down and wept on her hands and knees. Father was so pale I thought he would collapse. And that was after some weeks of fattening up. Of course you didn't know who I was."

"But how could I not remember?" she asked in bewilderment.

I rested my hand on her shoulder, but she took it immediately and held it in both of hers. "Everyone was looking away in those days. I wasn't the man you knew."

"But why didn't you say, 'Margaret, it's me, Ramsay!' I would've run to you, I would have —"

She faltered when she saw my eyes.

"It's not as if it would have made any difference."

I stubbed out my cigarette. "If we head back now, I'm sure we could catch the others."

I slid off the boulder and stumbled a few steps down to the trail, then turned to offer my hand.

"I don't want to go back now. I have to rethink everything."

"To what purpose?"

"Those years have been so fixed in my mind. But now —" She hesitated, then took my hand and slid down, and I held her awkwardly for a moment.

"Let's go along a bit further," she said. "I'm not hungry, are you?"

She trudged on swiftly, her mind obviously turning things over. The trail did become rocky soon enough, and while the late afternoon sun baked the open stretches, the shadows seemed to deepen on the turns through the bush. For the longest time I couldn't think of what more to say, and Margaret seemed determined to stride along in silence. She was not moving like any frail or failing woman.

"But everything has worked out for you," she said finally. "You have Lillian, and Michael, what a beautiful boy." She stopped suddenly. "What is Lillian going to think if we don't return with the others? She *is* jealous, isn't she? That's why she was so cold to me. We must go back!"

"She is cold to you, Margaret, because I am in love with a woman in the city."

The words just spilled out, without any sort of plan or discipline. I started to walk again, up the hill.

"And Lillian knows?"

I shook my head.

"Who is it?"

"A lovely woman I work with. We have been . . . on fire . . . for some years now." I could not say Dorothy's name, not to Margaret, and Margaret did not press. They were like two worlds, two separate refuges, that must not come together.

"And you are not . . . on fire . . . with Lillian?"

I felt as if I was almost running. We rounded a bend to a dip in the trail, my feet jolting with every step.

"I married the wrong woman! When I met her I got lost in some sort of dream of her beauty and her . . . youth and freshness. If you'd killed me on the first night of our honeymoon I would have died content." I slowed down to let her catch up, to think through what I was saying. "I never stopped thinking of you, Margaret. I had you like a fever from that week in London. In the camps . . ." A grouse suddenly exploded in the bush beside us and we both jumped back in alarm, then laughed as we saw what it was.

I held both her arms to look at her.

"I was put in solitary for three days. In a hole in the ground in the middle of winter. You'll say that I was hallucinating, but not only were you with me, you held me up, you marched me around, you told me stories, you flirted with me, we kissed, we made love . . . By all rights I should have frozen in that hole, but I didn't, Margaret. Because of a dream of you. *Nothing I'm saying now will go beyond us, beyond this afternoon.*"

She looked at me in alarm.

"Because this is a dream too, isn't it? You've dragged your family across the ocean, set this all up so that we can talk clear for once and then be done with it, yes?"

"Ramsay, you're hurting me."

270

I stared at my hands before releasing her.

"You can say anything to me," she said. "It will not go beyond this day."

We headed further up the trail — away from home, not back to it — and the silence stretched. The path was not wide enough to walk side by side, so I led; I tried to keep my pace slow enough not to tire her but quick enough to stay ahead of the bugs. As long as we were moving they seemed to bite less, and I heard no complaining from Margaret, just the regular rhythm of her breathing, her footfalls on the narrow trail.

At the next clearing we could see a span of fields down below us, the corner of a tiny lake, other hills stretching in the distance.

"We should have brought water, at least," I said, "if not a bite to eat. Why don't we rest here, then we'll head back."

Margaret looked away. "I didn't come just for this talk." She looked at me fiercely. "When England gets dragged into this Spanish war they're going to want to take Alexander, and he'll want to go. It's all happening again. I don't know if the world can bear it, but *I* can't. So you must talk to Alexander. Because you know. Tell him whatever it takes to make him want to stay out if it. I swear I will shut him up in a cave and roll a rock in front of the entrance and they will have to go through my body —"

She was breathing raggedly now, as if in a hard sprint.

"He's not exactly soldier material now," I said.

"Not any more than his father was, or you for that matter. Nobody should be forced into becoming an automaton to fire weapons and drop bombs on other humans."

"But the Germans —"

"We *created* the Germans! And the Italians, the Japanese

— the waters are poisoned now, and there's no way out except for another unbelievably bloody war. *I know this.* And I know there are enough desperate men all over the world to sign up today for any escape from this economic nightmare. The young men did it in our day and it's far worse now. *Just not my boy.* I will go mad with sorrow and grief." She waved her hat in the air to brush away the flies, then she reached for my hand again. "I did go mad. I could not say much in my letters — I felt horrible for writing to *you*, of all people, in such a state. But I was confined to bed for ages, Ramsay. Poor Father wanted to hospitalize me, he was so concerned. But I simply couldn't allow myself to take a spot that might have gone to a wounded soldier. What was I suffering, really, in the grand scheme of things?"

She waved the hat again, ineffectually, at the cloud of mosquitoes. I lit another cigarette and blew smoke at them.

"You're right," she said. "It would be good to have water right now. And I am starving." Once more she took my cigarette, but this time she kept smoking it, so I lit another of my own. "This woman you love so much. Why don't you just get a divorce and marry her? Mrs. Simpson manages to do it and she's still standing."

"Because I have a child. And I do care what the world thinks of me. To be frank I don't know what to do. I don't know if Dorothy" — it just spilled out beneath my guard — "that's her name, Dorothy. I don't know if she's even interested in marrying. She has been content to have me as is. Lillian would be smashed to pieces. At least in this state of frozen matrimony we can stumble through our days. It hasn't been unbearable." The sun now had moved beyond our little spot and it was either walk on or head back. "They'll be coming to look for us soon if we don't turn around now."

"*It hasn't been unbearable.* You don't know how heartbreaking it is to hear you say that."

"Why should the state of my marriage — ?"

"I agreed to marry Henry in my weakest days. Not for my own sake, but to stop his suffering. He stood by me, he visited or called every day, he spent his little trickle of pay on flowers for me, on chocolates, forbidden cuts of meat, old fancy teacups he thought might please me. If I didn't get better, if I didn't join myself to him, he would have crumpled. And if that isn't a terrible reason for marrying someone I don't know what is. But yes, it hasn't been unbearable. I have my children, and Henry is a good father to them and dotes on me. So I'm lucky. No indeed, it hasn't been unbearable."

We continued smoking in silence.

"Why didn't you insist on getting my attention until I knew who you were, Ramsay?" she said suddenly. "That was stupid of you. I'm sorry for saying it. But I was in another state. Emily's death was so sudden and so hard! I'm not surprised I walked right past you. But I never forgot you. I *never* did. You must believe me." She looked distraught. "At least you have your fire. I envy you that."

She stepped past me then, down the trail, back the way we had come.

Twenty

It was a silent walk, and then Henry and Rufus met us on the trail. Henry's face was over-baked, and he'd sweated through his jacket — it was absurd of him to still be wearing it on a hot day like that. But even Rufus, who'd remained trim and fit through the years, was drenched from the walk.

"There you are!" Henry gushed. "Are you all right, darling? I thought for certain you'd succumbed to the heat."

They had brought a flask of water, and we drank from it greedily.

"Shall we rest here for a time?" Henry puffed, and before we could answer he sank down on one knee and waved at the large cloud of pests we'd managed to congregate.

"If we don't keep going, we'll be eaten alive," Margaret said. "Will *you* be all right, dear?"

"I'm fine," Henry gasped. "I was just thinking of *you*."

Rufus took Henry's hand and pulled him up, then the four of us began to walk together.

"We heard the most disturbing news on the radio back at the house," Rufus said. "Spanish loyalist planes have bombed a German battleship in some rebel port."

"Iviza," Henry said.

"The Spanish government is firing back at last," I said. "It's not as if there hasn't been provocation."

"Exactly," Rufus said. "The loyalists claim the *Deutchs-land* — that was the German ship — fired on their planes. I wouldn't be surprised if they did. Of course officially it's part of the Non-Intervention patrol fleet."

"Will it be a European war then?" Margaret asked.

"We're waiting for the German reaction," Henry said. We'd begun walking more quickly now, as if the bad news had somehow changed the pace of the day, made it imperative that we return at speed.

"Won't this simply be an excuse for the Germans to pour all their troops openly into the fight on behalf of their brother fascists?" Margaret asked.

"The Germans have pulled out of the Non-Intervention Committee," Henry said. "But Hitler is just a lot of nasty talk, isn't he?"

When we made the river the sun had already fallen behind the trees, and the light on the water was completely different — the colours were darker and richer than in the heat of the day. How many times had I painted this very spot? And each time another shade of a subtly changed world.

Henry held onto Margaret's hand in the water, and as I watched from behind I had a hard time deciding who was supporting whom.

At the house the radio spilled its sporadic reports with all of us crowded around its staticky speaker, waiting to hear the worst — except Lillian, who was preparing chicken pies. It was Henry who had to have his ear closest to the set and who would sit up from time to time and announce, in headline form, what all of us could already hear.

"Twenty-three dead! Eighty-three wounded. The *Deutschland* is a 'pocket' battleship — whatever that is. The rebel siege of Bilbao continues! What's this? The *Deutschland* shouldn't have been anywhere near Iviza, since they were actually on Non-Intervention duty at the time! The Committee is meeting tomorrow."

I walked quietly into the kitchen to see if Lillian wanted any help. She'd strapped on her apron like battle armour and looked at my feet when I spoke.

"Should I get the card table out to add to the —"

"I've already done it."

I called out to Michael. "Would you set the table for your mother?"

"I've done that too," Lillian said. "You'll just have to wait to eat."

"There's no hurry. It smells wonderful," I said softly, backing away. Her eyes stayed down, her jaw welded shut.

I retreated to the front room, where Margaret was studying one of my paintings, a winter scene by the window that showed a winding section of creek in an open, snow-covered field. I watched her as she examined the sliver of silver in the middle where I'd hinted at the sun reflecting off a frozen patch of clear ice that couldn't quite be seen — it was mostly the reflection, the inference of ice.

"I would love to be here in the winter," she said.

"At thirty below you wouldn't love it for long."

"But we would be under a blanket by the fire, just the two of us," she said in a low voice, "and we'd talk enough to make up for decades of lost time."

"Yes, you and me. And your husband and three children, and house servants. You have house servants?"

276

"Just a couple. And there'd be Michael too, of course. And your wife and mistress."

"We'd all be very cozy watching the snow."

She turned to an old photograph on the windowsill of Father in his youth in the Far East, sitting in a studio rickshaw wearing a white pith helmet, with a dark, skinny coolie boy in a loincloth apparently about to pull him somewhere.

"What a marvellous moustache!" Margaret said of his handlebar.

She turned to me. "You will talk to Alexander. Promise me, Ramsay."

"Yes, I will."

It was an evening scramble to erect the tents. The old pine poles I thought I'd kept so well in a separate pile by the side of the meadow had rotted through over the years, so in the dying light I took Michael and Alexander with me back to the bush with an axe, and I cut several fresh ones, and then together we hauled them back. Michael talked all the way, especially when we passed by a swarm of fireflies spinning in the air like lighted fairies. Even Alexander laughed and ran after them then, but mostly he was quiet and kept within himself.

I asked him about school, and he replied, in as few words as possible, that he liked history.

"Is there a particular period that attracts you?"

After thinking for some time, he finally offered up the Greeks.

"What is it about the Greeks you find fascinating?"

He shrugged his shoulders — he and Michael were walking with a stack of poles between them — and Michael yelled out, "Hercules!" as if he might be able to summon the strongman out of the mist that very instant.

"Is it the first experiments with democracy? The struggles with the Spartans and Persians? The contrasting philosophies of Plato and Aristotle?" I remembered my father questioning me in the same way, but he would throw in Greek and Latin phrases as well — or French, German, Spanish, whatever the moment called for — and any remark I might summon would be greeted with cutting, penetrating further inquiry, designed to expose the depths of my ignorance.

I remembered, but I couldn't quite keep myself from doing it. "Was it the rise of Alexander?" I asked.

"You're Alexander too!" Michael called. Then he asked, "What did Alexander do?"

"He conquered most of the known world. For a time," I said.

On we walked, our Alexander remaining as quiet as he could get away with.

Well past dark the two tents were erected in the meadow and I'd found the cots in the crawl space under the house. Martha and Abigail put up a terrible racket when they saw that the boys were going to be allowed to sleep outside and they weren't. I left Margaret to try to sort it out, and when she couldn't I finally offered the second tent to the girls. "Lillian and I will sleep in Michael's room," I said.

"But there's hardly room for two adults there," Margaret said. "*I'll* take Michael's room. It will be fine for me. You and Lillian must stay in your own bedroom, of course, though it was most kind of you to offer it in the first place. I'm so sorry to be such trouble. We're all a family of temperamental sleepers. We oughtn't to be travelling at all."

But Lillian insisted that Margaret remain in the larger bedroom. "You deserve it," she said in an unbending voice. "You need more comfort."

"But this is silly!" Margaret protested. "At least Rufus and Vanessa must have it, and I'll take the spare room."

"Rufus and Vanessa are fine where they are," Lillian insisted.

It was a balmy evening, and the boys and Henry kept the flaps open, willing to brave the bugs for a spot of fresh breeze, while the girls tightened every knot, snuggled into their bedrolls and exclaimed at the comfort of the aging wooden cots. Margaret came out to sing the girls a lullaby, and as I listened to her soft, fine voice, I thought of Lillian singing in the cabin kitchen years ago when we were just beginning.

I found her inside, putting away the last of the great load of dishes used by this army of her husband's relatives who had descended upon her. I picked up a towel and set to helping with the cups.

"Do you remember that day I proposed?" I asked her.

Her face remained set with impatient annoyance. Finally she said, "Of course."

I'd been out at the river fishing, not where we were that afternoon but further downstream, near her father's old property. I'd taken to setting up my tent in their back field, and she'd come to ask me if there would be any fish for dinner. She'd done something with her hair — coiled it up with small white lilies. And she'd put on a new green dress she'd just made. It was the sight of her that literally made me lose my balance, not the fact that a fish had struck at the same instant. After she saved me from falling in she did not move aside. Her eyes did not sink to examining the rocks. And the kiss that we fell into — our first — felt as large as a chasm, as inevitable as gravity.

Later on, after dinner, when she was standing just like this in the kitchen washing up the dishes, I approached her from behind and just held her. Her father was sleeping beneath the evening paper in the front room, and I thought if I could not have her the storm inside me would blow my body to bits.

Now I tried not to drop the dishes. Lillian waited for me to finish my thought — I did have a reason, didn't I, for bringing up that earlier time?

Instead I said, "I hope we can manage tonight in Michael's room. It's just for one night."

"I thought they were staying the week."

"No. Their train leaves tomorrow afternoon."

"Are we not good enough for them?"

"They didn't want to overstay," I said quietly.

Rufus and Vanessa came in then. They'd had a moonlight walk down the lane and were leaning on one another like beautiful young lovers for whom the world has scattered its rose petals. But Rufus broke the spell immediately and honed in on the radio. "I wonder if there's been any more news," he said.

"Dear Mr. Crome," Vanessa said to him. "If Europe is in flames we'll hear all about it tomorrow. Would you just let the evening be?"

He looked at her as if reading some secret sign.

"Quite right, Mrs. Crome," he said. "It is a delicious evening, isn't it?"

Then came the slap of the back screen door and Margaret

entered as well. "What a blissful evening," she said. "I hope those brave children have earplugs. Henry tends to blow like a foghorn, especially when he's this tired. I must say I feel almost electric all of a sudden. Does anyone fancy a walk with me?"

Rufus's face lit with the possibility, and then he looked at Vanessa again and the possibility receded.

"We've just come back, I'm afraid," Vanessa said. "But look at you, all ready to go even after your long hike this afternoon."

Margaret turned to Lillian, who was furiously wiping the table. "Would you like to come for a short stroll? I feel as if we've hardly had a chance to chat."

"Not tonight," Lillian said shortly.

"Oh dear," Margaret said. "I know I'll pay for it later, but right now ..." She turned to me. "Ramsay? Just a short walk?"

"I need to turn in," I said grimly.

"Yes, it must be time," Vanessa said, gripping her husband's hand and exaggerating a yawn. "We're over here in the spare, is that right?"

Once again the sleeping arrangements were discussed. Margaret wanted to cede the big bedroom, but Lillian was adamant. So it was decided. Vanessa and Rufus slipped off to the spare room, and Margaret went out alone for a short stroll just to the end of the lane, she said, while Lillian cleaned up the last invisible traces of the dinner. I retreated to Michael's room, where I sat in the shadows staring into the night. The moon hung like a paper lantern partially obscured behind a fan of thinly ribbed clouds.

Eventually Lillian stepped into the room and snapped on

the light. She had brought her nightclothes down from the upstairs bedroom, and when she shut the door she quickly began to disrobe.

"I hope your cousin didn't get herself lost."

In the cold light of the overhead lamp, the skin of her fine belly and breasts seemed paler than moonlight.

Soon the light was snapped off and she was in bed.

I looked out the window again and considered, absurdly, spending the rest of the night sitting with my eyes open like some cat or owl. I wasn't going to sleep anyway. Not in this state.

But the charade of marital normalcy had a powerful pull. I found myself walking to the bathroom and cleaning up as if this were simply any other night and returning to where Lillian had already settled in. She was facing the wall with her back to me, leaving only a pitiful few inches of bed to which I was supposed to cling while asleep.

It really was ridiculous to think of the two of us sharing Michael's bed. We could hardly seem to share the house anymore.

"I'm afraid Margaret's not back yet," I said to my wife's shape in the gloom. "I should have gone with her, of course. I'll just step out and find her quickly."

No reaction.

"Lillian?"

"Do what you must," she snapped.

Outside, the night air was still warm on my face, and the sky, so strikingly lit, stretched clouded and star-pricked like a huge dark canvas above me. It was a relief to walk, to feel my limbs move. I headed down the lane where Margaret had said she'd be, the trees silent, brooding witnesses. From the meadow I could hear one of the girls — I wasn't sure which — say, "If you stay beneath the covers they can't get you!" I walked more softly, wanting to be invisible, to melt into the air and blow away.

Margaret was sitting in darkness on a stump near the join of the lane and the larger village road, which were both quiet now, and still. I didn't see her at first but was set to sail on past when she remarked, "There are a lot of frogs on the road."

I followed her gaze and made out two or three dark frogs on the lane and road, leaping about, then stopping to disappear into tiny lumps before heading off again.

"You should come back to the house," I said, more abruptly than I'd meant to.

"Yes, I'm sorry. I didn't mean to tarry here."

But she didn't move.

"They have the most wonderful voices," she said. They were singing, not the ones on the road but hundreds of others in the small pond not far off on the other side of the wood. "It all sounds hopelessly complex and mysterious. They're mating, I suppose?"

"I don't imagine they're talking about the Spanish Civil War. Or maybe they have an equivalent we just don't know about."

The crickets were singing too, and the combined songs seemed to rise and fill the air then, to make further talk impossible. I didn't step any nearer, although there was room on the mossy stump where I might have sat beside her.

"You have a lot of nerve," I said, suddenly feeling reckless, "telling me to divorce my wife."

"I said no such thing." She turned to face me. "I asked you why you didn't. You sounded so unhappy with your situation."

"Maybe you should divorce your husband. You hardly seem to be happier than me."

"You know that's impossible," she said soberly. "I could no more prove adultery or habitual drunkenness or cruelty or any of the other proposed new grounds than you could prove them against Lillian. Oh, I suppose if I asked Henry, if I could be so cruel as that, he would arrange to be found adulterous for me. But I might as well put a gun to his head. You already have your grounds. You'd just be acknowledging a reality. And you would continue to provide for your family through alimony."

We lapsed into a strained silence. Finally I said, "I promised Lillian I would be back with you straightaway."

"Yes, I'm sorry." She stood abruptly, suddenly so near to me I could feel the heat coming off her skin. Her hand brushed my arm as she stepped past me, and I grasped onto her wrist. She stopped but held herself still at a distance.

"I thought you said Lillian was waiting?"

"I want you to see some paintings," I said. "They're in a storage room in my studio off the upstairs bedroom. The key to the door is underneath the large mug on the window shelf that holds my brushes."

"*You* must show me," she said.

"No."

"Why not?"

But she knew why. I couldn't go to her bedroom with her,

not alone at night when everyone else was asleep. I shouldn't have been with her now.

"When the house burnt a few years ago I lost every painting. But I've redone the ones that stayed most fixed in my head. They changed, of course, many of them. If you're shocked or offended by what you see, I'm sorry — I apologize in advance. I could not keep myself from working on them."

I started walking and she fell in beside me.

"Are they disreputable?"

"Some are from the war. Some contain the most beauty I could summon and concentrate on canvas." The house loomed white and ghostly before us. How long had we been gone? I was seized with the thought that Lillian would suddenly wake the house with a screaming, raging fit in front of everyone. The children would come running; Henry would look at us, guiltily together; Vanessa and Rufus would stumble out in their nightclothes, gaping at the commotion.

But all was still.

I closed the door quickly and hurried in some paces ahead of Margaret. No lights were on, but it was easy enough to pick our way through the shadows.

"Good night, Ramsay," she said at the stairs.

The door to Michael's room squeaked. I pushed myself through. Lillian lay in exactly the same position as I'd left her. She looked to be in a deep and unrelenting sleep.

I shucked off my outer clothes and climbed in behind her. I was warm still from the walk, and it didn't matter that Michael's sheet and thin blanket barely covered half of me. I put my arm around my wife and found her body rigid, as if she were holding herself intact.

Lillian, I imagined myself saying. I'm in love with someone.

I imagined the winds suddenly blowing out the windows,
tearing the roof off the house.

Her body softened slightly and moulded itself to me.

Lillian, I imagined saying in a voice I would have to summon from somewhere. I can't go on, I'm sorry. I can't.

I closed my eyes. What does it matter, at night, whose
body you lie beside? We are so similar in the dark, and most
of the night passes in sleep.

I listened for the sound of Margaret's feet on the floor
above us. By now she would have found the key. Had she
found the light too, or was she grabbing about in the dark?
I thought I heard shuffling. Lillian tensed and tried to move
away from me, but there was no place to go.

She screwed her face into the one pillow. Against all of
my rational will, I started to harden just from the heat and
proximity of her, and perhaps from the close call with Margaret. Why hadn't I simply kissed her out on the lane? No
one would have seen, and certainly Lillian believed I did kiss
her. That's why she was coiled so tightly in the bed, ready to
lash out at me. Margaret would be gone tomorrow. Europe
was coming to pieces. I might never see her again.

Lillian turned her face to me, wet with tears. "You used
to love me," she said in a little voice. She pulled up her nightdress and took me suddenly between her legs. "Is this what
you want me to do?"

"Shh."

"Tell me what you want."

She was rocking against me now. I was balanced on a bare

few inches of bed. Overhead I heard a soft thump. Lillian froze. "What's she doing?"

"I don't know. Moving her trunk?"

I began to subside. I tried to think of Margaret sitting in the water, the sunlight favouring her right breast, a reed brushing against the whiteness of her belly, her hair falling across her face. She might be looking at that painting right this moment, I thought.

Lillian clutched the pillow and let out a low, pained breath. I held her, tried to keep her from shaking.

"Why am I nothing to you?" she moaned.

"That's not true."

"I can smell her on you!"

"No. No, you can't."

She elbowed me. "Why don't you go up and sleep with her now," she hissed. "*It's what you want.*"

"It isn't. Lillian, I swear."

She felt and found my cock soft as a bag of sawdust.

"Swear all you like," she said bitterly.

Then we both froze to listen to new noises: a gentle rhythmic squeaking, like a metallic sign swinging in the breeze, and then a thumping on the floor in the spare room next to ours — a galloping bed — and hard breathing that seemed to go on and on forever.

Rufus and Vanessa.

"Damn them all! " Lillian said. She rolled over me and onto her feet. "I'm going to sleep in the sitting room."

She disappeared with the sheet, the blanket, the pillow and all peace.

Twenty-one

The next morning Lillian was up before any of us, clattering around the kitchen with a vengeance. My head felt stuffed and fragile from lack of sleep. By the time I walked out of the bedroom she had cooked up a whole side of bacon — rations for some weeks if it were just the three of us — and all the eggs in the house and enough coffee for a political rally. She had folded up the blankets on the chesterfield, and as soon as she saw me in the hallway she hurried past and into Michael's room, where she changed quickly back into yesterday's dress.

The children charged into the house from outside, Martha and Abigail wrapped primly in housecoats, Michael barely clothed in a torn pair of underpants. Alexander slouched in wearing pyjamas, his hair as squashed and tired as a bird's nest wintered over.

"So how was it in the wilds?" I asked Martha.

"I could not sleep a wink for the parasites! Even when I burrowed down they bit me through the coverings! Look!" And she showed us all several small red marks on her arms, neck, legs and ankles.

"I wasn't bitten at all!" Abigail declared.

"Well, I would have slept despite the bugs if you hadn't squirmed all the time," Martha said to her.

"I did not!"

"Now, young ladies," Margaret said, and I turned to see her coming down the stairs. In a shaft of sunlight from the landing window, in the soft white dress she was wearing, she looked as radiant as I'd ever seen her. "You wanted your wilderness experience, so you mustn't grumble over any physical hardship."

"I didn't get bites!" Michael announced. "Well, just a few."

"There, you see — frontier stoicism. Let's try to exhibit a small portion of it, at least."

Henry came in then. His eyes were puffed and red, and his thin hair pointed limply in several directions. "Oh, my dear," he said as soon as he saw Margaret. "You look as if you've slept a century in a glass room and emerged more resplendent than ever!"

Margaret beamed at him. "And you look as if you've been dragged behind a horse. Did you not sleep well?"

"I dreamt we were on board the *Hindenburg*," he said. "The fire was raging all around us, but you wouldn't jump out. You thought the children were in the back somewhere, but in fact we'd left them in Munich."

"What were they doing in Munich?"

"I don't know, but they were quite safe."

"Being raised by Nazis, no doubt."

He crossed the floor and kissed his wife lightly on the forehead. "Now I see that you floated out, safe as an angel. What a relief!"

Margaret asked Lillian if there was anything she could

do to help, but Lillian replied, with a terrible summoning of goodwill, that everything was in hand. "I think I'm ready to serve," she said. "But we don't have everyone."

We waited for Rufus and Vanessa. Henry started playing with the radio, trying to get news. The reception was quite bad most mornings. Together we sat before the receiver and twiddled with the dial like amateur safecrackers, getting little but static and dead air.

Then Rufus and Vanessa emerged, looking sunny. Rufus had on a navy blue jacket with white pants, a maroon cravat around his neck, Vanessa a creamy pair of athletic slacks and white shirt with turned-up cuffs, and a maroon scarf matching her husband's, not around her neck but in her hair.

"What a wonderful morning!" Rufus said. "I haven't slept like that in ages."

Without saying a word to Lillian, Vanessa stepped past her and began to pour coffee for all the adults. Rufus joined Henry and me to struggle with the radio. As soon as Rufus put his hand on the console a voice said, "...worst European crisis since the onset of war twenty-three years ago."

Rufus lifted his hand and the voice degenerated into static.

"What's that?" Margaret exclaimed.

Rufus put his hand back exactly where it had been, but this time the sound did not improve.

"Darling, stand where you were!" Vanessa ordered. Rufus lifted his hand, then put it back again — nothing.

"You were over *there*," Vanessa said. She strode to Rufus's side, moved him over an inch and faced him towards the living room window.

The radio crackled to life again.

"... estimates there are more than a hundred dead. The

town itself has been completely reduced to rubble, with fears that . . .”

Once more the sound faded to crackles and burps.

"Is that Bilbao?" Margaret asked.

"It would be thousands dead, not a hundred," Henry said. "Tens of thousands. Think of all those refugees." He moved the tuning dial slightly, and, with Rufus still standing with his hand on the set, we managed to pick up the ragged strains of far-away fiddle music.

"Turn it back! Oh, you're losing it!" Margaret said.

While we ate breakfast, Henry and Rufus continued to work at the radio, bringing in bits of news. "It's some smaller place called Almeria," Rufus said. "An ancient town in Andalusia. Germany sent five warships to bomb it to rubble in reprisal for the *Deutschland*."

Later Henry came in and grabbed at some coffee. "Both Germany and Italy have pulled out of the Non-Intervention Committee. They might be set to enter the war formally if Spain declares against them."

We chewed our breakfast over mounting gloom. The children were all quiet, impressed, apparently, with the degree of alarm among the adults.

"How old are you now?" I asked Alexander. I could feel Margaret's eyes burning my face.

"Sixteen."

"Your mother wants me to talk to you about war."

Alexander looked at Margaret reprovingly.

"I hardly ever talk about it. But maybe this is a good time."

I'd had my fill of eggs and toast. A great plate of bacon sat cooling still on the table. Lillian was already up washing the first of the dishes. But she was listening. Everybody was listening.

"I was in the Great War. Let me just tell you about one day. One particular afternoon just after I'd been captured. As a young soldier, you think you'll win or you'll die. But taken prisoner? I never considered it."

I poured myself more coffee.

"I was in a church in a place called Roulers. Or at least it used to be a church. But God had decamped —" I couldn't help myself, I looked at Lillian. "Forgive me, but I haven't felt a whisper of Him since. That church was now a collection and feeding centre for new prisoners fresh from battle. There were maybe fifty of us. A lot of wounded men lying on the ground bleeding, not likely to survive. And all of us in shock. A tiny old Belgian man came by with a bucket of what we came to call sandstorm soup. I don't know what was in it. Ground acorns. Bits of dirt. Greasy water. And most of us had no mess kits — no containers. We used old helmets. Some men used their boots. One fellow got so angry he took the old Belgian's pot and hurled it across the pews. What do you imagine happened?"

Alexander looked down at the table, his cheeks red. I pulled Michael to my knee and held him.

"First, several of the prisoners who were most starved ran like rats towards the spilled soup and began to shove it into their mouths as if it wasn't one step above sewage. Even the German dogs stayed away from that soup. But the guards got so angry they started rifle-butting all of us to the ground. We were in defeat, but we were all fighters, you see. We fought over everything. We fought over drinks, we fought over line-ups to go visit prostitutes —" I glanced over at Margaret. "I will not gloss this over. I want you all to know. We fought, at times, for the pure pleasure of being young men and fighting. But that day, as broken prisoners in Roulers, we didn't fight. I got hit on my bad arm and spun onto the ground. I thought I was going to get up again and smash someone and then get killed. But instead I huddled on the ground and heaved up the sandstorm soup. You can imagine it. We've all vomited. But I was so frightened I held it in my mouth. I swallowed it down again."

I looked around at their expressions of disgust and amazement, of incomprehension. Margaret, especially, appeared close to tears. A gentle breeze was blowing warm air past Lillian's yellow curtains, and suddenly I longed to be outside, to have all of us feel the sun and enjoy the day while it lasted.

"That isn't war," Alexander said finally, his voice more belligerent than perhaps he'd meant it to be. "That's being a prisoner. It's not defending your country. It's not standing up to people like Mussolini and Hitler. It's just a little part —"

"Yes, it's a little part," I said quietly. "All I can tell you about . . ." The thought trailed off. I felt extremely weary, from the bad night, no doubt, from all the emotions this brief visit had dredged up. It was all too much to try to say at once. Anyway, the young insist on making their own damn mistakes.

"When do you give your life?" I asked, looking from Alexander to Michael, from Martha to Abigail and back to Michael again. They were too young to hear most of this, and yet the world wasn't waiting for them to grow older. "Only . . . *only* to protect people you love. Not for your country, not for your God, not for somebody's idea of empire, not for democracy or any other ideal, or worse yet, some kind of thrill or adventure. Risk your life only for those you love."

I rose then and washed out my coffee cup in the sink. When I turned again they were all looking at me as if collectively holding their breath.

"What time is your train?" I asked. "What shall we do with this day?"

Twenty-two

Rufus had brought badminton rackets and shuttlecocks, of all things, in his luggage, and insisted that we repair to the meadow for a tournament. We struck the tents and used two of the poles to string a hastily constructed net — of ribbons and twine — and my brother paced out the court and marked the edges with twigs stuck in the grass. Then he picked up a racket and started sending a bird high into the air over and over with quick snaps of his wrist.

"Mixed doubles, then!" he said gleefully. "Vanessa and I are a team. Who's against us? Ramsay and Margaret?"

Vanessa picked up another racket, and the two of them began batting the bird back and forth ferociously.

"This is far too strenuous for Margaret," Henry insisted. As soon as he said it Margaret picked up the third racket.

"That's nonsense!" she said.

"But your *heart*, darling!"

"A little regular exercise will do it a world of good," she insisted. "And that's a direct quote from the doctor. Now if you don't want to play with me, I'll ask the other man in my life." She turned — her gaze strayed right across me — and looked at Alexander. "Come on, dear. Let's show these North Americans how to play our game."

They warmed up for a minute or two, and then Rufus insisted that they get on with it. Vanessa had a delicate, ladylike touch, time and again able to nudge the bird over the net by the barest of margins. But in moments of excitement she also had a withering smash. Rufus too had obviously spent some years of his life on comfortable lawns developing his skills, and the two together were unbeatable.

Margaret and Alexander gave them a run, however. Though a quiet boy, in competition Alexander threw himself about the court trying to chase down his opponents' shots. For the most part Margaret simply got out of his way or tried to encourage him, but she did hit several fine shots, while Henry worried from the sidelines.

When the game was done Rufus turned to me. "You and Lillian, now, Ramsay!" he said, in something like Father's old tone when he was organizing us for boxing or baseball. "Where's your bride? The tournament is on the line!"

I retreated to the kitchen where Lillian was furiously at work on lunch, cutting and buttering bread slices while chicken soup boiled on the stove.

"Come on," I said gently. "We've all stuffed ourselves from breakfast. Rufus has ordered us down to the meadow to play badminton."

She could not seem to look at me.

"It's mixed teams and we're supposed to play together."

"You never told me that story," she said fiercely. She turned with the breadknife in her hand and walked past me, then picked up a ladle and began angrily stirring the soup. "But you told *her*."

"I told everyone."

"You were talking to her." Now she slammed the soup ladle onto the floor. "You love *her*. It's all over your face whenever she's there!"

"Let's not talk about this now," I said. Soup had stained her apron and was dripping down the side of the stove, puddling onto the floor.

Rufus called from outside, "Where's Lillian? Come on, Ramsay! Can't you get a grip on your own wife?"

Lillian looked at me through hard tears. "We never talk about it." She reached for a rag then from the sink and started to wipe up the stains.

I left her there and steamed out the back door.

"Where's Lillian?" Rufus asked jovially.

"She's not much for games," I replied.

Back in the meadow the children had got hold of the rackets now and were flailing away. Michael swung his with both hands, like a baseball bat, and Abigail and Martha seemed to be chasing butterflies with theirs.

"Lillian's not still back in the kitchen, is she?" Margaret said.

"She didn't want to play." I shoved my hands in my pockets and looked elsewhere. A flock of sparrows was performing daring feats over the fields in the distance, speeding black spots against an impeccable blue sky.

"Well, I must go and help her, then," Margaret said. "She has done everything for us." She began to step off towards the house, but I put a hand on her shoulder.

"Best leave her for a while."

"Oh dear," she said, scanning my face for clues. "Have I — ?"

I shook my head, not in denial but frustration.

"Oh dear," she said again.

Rufus insisted that he and I play singles. I felt like smashing him over the head with the racket, he was so relentless in his goading. But I finally convinced him to take on Henry. "He'll give you a much better game than I ever could," I said. "I don't know the first thing about badminton."

"He'll not want to play *me*!" Henry called out, but he already had the extra racket in his hand and was swishing it experimentally through the air. After his wife's creditable showing he seemed to want to impress her. So the court was cleared of children and we all watched Henry huff and slash at the empty air, and smash himself in the knee, and fall and kick at his hat clownishly, his face wreathed with smiles. Margaret said to me, when her husband was on the grass searching for his fallen glasses, "I *must* go talk to her."

"No."

"But I can't have her feeling so wretched on my account!"

"It has almost nothing to do with you," I whispered.

The game continued. At one point poor Henry fell backwards and lay, very still, gazing up at the sky. Margaret ran to him on the court. "Are you all right, dear?"

He pulled her down and kissed at her — she turned her head in reflex and he grazed her cheek — and then he said, "It's very pleasant just looking up at nothing, now, isn't it?"

And the hours slowly passed. Rufus and Alexander played game after game. Vanessa drifted off to the garden with the children, and Henry crawled over to the edge of the wood and lay on his belly examining some ant works. Margaret and I found ourselves sitting in the shade not far from the court but at a distance enough to talk in confidence.

"I looked at your paintings," she said quietly. "Thank you for seeing me with so much love."

She was sitting back against her hands, and I allowed myself to run my fingers over hers in the grass.

"And for what you said to Alexander. Thank you," she said. "I know it can't be easy for you to talk of those years."

I laughed ruefully. "I talked of only the smallest bit."

Later Lillian, without a visible trace of anger, served us all another fine meal, which we ate as if it would be a sin not to satisfy ourselves when the food was so good.

The afternoon slid on, and then it was time to go. The sky above continued to blow bluer than a dream, and the sun shone kindly down, and the wildflowers seemed to be waving to us from the roadside. Even Charles was in a sprightly mood as he trotted us up the hill, the hay wagon behind loaded down with relatives and their travelling goods. We were not early this time. Already other cars and wagons had gathered in the lot. I parked Charles in the shade where I'd left him just the day before.

How ridiculous of them to stay for such a short time. We discussed it again, but the tickets had been purchased, plans were set. Rufus filled me in on the itinerary: the Basilica, of course, and Mount Royal, and staying at the Ritz-Carlton.

"If you're going to be working in Montreal this week, then perhaps we could get together for a lunch," Rufus said.

"I'll have to see about it," I said vaguely. I was suddenly looking forward to a return to the office and perhaps for a little while sitting in sanctuary on Stanley Street, holding my Dorothy. It seemed like ages since I'd last seen her.

Then, as if reading my thoughts, there was Margaret, standing a little off from the others, looking at me, waiting to be approached.

"Are we to meet then only every twenty years?" she said, when I finally walked over to her.

"You look as if you're in your twenties still," I said, "and I'm a hundred and four." Henry popped suddenly into view behind her, wrestling with the girls' bags. Margaret kissed my cheek as a cousin will. A cousin who is travelling on with her husband and children, who is holding herself very much in check.

"You're a marvellous specimen for such an advanced age," she said quietly. "You had such a reckless intensity to you back then. Now you seem ... quite formidably calmer. Are you, Ramsay?"

All the people around us seemed to begin moving at once, and then in the distance we heard the first rumblings and whistles of the train.

Gently I stepped past her to help with the mountain of luggage. Suddenly there were too many people to deal with: goodbyes to say to Rufus and Vanessa, to Henry and the girls and Alexander, and all these suitcases to manage, and Margaret's trunk, and this herd of relatives to move through the station and onto the platform and down the way while the train eased into place. Breathing became harder, tears seemed set to wash me over.

"I'm sure there won't be war," Henry said, grasping my hand. "This is just another tempest. And I have met Chamberlain. He's very able. I'm sure level heads will prevail."

"We can only hope," I said to him. "Safe travels."

"And work on your badminton!" Rufus said jovially to him, as if seeing him off, but of course Rufus was going along for the holiday as well.

"Yes! Yes, we all must work on our badminton. Except for you and Vanessa!"

The children now were boarding, and I looked around but couldn't see Margaret anymore. Had she already stepped on?

"Thank you for your story," Alexander said to me, somewhat formally. His mother must have put him up to it, I thought immediately, but he stayed gripping my hand and seemed to mean what he said. "It made me think."

"Thinking is good," I said, somewhat stupidly. Where had Margaret gone?

"Would you fight against Hitler?" he asked.

I thought I'd seen her, but it was someone else in white.

"If Nazi planes were threatening someone you loved —"

He was still gripping my hand. Most of the platform now was clearing.

"Pray it doesn't come to that," I said. "Just remember, you'll break your mother's heart if you go to war and Hitler's planes are not already sounding in the distance."

He ducked his head. "It would be too late by then. And I *would* like to be a pilot," he said quickly, and stepped on board.

The platform had emptied considerably. Michael and I stood together looking at all of them leaning out the window — little Abigail and Martha, with Henry squashed between them and Rufus just behind. The conductor called and the car bumped forward a first tentative lurch . . . and then she

301

threw herself upon me, a flash of white bursting from the train. I had to take a step backwards to keep from falling over. And she kissed me in front of everyone — a hungry, hard, gasping kiss.

Henry was watching from the train window just a few feet away.

"This is yours!" she said, and she handed me a scroll of paper done up in a faded old ribbon. "I'm giving it back. But only if you promise to write from now on, *faithfully*, about everything that happens. Do you understand?"

We started walking beside the train.

"Yes, of course."

She disappeared back onto the car.

Michael and I kept walking to the end of the platform, then we stood and waved until the train rounded the corner.

My heart was running downhill on gravel.

"What did she give you?" Michael asked.

I picked at the tight little knot of the ribbon until the scrolled sheet came free. It was an old pencil sketch — of Margaret, a young, very beautiful Margaret.

"Did you draw her?"

"A long time ago," I said. Her hair was piled up on her head in the old-fashioned way, and her cheeks, her throat, her eyes especially, were young and full of life. "I was sick one night when I stayed in London as a soldier, and Margaret sat by me the next day for a while. So I drew her."

At the bottom of the paper, in pencil, she had written something new: *I believe that the love we hold helps us through the worst of times.*

"Will you draw me?" Michael asked.

302

We started walking back towards Charles and the wagon. I looked up again, as if expecting the train to be bringing her back. But the track was clear, of course.

"Certainly."

"Because it has been a long time since you drew me. I've grown a lot."

Every inch of the sky was immaculate still, without a mark or hint of warning.

On the wagon Michael stood before me and held the reins. He chattered most of the way about Abigail and Martha. He said straight out, without a hint of embarrassment, that he thought Martha was beautiful. "As soon as I saw her I felt all wobbly," he said.

"Really?"

"Like this," he said, and he half-turned and wobbled my stomach with his little hand.

"Watch the road, sonny-boy."

"Have you felt like that?" he asked me, his voice very serious. "It's like . . . there's a dizziness inside you."

"Yes. I've felt that."

Once we made it through town the wind picked up and blew dust into our eyes, and Charles snorted and snuffed. I took over the reins, and Michael whistled between his thumbs and turned his head away from the breeze. I whistled too, and the clop-clop of Charles's huge hooves and the groaning roll of the wagon wheels turned us into a small moving symphony. Finally we made the Bretton farm. I unhitched the wagon and together Michael and I towelled and brushed down Charles. Michael got him a bucket of water and fed him oats, and I talked with Bretton for a time about the weather. He was sure that the endless prairie drought was moving east, hoppers would take every crop, and soon dust would parch every stream in the area.

His property couldn't have been more lush — every inch of it seemed verdant and full of life, with plants growing even out of the fence posts where we were, in the shade by his barn.

"Pretty serious news out of Europe these days," I said.

"What's that?"

I told him that the Germans had flattened Almeria and were threatening to enter the Spanish war.

"Oh, that business. I haven't been following that."

On the walk home Michael asked me if there was going to be another world war.

"I don't see how we can avoid it."

"Will you be a soldier again?"

"No, not me."

"Why not?"

"I did my bit."

He wanted me to tell him all about the news of the last few days. He'd been listening, and trying to understand, he said, but he couldn't follow it all. "There are antichrists and —"

"Anarchists," I said.

"And loyal ones and commentists —"

"Communists."

"But who are we cheering for?"

I couldn't answer right away. A pair of red-winged black-birds swooped beneath low-lying limbs some feet away and then skirted off. "For peace, Michael. Peace is the underdog here."

As we approached the lane to the house I stopped him. Nothing had changed, really — the sky was the same as a few minutes before, the road as dusty and worn as ever, the summer weeds and flowers were still slowly fighting it out in the ditches around us — and yet the air felt thicker. I had the beginnings of a dreadful sickening in the pit of my stomach.

Not the dizziness Michael had mentioned.

"No matter what happens," I said to him, "if there's a war or . . . something else —"

His face was so grave, his eyes so large and trusting.

"We are in this together," I said.

"In what?"

"This life, kiddo." I knelt down and hugged him and tried to keep my tears from soaking the shoulder of his shirt, but I was gasping suddenly, shaking with sobs.

A car came by. It was Blaine Williams, a man from the village I did not know well. He slowed and leaned out his window. "Everything all right?"

I couldn't speak. But I wiped my face away from his view, then nodded to him and straightened up in a familiar way. He tipped his hat to us, then drove on.

"What's wrong, Daddy?"

"Nothing," I whispered. "You go on ahead."

Michael was only too happy to sprint up the lane by himself. When I got to the house he jumped out from behind a bush with two badminton rackets in his hands.

"Uncle Rufus forgot these!" he squealed. "And the birdies. Will you play with me? *Please!*"

"All right."

I glanced through the window and saw Lillian, not in the kitchen, not rolling out loaves of dough or stitching up someone's torn trousers, but sitting alone in the front room, her spine quite straight, not resting against the back of the chesterfield, not even close. She was staring at nothing, with a face that looked spiritless and bleak.

"Come on!" Michael said, and pulled at my hand.

"You go ahead and practice. I'll be there in a minute."

"*I can't practice by myself!*"

"Just . . . just a few minutes," I said quietly. "You go down to the meadow."

He caught my tone then, and the stricken expression that must have been on my face registered on his own. One of the rackets dropped from his hand, and he didn't pick it up. "Go down to the meadow, Michael," I said more firmly.

Off he ran. If Lillian heard the exchange her face didn't betray it. She seemed to be braced and waiting for me to come in and do the unspeakable.

I looked at the door but my feet didn't move. I imagined myself taking first one step, then another. I saw my hand on the screen door — the door I'd cut and planed and sanded and hammered together, painted and fit into that space, twice — I saw some ghost of myself walking into the gloom and standing before the sad, sad lady sitting so all alone.

Lillian, the ghost called — suddenly the voice seemed to surround me. And then my mind was filled with all manner of things that might be said — little, innocent words that could be stitched together in so many ways. Soft and tiny strings of sound to set the world to war.

I don't know how long I stood looking at the future, so full of certain pain and fog before there could be any hope of getting past it. Yet finally, without a conscious command, my feet *were* moving, my hand was on the door, the door fell open, and it seemed impossible to keep from striding through.

Author's Note

The author gratefully acknowledges the financial support of the Canada Council for the Arts and the Ontario Arts Council in the preparation of this manuscript. Thanks too to Elizabeth Hay, Laura Brandon, Susan Whitney, Kathy Bergquist, Dave Murray, Kate Preston, Helena Spector, Frances Dawson, Michael Dawson, and Reinhard Pummer for their help with early drafts, and to the many other friends and family who likewise offered advice, support and encouragement; to the staffs of Library and Archives Canada, the Canadian War Museum, the Imperial War Museum, and the McCord Museum for their help on research matters; to Laurel Boone and Bethany Gibson for their inspired editorial guidance; to my agent Ellen Levine for never faltering; and to my wife, muse, partner and first reader, Suzanne Evans, for everything.

Like *The Sojourn*, this story draws on a few threads of family history and mythology. I am indebted to Philip Cumyn's memoir and family history *The Sun Always Shines*, and to various family papers and remembrances shared by Joan Matthews and my mother, Suzanne Cumyn, among others. But *The Famished Lover* is entirely a work of fiction, and, except